HER UNBROKEN SEAL,

MIDNIGHT DELTA SERIES, BOOK 11

CAITLYN O'LEARY

PASSIONATELY KIND PUBLISHING INC.

To the men and women everywhere who have dealt with traumatic brain injuries whether mild or catastrophic.

SYNOPSIS

What happens when the man you love is now a stranger?

Lydia Hildalgo has been engaged to Clint Archer for five years. He'd been the love of her life since he'd carried her on his back out of the Mexican jungle. She knew the risk of loving a Navy SEAL, and she'd been happy to take it.

After a harrowing mission, Clint wakes up with no memory of what happened, and a brain that doesn't feel like his own, he doesn't know what to do, or who to turn to.

When one of his teammates needs his brand of help, he can't turn him down, but he doesn't know if he's the same man he once was. With his mood swings, can he be trusted to do the job? And what about Lydia? What happens when the man she loved with all her heart, is not who he once was? Is there any way that they can find a way back to one another and finally create the future of their dreams?

This is a stand-alone, but having read book two, Lydia and Clint's first story in the Midnight Delta series, will enhance your enjoyment.

1

"MASON, COME IN. TIME TO CHECK IN." CLINT SHOVED HIS fear and anger down deep, the way he'd been trained. Still, there were times he hated being the computer/communications guy on the team. He wanted in on the action, but no, he had to be in the back, coordinating things. And now he couldn't get his best friend and Lieutenant to answer on their team commlink at the agreed-upon time.

What the hell? I'm going to rip them a new one when I see them. I better damn well see them, they better be okay!

He might be working to channel calm from heaven, but he knew deep in his gut that this was going to be one of *those* missions. He'd felt it three times before in his career as a SEAL, and he'd been right *every single* time. There was some bad juju going on, he just knew it.

He'd known it when they'd filed into the briefing room back in California to hear about the mission. He'd known it when they'd touched down here in Syria. He sure as hell knew it now that his team, his best friends, were suddenly not talking to him as they were all spread out along the streets of Idlib. The men were all over the place—in between shelled-out buildings, long lines of cars and not to mention the streets filled with carts and people trying to flee to the Turkish border for safety.

Yeah, there might not be bullets flying, but this was going to turn into a clusterfuck. He knew it to the marrow of his bones.

"Somebody better damn well check in or your ass is grass and I'm the lawnmower," Clint gritted out.

"I'm here, I'm here. Sorry about that, it's crazy down here." His lieutenant didn't sound as contrite as Clint felt the situation warranted.

"Dare, say you have something," Mason commanded his medic through their comm system. Finally, Clint relaxed a small amount. The fact that Mase was demanding that Darius pull information out of thin air was damned ironic, considering they were surrounded by thousands of fleeing refugees, and Clint had been doing the same thing for twenty minutes.

"Nothing so far, but I'm doing more doctoring than I am gathering intel. It's brutal out here." It was sub-zero conditions and Clint had seen plenty of displaced Kurds walking with small children and babies. *Of course,* Dare was doing triage.

"What the fuck were these numbnuts thinking coming to Idlib?" Drake demanded to know for the four quillionth time. "I mean I know politicians are, by nature, self-serving and stupid, but this has to take the cake."

"Can it, Avery," Mason clipped out. Apparently, he was as sick of hearing Drake's complaining as Clint was. "This is the mission. We locate the Senator, his entourage, the poor reporters he strong-armed into coming along and get them the hell out of here. More importantly, before whichever terrorist group is up to bat, finds them."

"That'd be Hayat Tahrir al-Sham," Finn said through Clint's receiver. "They have the stick this week. Next week my bet is on al-Qaeda."

"Doesn't fucking matter," Drake grumbled. "They're all the same, they're killing innocents and they will kidnap Senator Leonard and his little team, and why in the fuck did he take two women with him? Why in the fuck did he leave Damascus? Why in the fuck did he come to Syria in the first place?"

"This is the last time I'm telling you, Drake, shut it." Mason was pissed. "Dare, start asking questions."

Clint knew that Mason was relying on Dare Stanton to find out information because he was doing field medic work on the refugees. However, Clint would bet his bottom dollar it would be Finn who would come up with answers. Darius would end up trying to save the entire caravan of people from freezing to death, especially the children. He could never pass up helping a child; it wasn't in his make-up.

"Guys, we have to make this fast. I have rumors that tanks are coming this way on the M-5 highway. You know that means they're intending to clear the way so this week's bad guy of the month can come in and scoop up the senator and his party," Clint said as he looked down at his tablet. "I'm still trying to get the intel verified," he told his team.

Clint was positioned on top of what was once an apartment building, but was now a bomb-shelled husk of rubble. He had tracking on each of his men but having eyes on them amongst the chaos was impossible, that's why he'd been so concerned not hearing from them.

"Well, good luck to the terrorists, they first need to find them," Finn said drily.

"Considering how much that bastard likes his media coverage, you would have thought he was on the back of some truck hollering through a bullhorn," Jack Preston's Texas twang came through Clint's receiver.

"Clint, did you ever get a total count of how many people he had here in Idlib and how many stayed behind in Damascus?" Mason asked.

"We have two reporters from the Associated Press here. I keep hoping that they will broadcast something so we can pinpoint the senator's location. Then we have Senator Leonard and three aides.

"So, Leonard basically—" Drake started.

"Yes, we know Drake, he took a circus with him," Clint cut in wearily. "The good news is that two of them speak Arabic."

"Won't do them a bit of good if the senator is doing everything, he can to paint a bullseye on them for the terrorists," Finn said wearily. "I'm with Drake on this one."

Clint rolled his eyes when he heard Drake's self-satisfied laughter. There'd be no shutting him up now.

"We've been doing this wrong. They had to have split up. There is no way that a group that size would have gone unnoticed. But if they've split up, then they would have blended more easily. Shit, I should have thought of this sooner." Clint could hear Mason beating himself up.

"The senator would have taken the reporters with him. He'd want the publicity," Clint said.

"You got that right," Drake agreed. "He'd be keeping out of the way of the US forces, not that there are many left, he'd be in with the refugees. Hell, he's probably looking for a baby to kiss." Drake's voice was thick with disdain.

"What about the others?" Jack asked.

"If they have the sense God gave a gnat, they'd be

looking at any of the remaining servicemen as a way to get back to the States," Drake said.

"There aren't any US Forces in this part of Syria, that's the problem. This area was taken over by ISIL, Hayat Tahrir al-Sham, and Al Qaeda months ago. We were forced to leave in total. That's why everyone is getting the hell out. The only reason we're walking around without question is that the Kurds are just hoping we're the first wave of US troops coming back in," Mason explained.

"Good, then maybe the senator's group will flag us down." Once again Clint could hear Drake's voice filled with self-satisfaction.

"Yeah sure, amongst tens of thousands of people clogging the streets and highway to get the fuck out of the city. Jeez, what world do you live in? Has Karen got you believing in fairies and unicorns?" Clint asked.

"Like Lydia doesn't have—" Drake started.

"Stop it!" Mason interrupted. "Especially you, Avery. I don't need this shit. We're here to get these civilians the hell out of here. Clint, do you have us all pinpointed?"

Clint looked down at his tablet. He saw all of the signals for the six men of Midnight Delta, which included him.

"Yep. Mason, you're good where you are, you're hitting the northwest side of the square. Jack, you need to veer southeast, you're too close to Darius. Drake, just continue on where you're going. Finn, move a little more to the south. I'm looking for any significant clusters that might indicate the refugees are surrounding some Americans. So far, nothing."

"I've got something," Darius said. "One of the kids just told me that his mother is cooking dinner for some honored guests. He said they're foreigners like me, but they don't have guns. She's not leaving. Probably either her husband or her sons are part of the rebellion."

"I'm down with some home cooking," Jack drawled before Drake could get himself in trouble by opening his mouth.

"I'm already working that angle," Darius said. "Let me patch the boy up. I think that a little triage and a little chocolate for him and his mom should do the trick."

"Always does," Finn agreed. "Clint, guide us to Dare. Not Drake, he'd ruin the invitation."

"But I'm hungry." Drake's whine was half-hearted. Clint could tell he had his sights on something.

"Finn and Jack, you head on over to Darius," Mason directed. "Drake, you stay on whatever you've got going. Clint, anything yet?"

Clint did another slow sweep of the city square. Finally, he saw something worthwhile, and it wasn't where Drake was located. There was a huddle of people with their arms waving. "Mase, could be that what I'm seeing is nothing more than people bidding on some provisions, but they're looking pretty worked up. They're close to you. You need to just go about twenty meters east of your position and you'll run into it."

If anybody could figure out what was going on, it was Mason Gault. Clint couldn't ask for a better leader and best friend.

2

Along with tracking the movements of his team, and sweeping the city square in Idlib, Clint had also been listening into Hayat Tahrir al-Sham radio chatter that US Intelligence had patched him into. Luckily, multi-tasking was his middle name. Now it was beginning to get interesting.

"Jack, no home-cooking for you, you're following me."

"On it," Jack answered Mason. "Clint?"

"You need to go about seventy-five meters northwest. About twenty-five meters past the big clock in the middle of Idlib Square. If you miss it, then I'm kicking you off the team."

Jack laughed.

"When you get closer, I'll guide you," Clint promised Jack.

Now that everybody had their orders, Clint listened to the terrorist chatter more intently. Yep, he definitely heard them talking about Americans.

Goddammit!

The only good news is they decided not to deploy

helicopters—they were coming in alongside the M-5 highway via tanks. That gave them some time. Just a tiny bit of time. He got on the horn.

"Klein here."

"It's Archer," Clint responded. "Need some help."

"I thought you SEALs could take care of everything all on your own," Felix Klein laughed. "What do you need? Is this about the Hayat Tahrir al-Sham tanks moving toward Idlib?"

"You've got it in one." He loved Felix, the man was always on top of his game.

"I've got you covered. We're deploying a drone right now. We'll let you know how many and where they are so we can get you an ETA."

Clint felt his shoulders relax. It was good to have *some* friends here in Syria, even if they were far away. The few US troops left were next to the Iraqi and Jordanian border.

"I'd talk freely, but I can't. So, with that said, any luck finding our esteemed senator?" Felix asked. His words might be respectful, but his tone was anything but.

Clint grinned. "We've got some leads. But the last thing we need is hellfire raining down on us, so thanks for checking things out for us, I owe you."

"Man, you're already paying. I'd sooner dig a latrine or clean a latrine than take your duty."

This time Clint laughed. He couldn't help it. Seemed this senator had not made any friends overseas.

"I'll have info for you in fifteen or less."

"Let's hope it's good," Clint prayed.

"Here's hoping."

"I'm going to stay on the line to continue monitoring in case something comes up," Felix said.

"Sounds good," Clint answered.

"The rumor is verified," Clint said into his mic to his team. "Hayat Tahrir al-Sham has tanks coming this way on the M5 highway."

"What's the ETA?" Mason demanded to know.

"My contact with a Marine unit here in Syria is sending a drone to scope things out. We should know the ETA and number in a half-hour, but we don't have that much time to waste."

"Guys, we need to speed this along," Mason commanded.

Clint saw Mason's beacon coming up on the huddle of people. Jack was further out. Drake was still in the same spot he had been for the last five minutes.

"Drake, what's up?" Clint asked.

"Men with guns. They're questioning everybody who goes by."

"Why haven't they noticed you?"

"I'm tucked in the back of one of the burnt-out vehicles, they don't see me."

"Who are these men?" Mason demanded to know.

"My guess is Kurdish rebels. None of the refugees are scared of them."

"Can you make out what they're saying?" Mason asked.

"Yep, they're looking for a group of Americans in civilian clothing. Men and women. They were driving in two Range Rovers."

"Well shit, that's more intel than we had," Clint bit out. He'd been scanning the area for almost forty-five minutes and there hadn't been a sign of a Range Rover. It would have stuck out like a sore thumb. "Meanwhile, what we had been told is that they were planning to hold a press conference Idlib Square also known as Clock Square, go figure. I'm going to need to move positions, see what I can, down some of the streets feeding into the square."

"Negative. We need you concentrating on the square," Mason said.

Clint eyed the next apartment building to the right of him. If he could jump over to that one, he could see down the large avenue that fed into the square. It was the same path that the tanks would take, and the same path someone from Damascus would have taken. Chances were the senator's party would have taken that road to get to the square.

"I can do both," Clint said as he gathered together his pile of supplies and tucked them into his vest and backpack.

"Then do it," Mason agreed, trusting him.

Clint ran to the edge of the roof and looked down. It was easy. Only a four-story drop, he'd be fine if he fell.

Not.

But it had to be done.

He looked over at the other building. Lucky for him the top of the building had been blown away, leaving it with only three stories. Clint took a running jump and landed perfectly.

Lydia would probably say it was the yoga that was keeping him limber. He grinned as he rushed to the side of the building that faced the avenue. He pulled out his binoculars and God bless the little baby Jesus, what did he find? Two black Land Rovers.

"Got the Land Rovers sighted. Somebody has the hood up on one of them. My guess is that they're trying to hot-wire it. They're about one kilometer south from the square on the main boulevard coming in from Damascus."

"Who's free to head that way?" Mason barked into his mic.

Jack and Finn immediately volunteered. Clint saw their beacons on his tablet, but he couldn't make them out in the crowd, which was a good thing.

"Archer, you there?" Felix tagged him.

"Yep. What's the scoop?"

"You're not going to like it. They've got four tanks headed your way. They're moving at top speed. The drone clocked them with an ETA by sunset. You need to find the senator and his pals and get the hell out of there. Seriously, Clint, what's been taking you so long?"

"Fuck you, Felix," Clint said without any real heat as he kept his eyes peeled on the scene below. "Sundown is when?"

"You've got an hour and forty-five minutes. Maybe two. Seriously, man, you've got to get this done."

"I hear you, so quit talking to me unless it's important. Archer out."

Clint relayed the information to his team.

Once again, he was left with the frustrating but necessary job of scanning the crowds for Americans. He huffed out a laugh when he saw Jack, head-and-shoulders above others in the crowd wearing a thobe and a close-fitting white turban to cover his blond hair. The slightly smaller man beside him was dressed similarly. That'd be Finn, who Clint would bet his bottom dollar had acquired the disguises. Not that unheard of, but with men asking questions about Americans in their midst, it was best to lay low.

He still hadn't spotted Drake, but he was pretty sure he knew which burnt-out vehicle he was hiding in. He could see the huddle of people around Darius, even though he couldn't see his teammate who was likely crouched down with a small patient on his knee. That left Mason.

"Mase, Whatcha got?"

"You were spot-on, Archer. We've finally found three of our targets. No senator, but I have the cameraman and two of the congressmen's aides."

Clint listened in as Mason explained the urgency to get them the hell out of Idlib.

"Sign me up," said someone. "Where's our ride out of here?"

"We can't. We have a job to do," another male voice spoke up. Clint assumed it was one of the senator's aides. "We have to get footage of the senator talking to some of the Kurdish refugees, then he needs to talk to some of the Kurdish rebels. He needs to broker peace between al Assad and the rebels."

"The first part is utter bullshit." The first man spoke up. Now Clint figured out it must be the cameraman. "He just wants his name in lights. Everybody knows what's going on. Now if you said he was going to get them more US aid, that would be a whole other thing. The second part is lunacy. He's going to end up getting himself and the rest of us killed. Why weren't we informed of his intentions from the get-go?"

"It wasn't your place to know, you're just a reporter. So, you report."

Clint didn't like the guy. He was an asshole.

"Quit arguing," Mason growled. "I need to gather everyone who was part of your group so we can get out of here. We don't have much time."

"Sure, we do," piped up a woman's voice. "The senator was told by one of the ambassador's top people that this was a safe excursion."

Jesus. Who was running things? Dora the Explorer?

"Well, his information was wrong. We've got terrorists with tanks headed this way. We have less than ninety minutes to clear the hell out of here, or risk being killed. Or worse yet, captured."

"What do you mean, worse yet?" the second man asked.

Clint pictured Mason's head exploding.

"Clint, you're going to be our landmark. I'd use the clock, but that's too exposed. Instead, I'm bringing these three your way."

"Got it."

"But—" the woman started.

"Shut it, or I'll explain in very specific detail what the soldier means by worse. Especially for a woman," the cameraman said. "We need to follow him and shut the fuck up, you got it, Kelley?"

"Dare, quit with the doctoring. I need you to meet me at Clint's location. We're going to get details from this group and go out and find the senator and the rest of this hippy-dippy group."

"Got it," Darius agreed.

Clint packed up again and climbed down to the back of the second floor of the shelled-out building. There were enough handholds for everyone to make it up to meet him. That way they would be out of the melee.

Dare was the first to arrive. He looked grim.

"Wanna talk?" Clint asked.

"What's the point? It's not going to change a damn thing. I worked on at least three people who aren't going to live out the week."

It had been a couple of years since they had seen so many desperate innocents. Clint knew better than to offer any platitudes or ask any more questions. He watched as Dare heaved out of his backpack like an old man. Certain things tended to age you.

"When are the civilians going to be here?"

Clint did a head tilt and Dare looked over to the square. He could see them making their way towards the apartment building, with Mason pushing them along. It was going to take them forever to get to the apartment building at that pace.

"Finn? Jack? You got anything?" Clint asked over their comm system.

"Give us a sec." Finn's voice was a whisper. Sounded promising.

"Drake, what are we waiting on?" Clint wanted to know.

"Whoever these guys are, they're showing pictures of Leonard and his two aides. They're also waving cash around. I was wrong; these aren't Kurdish rebels, they're either Hayat Tahrir al-Sham or Al Qaeda. They have to have moles in the American embassy."

"Great, just fucking great. Has anybody stepped up and taken the bait?"

"Not so far."

"I still have a dinner date with Rebin, his two sisters, and their mother. They really need to leave Idlib, but they're determined to stay." Darius said. "When these yahoos get here, we'll see if that's them, or if it's the rest of the delegation. I get the feeling the kid's family are rebels."

"Drake, get back here. You've found out all you're going to," Clint said into his mic.

"Already on my way."

Clint glanced back into the crowd and saw that Mason and the three others had made some progress.

"Archer!"

It was Felix.

"What?"

"You've got another problem."

Great.

"Tell me."

"We've kept the drone over the convoy. Two trucks with mounted RPGs linked up and are now moving ahead of the tanks. They should be there in thirty mikes. Whatever you're doing, do it double-time, man."

I knew this was a shit-sandwich. I just knew it.

"Got it. Can your drone keep an eye on them?"

"Negative. Doesn't have the fuel. It's got to come back to base."

"Understood."

CLINT RELAYED THE INFORMATION TO EVERYONE. HE WATCHED as Mason grabbed the arms of the two aides and started jogging them his way. One of them seemed to be pulling back like he didn't want to go.

Was he for real?

The man holding the camera followed. At least he had the good sense to follow at a fast pace. *He* didn't want to die.

"What do you need?" Drake asked as his head showed over the top of the second floor. Now *he* had made good time.

"I need more eyes on the crowd. But my gut's telling me that Finn and Jack are going to find the senator and the rest of them. But we'll question the people that Mason is bringing in."

"I still worry that some of them might be going with Rebin's mom for dinner. It's a damn good photo op." Darius reminded Clint.

"But they don't have their cameraman."

"There's always a phone to video it."

Shit, his friend was right. He needed to keep his head in the game.

"Dare, we only have a half-hour to get the senator. If, and this is a very big if, the civilians Mase is bringing in can't tell us anything, you're taking Mason with you to the house. I'm assuming they told you where?"

Dare nodded.

"Why not me? I'm sociable."

Dare and Clint stared at Drake, who finally held up his hands. The man had the manners of a bull in a china shop —when you needed finesse, you sent in Mason.

"Need some help," Mason yelled from the bottom of the apartment building.

Drake scrambled down and soon had the woman up to the second floor. He had carried her on his back. She looked terrified.

Next came the cameraman. You could tell because he was still clutching his video camera close to his chest. Mason brought up the rear with a man wearing chinos and a polo shirt who didn't look terrified. Instead, he looked put-out.

Great, he was one of those. The entitled type.

"This is unnecessary. We have diplomatic immunity," he was saying to Mason.

"You know what? How about we leave your ass down there, in your little American preppy clothes, and see how far your immunity goes when the terrorist tanks show up. Shall we?" Drake rumbled at the man as he helped the woman to her feet.

For once Mason didn't stop Drake's tirade, he just let it rip.

"Terrorists don't have tanks," the little snot said.

"These guys have an army. Don't you do any kind of

research?" Drake derided him. "Mase, can't I take him back down near the clock in the middle of the square?"

That seemed to quell the little shit's attitude.

Mason turned to the civilians. "Do any of you have any idea where the rest of your group might have gone too? We need to gather them up and get the hell out of here."

"How are we going to get out if they have tanks coming to kill us?" the woman whimpered.

"If we get out of Idlib and quickly reach our rendezvous point, we'll be helicoptered out of here," Mason explained, far too kindly in Clint's opinion. "Now, where do you think the senator went?"

"He was trying to find one of the Kurdish rebels who might be willing to come back to the Syrian embassy with him. That way—"

"What kind of dumbfuck idea is that?" Drake broke in. "In all my years of trying to understand politicians, this has to take the cake. Like a Kurdish rebel is going to go talk to al Assad. He's been trying to butcher the Kurds."

"He wants to try to broker a peace deal."

"Holy mother of God," Darius breathed. Then he spoke louder. "Was he planning on going to dinner with a family that might have some rebels there?"

"How'd you know?" the male aide asked.

"It's our job to know things. You would have thought that before walking into this hellhole you would have done *some* homework."

"I hope to God you do know," the cameraman spoke up. "My partner, Shelley is stuck with the senator. We were assigned to this mess, it would be a Godsend if you knew where she was and could rescue her."

"I should go with you. The senator needs my expertise," the little pissant spoke up. Clint felt a headache coming on.

"All three of you are staying here. The last thing we need is more of you to go missing."

"But—"

"Drake, you will stay with them." Mason grinned at his second in command. "Coordinate with Clint what needs doing. He's coming with us."

Drake crossed his arms and stood up straighter. Suddenly he doubled in size. "Gladly."

Thank God, no babysitting.

Clint quickly explained what was going on with Felix and gave over his tablet and headset to Drake. "Good luck with the 'experts.'" He grinned. Then he, Dare, and Mason headed on down into the crowds.

IT TOOK Dare fifteen minutes to find Rebin, which was fifteen minutes too long in Clint's opinion.

"Doctor!" the kid yelled in Arabic. He ran up to Darius and grabbed his hand. "Mama has made dinner. There are many guests." As he attempted to pull Dare along with him, he then saw Clint and Mason following along.

"Who are they?" he asked.

"They are here to help. They also know medicine."

Which was true, Clint supposed.

"Good, good," the kid grinned. "Come, come."

He wound them through many twists and turns in the back alleys of Idlib to get to his home. Clint took up the rear and surreptitiously marked the way with chalk and prayed that Rebin's male relatives wouldn't be eating dinner there, because if they were, this was going to be a total clusterfuck.

The only good thing they had going was that the kid was moving at breakneck speed. They might just outrun the

Hayat Tahrir al-Sham at this rate. *If* they threw salt over their shoulder, knocked on wood, and kissed a leprechaun.

Door after door lined one long wall, indicating different people's homes. At the seventh door, Rebin stopped. As soon as the boy opened the door to his home, all thoughts of luck went out the window.

"Papa, no!" Rebin cried.

Clint didn't have a real good view, but he could see a little past Dare and Mason and it wasn't good. An older man in a tight turban and robes had a man, who Clint assumed was the senator, held against his chest. He had a gun to the man's temple.

Clint stepped backwards so that his back was to the outside wall of the home. "Finn. Jack. We've found them," Clint said into his mic. "Get back to the apartment building with Drake. We're bringing them in."

"Do you need back-up?" Finn immediately asked.

"Negative." Hell, one more person in this situation would blow it apart for sure. He knew Finn, Drake, and Jack would be quiet as they listened in to what was going on with their situation.

While he had been talking to Finn, he'd also been listening to Mason talk to the Kurdish rebel in Arabic. "This isn't going to accomplish anything. You need to let the man go."

"He's spying on us."

Clint rolled his eyes. The senator was too stupid to be a spy.

"He wanted to do a news story, not spy. You need to take all of their cell phones away from them to make sure no pictures were taken." Mason said.

One woman's voice immediately began protesting. She must be the aide named Priya who Clint knew spoke Arabic.

"You can't take our phones away from us. We need them," she practically shrieked.

God, are none of these people reasonable?

"What's going on?" A man asked in English. His voice had a distinct tremor. It was probably the senator.

"They want to take away our cell phones," Priya answered.

"Here," another woman said. "You can have mine."

Hallelujah, another smart journalist!

He blew out a breath.

"Don't give your phone to them. We need to have a record of this," the senator protested.

"Sir, do you want to get out of this situation alive, or not?" Dare asked in a calm voice.

Obviously, Mason had given Darius point on this since he had already established a rapport with the mother and son.

"What did you say?" the young boy asked.

"I am telling this man to cooperate with your father," Darius said in Arabic. "Nobody here is a spy. My friends and I were sent to help people like you and your mom. We were also sent to find these people and take them home. They are not spies, they are journalists who need to hand over their cameras and notes so that your family is protected."

"Son, these people cannot be trusted."

"Yes they can, Papa. He fixed my arm. Look." He shoved up the sleeve of his shirt and showed a bandage that Darius had applied. "He helped a lot of people," he said as he pointed to Dare. "Please Papa, don't hurt them. He is my friend."

Clint watched as the man looked at his son. For just a moment his eyes cut over to look at his wife. He must have seen something in her eyes, because he started to talk to Darius.

"I will release them, if they relinquish their phones and notes, as you have suggested. But they must leave Idlib immediately. The enemy is headed our way, I must get my family to safety."

"What did he say?" the senator demanded to know.

"Give me your cell phone and any notes you took," Mason said, holding out his hand.

"No."

Clint walked in, holding his rifle at his hip, his expression fierce. "Lieutenant, I've gotten word that the Hayat Tahrir al-Sham are on the move. They are looking for the senator. If he's taken, they'll make an example of him. We have to leave now."

"Rebin's father won't let them go until they relinquish their notes and phones. They seem reluctant. Maybe we should just leave them," Mason replied.

"Not me," the reporter spoke up. "I handed over my cell phone. Here's my tape recorder, and all my notes." She thrust them at one of the other men who were standing beside the Kurdish rebel who still held the senator by his throat. "If you had any sense, you would too," she said as she looked at Priya and the senator.

The other woman, the aide to the senator, looked to him for direction. Talk about a lemming, she'd definitely follow him off a cliff.

Their job was to rescue the senator, but really, was this bright bulb worth it? He took a deep yoga breath, but before he could say something, Darius spoke up.

"Sir, you now have firsthand accounts of what this was like, even without notes and video, imagine what people will say when you go back and tell your story. You will be a hero."

Clint was pretty sure he threw up a little bit in his mouth.

"You're right," the senator said. "Tell the man we'll give him everything."

Clint looked at his watch. They now had fifteen minutes before the trucks with the RPGs would be to Idlib, it would take much more than a minute to make it to the city square.

Darius repeated the Senator's words to the Kurdish rebel. Rebin pleaded with his father to listen to his friend. Slowly, Rebin's father released the senator, but he kept his pistol trained on him. The senator and his aide emptied their pockets and the aide scrambled through her purse and pulled out two notepads and two phones and handed them to the man.

The rebel barked out orders to his wife as he started to pat down the senator. Rebin's mother patted down the reporter and the aide, as one of the other rebels tipped over their purses onto the floor to look for any other recording devices or notes. When the aide was found with a tape recorder, the young man slapped her across the face.

Clint, Mason, and Darius rushed into the small house and raised their guns.

"Enough," Mason shouted in Arabic. "You have everything now. We will be out of Idlib in less than an hour.

"How do we know we can trust you? Once you were on our side. Not now."

"I know that we have four Hayat Tahrir al-Sham tanks on the way here," Clint said. "We had a drone do a flyover. They'll be here in less than an hour and twenty minutes, but what's worse—two trucks with RPGs mounted to them will probably be in the city square in less than ten minutes. You've got to make yourself scarce."

It was a long tense moment as the man considered Clint's words. Then he shoved the senator at Mason. "Take him."

Darius grabbed the woman who had been hit and put his arm around her shoulders.

"We've got to leave," Mason said in English. "Now."

The reporter was the first one out the door.

Clint followed closely behind her. Mason had the senator by his arm and pulled him out of the small house. None of them wanted to stay a second longer than they had to.

Clint had to hand it to the aide; she didn't make a peep, and her face was swelling. Dare was whispering to her. He was good at that shit. Right now, Clint just wanted to make it to the evac point and get everyone out of there. Something was off about this mission. He had to make sure his team stayed safe.

Clint led the way back to the square following the trail he'd left. People got out of the way when they saw the American soldiers. Even better, the civilians kept up with Clint's pace.

"Guys, we have a problem," Drake said through their headsets. "Chatter coming in that the bad guys' trucks have made it to the city. They're saying they'll be at the square in minutes. Head straight to the helicopter rendezvous point. We'll meet you there."

Clint thought about Drake having to wrangle the three others by himself. "Have Jack and Finn made it to your location?"

"We were slowed down by some insurgents," Finn

answered. "By the time Drake reaches the edge of the square, we'll be there to help."

"Got it." Clint breathed out a breath of frustration. Not good enough. They were at the entrance of the town square, opposite the apartment building to Drake. "You guys go to the west," he said, pointing to his right.

"Meanwhile, I'm—" Clint started. Darius nodded, so did Mason. Clint grinned. He hadn't needed to even tell him his plan, they both just knew.

Darius locked arms with the reporter. "Come with me, ma'am."

Clint began shouldering his way through the throng of people as he made his way to the opposite side of the square toward Drake and the three other civilians. "Drake, I'll be there in just a minute."

"Gotcha."

4

_____

EVEN OVER THE CACOPHONY OF VEHICLES, PEOPLE, BABIES, AND young children crying and adults yelling, Clint still heard the distinctive rumble of armed vehicles entering the square.

"Drake, we're going to have to be quick. Trucks have arrived."

"Fuck, man, I see them. I'm bringing the people down to the square pronto."

Clint was too busy pushing himself through the mass of people to respond.

"We'll cover you when you get to the far west edge of the square," Finn said. He sounded out of breath. What in the hell happened when they had gone down the other avenue?

"We've got them, don't worry," Clint assured him. He arrived at the bottom of the apartment building as Drake was helping down the female aide. The male aide, Devon something-or-other was looking antsy.

"Where's the senator? Why isn't he with you?"

Clint saw that he had his cell phone trained on Clint's face. He slapped it out of his hand, watching with great satisfaction as it shattered on a cement block. Devon yelped in outrage. "What the fuck man? I'm going to report you!"

"Try it," Drake and Clint said in unison. This time Clint knew that he was the scary one, because the little shit was looking at him like he might just piss his pants.

"You didn't tell me where the senator is."

"Darwin, I don't owe you any answers. Now do I have to search you for any other recording devices?" Shit-for-brains shook his head as he looked down at the rubble. Clint shoved him at Drake and did a fast pat-down. Yep, he was just like the senator he served. He found another cellphone in his breast pocket.

"Allow me," Drake said as he held out his hand. "I'm the one who was too stupid to search him." Clint handed the phone to Drake and he then threw it to the ground, then stomped on it with his boot. No way was that ever going to work again. Still...

Clint picked up both phones and picked out the SIM cards and crushed those just to ensure that no recordings would be passed along. That was the last thing he and the other SEALs would need. They'd had that happen to them once, and to this day the consequences still made Clint shudder.

Drake turned to the cameraman. "Clint, he hasn't turned that camera on or pointed it at us since we got here. He's Associated Press, he knows the rules."

Clint stared at the reporter. Who immediately started speaking as he pulled out his film. "Here, have it all. I'm sick of the senator and his whole bullshit plan. I want you to feel good that I haven't filmed you."

Clint took the film, put it into his backpack, and then did a quick pat-down of the reporter. He was good.

Drake questioned the female aide, checked her purse, and determined she was good to go.

"Let's move." Clint grabbed Delwood's arm in a tight grip and headed west. They stayed close to the buildings, which was a little less jammed with people.

"Y'all, the trucks are advancing to the clock in the center of the square. They're doing a three-sixty with the guns. Stay low," Jack advised.

Clint pulled the weasel into a duckwalk. He didn't need to turn around to know that Drake was doing the same with the others. It was going to slow them down, but it would ultimately save their lives. They went a quarter of a kilometer when Drake told him to hold up. He looked back and saw the woman on her knees. "I can't go anymore. My legs can't go on. I need to stand up."

"You can't, ma'am," Drake told her. "We'll be targeted. You have to stay low."

"I can't." Her face was red, and Clint could see her legs trembling as she was kneeling.

"Leave her behind," the snot-nosed aide sneered. "I'm not dying because her fat ass can't keep up."

"Nobody gets left behind." Drake bared his teeth. He turned back to the woman. "I'm going to help you. You need to trust me." Drake put his arm around her waist and had her do the same to him. "Let me take your weight. You've got this."

"You, me, and the reporter need to get out of here quicker," the asshole aide said to Clint. "We'll leave them behind."

"You're doing what I tell you to do. I'm in charge." Drakes' voice was deadly.

"I'm just—"

"One more word out of you, and I'm dragging you into

the middle of the square with a bullseye on your forehead. You'll just be one sad casualty in all of this. Got it?" Drake snarled.

"You do that and it's murder, plain and simple," the dweeb cried.

"Like I care. You just suggested the same thing for her, now didn't you? So shut the hell up so I can save all of you."

"But..."

"I'll throw you in front of those trucks, is that what you want? They would love to take you hostage. You wouldn't last two days." Drake's smile was scary.

Deadwood gulped. "I'll do what you say." Finally, he got it.

"Drake, you go first, *this guy* and I will follow."

Drake moved forward with the injured woman and the reporter moved in behind him. Clint nudged the mouthpiece in front of him then took the rear position. With every step he took, he swore the rumble of the trucks got louder. He kept looking over his shoulder, but there was no sign of them.

Quit with the overactive imagination. Got it?

"We're almost at the public park, halfway to the rendezvous point. We're calling in the helicopter," Mason informed his team.

Clint knew that the trek was nearly three kilometers west from Clock Square to the rendezvous point. "Made good time, Lieutenant," he complimented.

"How far are you?"

"We're still another fifty meters before we'll be out of the square," Clint responded.

"Hurry your asses up," Mason's words were clipped.

"We *are* hurrying." Drake's words were grim.

"Where are you? We're at the west entrance to the square. Do you need help?" Finn asked.

"Stay there, give us two minutes, and we'll be with you," Clint said.

As soon as he stopped talking, Clint heard the ominous rumble of the trucks. He turned around, his rifle at the ready. Squinting, he saw the tip of the guns on the truck.

Fuck me.

They weren't grenade launchers, they were Vulcan anti-aircraft guns. Those things could tear you up. They were good at blowing off the top of a building.

"Jack, Finn. The trucks are armed with anti-aircraft guns."

He could almost hear everybody wincing over his receiver.

"Did you see them, or have they started to blow things up?" Mason sounded so tense and tight he could probably turn coal into diamonds between his butt cheeks.

"Just saw the top of the gun. None of the Hayat Tahrir al-Sham have spotted us...yet."

"And before you ask, we're going as fast as we can," Drake spoke up.

"You go on ahead," Clint told Drake. "I'm going to get closer to the trucks and make sure they don't point anything your way."

"Negative," Mason spit out. "You stay with Drake and the civilians."

"And let them be sitting ducks? That's just plain stupid. I'm just going to get a little closer to them. If they start sniffing toward Drake's band of merry men, then I'll create a diversion. But you know me, I'm not going to put myself in harm's way. Lydia would stomp all over my ass."

That got a short laugh out of Mason, longer laughs from

the others. "Fine, Clint, I trust your judgment. Do what you need to do, just don't get your ass shot."

"Roger that."

He turned to Dipshit. "You're following Drake and making yourself useful. If you leave his side, you're going to get lost and there's a good chance you're going to end up dead. Ultimately, it's your call. We get paid if we bring home five people or six people."

The young man glared at Clint.

Bring it on, little buddy.

The kid must have seen Clint's determination. He nodded. "I'll stay with them." His voice was still snotty and sullen.

Who in the hell raised him? Wolves?

Clint gave Drake a chin tilt then headed toward the trucks. This time he didn't push his way through the crowd; instead, he melted into it. He twisted and turned so that there was no disruption amongst the flow of people, leaving nothing that would show the Hayat Tahrir al-Sham that there was an anomaly in the crowd.

When he got close enough to see the actual soldiers on the truck, Clint looked around for a reason to pause. He saw a woman whose wheelbarrow had tipped over and all of her belongings had spilled onto the cobblestones. She had one baby crying in her arms and two youngsters toddling beside her.

He offered to help her, and she smiled gratefully. She seemed awfully young to have three children. Clint wondered if she was already a widow. As he helped to re-load the wheelbarrow, he counted how many men were on which truck. There wasn't one piece of good news. The anti-aircraft guns were well-manned; as a matter of fact, men were hanging off every available spot on the trucks. Clint was surprised they weren't going into the crowd to strike even more terror amongst the people.

When Clint was done helping the young mother, he offered to push the wheelbarrow and stayed bent low over it. He would have held one of the toddlers, but if he were spotted and had to run in an instant, he didn't want the child to possibly get hurt.

The mother continued to thank him as he maneuvered the wheelbarrow at a slow pace back east toward the clock tower, which allowed the trucks to come parallel with them. That's when he saw it. There was a great deal of chatter going on in the first truck, then he saw them lowering the gun. Clint couldn't figure out where they were aiming, but it was toward the area where he had left Drake and the others. He turned his radio to a different channel in hopes of hearing any kind of chatter from the trucks.

As he continued his slow pace, he listened intently.

There it was. They were looking for the American officials too. Somebody had tipped them off that they were in the square somewhere. Clint saw five men jump off the sides of the trucks and start shoving their way through the scared crowd. Their brand of questioning was brutal. People were getting beaten and pistol-whipped, didn't matter if they were man or woman. Clint moved the little family he was with in the opposite direction and then told them to huddle under the little outcropping of a storefront.

"Wait here until the Syrian soldiers have left the square. Then you'll be safe," he told the mother. She gave a scared nod, and he left her.

He felt fear as he saw the trucks aim for the street that would eventually take his team to Hwy 60 that would lead them to the Public Park and beyond that to the rendezvous point.

"The trucks are heading your way, they're taking the east street out of the square that'll then take them to Hwy 60. I'm going to divert them."

"No, you're not," Mason ordered. "Unless you've thought of something that you can live through, you're commanded to stand down."

There were twelve Hayat Tahrir al-Sham soldiers, two trucks, and two anti-aircraft guns all headed after his team and the civilians. There was only one thing that Clint could think of that might, just might, divert them and keep his happy ass alive. It was worth a shot.

"Mase, it goes against my personal beliefs to commit suicide, so this has a good shot of me changing their direction, while staying alive. It's a twofer."

"I've met up with Jack and Finn. Tell me your twofer so I can help," Drake demanded. "I've already started back into the square, so don't fucking argue with me."

Clint was already running toward the first apartment building that he had set up a command post. "Head to the apartment building where we met. I'll be jumping over to it."

"What the fuck do you mean, jumping over to it? What the fuck are you doing, Archer?"

Clint didn't bother answering Drake. He kept his body as low as possible and kept the speed on so he could get to the apartment building and make his way to the top. Then he would start making a ruckus. Anything to get the terrorists' attention and truck guns pointed his way, and away from his team.

Clint raced inside the bombed-out building and was making his way from the second to the third floor, intent on getting to the roof. That was when the entire building started to shudder with incoming fire from the big anti-aircraft artillery. Luckily, the stairwell was deep enough in the building that besides the shaking he was just getting dust falling on him, no bullets were making it through to him.

"Clint, are you in the building next door?" Drake asked. "Or do they just have shitty aim?"

"I got what I wanted. Now they're pointed in the wrong direction. Now I just have to hop over to the neighbors without being seen, and I'm Scott free."

"Well don't go up to the roof, because then you're toast."

"Thanks for pointing out the obvious." The dust was coming down thicker. Had they already blown through the front wall of the building?

Clint stopped on the fourth floor, not bothering to head to the roof—that was just a quick way to get dead. He ran down one of the building's corridors and pushed open a door that had an apartment that would have a window facing the building Drake was in.

Once he was inside the empty apartment, he broke the glass and was staring down at the roof where Drake was standing.

"Hiya," Drake said over their comm system. "Fancy meeting you here."

"Can the bullshit. Can Clint make the jump?" Mason demanded to know.

"Sure, he can," Drake answered easily. But when Drake met Clint's eyes, they knew it wasn't going to be easy. The window started a half meter off the ground, so Clint would have to clear that before spanning the distance between the apartments and landing on the nearby rooftop.

Since they were on the backside, they were away from the street and the bullets from the guns, but that was the only thing they had going for them.

Clint found a pillow and used that to cover his arm while he broke out the remaining glass from the window. He grinned when Drake squatted down in a classic catcher's position and pretended to hit his fist into a mitt. Clint moved back as far as he could from the window then started to run toward the window.

He leaped over the ledge.

Whap. Whap. Whap.

Fuck!

More glass shattered. Clint was buffeted with concussions as parts of the building behind him exploded. For a split second, he felt his right foot hitting the other rooftop, while his left foot snagged the ledge.

His vision blurred. He thought he felt a hand gripping his arm.

Then his world went black.

5

"CLINT!"

He was underwater.

"Talk to me."

It was Drake. He sounded worried.

"HE'S BLEEDING FROM HIS EARS."

Drake again.

"Come on, Clint, talk to me." Was Drake pleading?

"Hand him to me." That was Finn's voice. "I've got you, Clint. Are you with me? Can you hear me?"

I'm fine.

Wait a minute. Why can't I feel my body?

Why can't I open my eyes?

"The terrorists are still focused on the apartment building. We've got to get to Mason at the rendezvous point."

My plan worked!

"Not too fast, we can't jostle him," Drake said. He still sounded worried. That wasn't right.

"Drake, we've got to get to safety. The sooner we can get him to a hospital, the better. We need to get over the border to Turkey."

I'm fine. You can go fast.

"I said don't jostle him. We're going slow. I'm the second-in-command, you're going to listen to me, you got it?"

Jesus, Drake, you need a chill pill. I'm fine.

But am I?

He couldn't see. He couldn't feel anything. Apparently, he could only talk in his head. What had happened?

"Drake, Mason just said the helicopter is almost to the rendezvous point. We don't have a choice, we've got to motor."

"Listen to me, Archer. You don't die on my watch, got it!"

Die?

Must be bad.

"Clint, think of Lydia. You gotta be strong," Drake whispered.

Lydia.

Clint had trouble picturing her face. Then everything went dark again.

"CHIEF, CAN YOU HEAR ME?" a woman's voice asked. "I'm Doctor Klaus. You're here in Germany. I need you to squeeze my hand if you can hear me."

Germany?

"Chief?"

"Syria," Clint said roughly. His throat felt like it was filled with barbed wire.

"Can you squeeze my hand?" The woman's voice asked kindly.

"Am."

Is that my voice?

"Drink?"

"Squeeze my hand and I'll get you a drink."

His head hurt. His throat hurt. And he *was* squeezing her damned hand. If he hadn't been raised to be a gentleman, he might have cursed at this woman. Clint tried to open his eyes so he could glare at her, but he couldn't.

Dammit!

"That's good. I felt that. You're doing good. Let me get you some ice chips."

"Water." He croaked out.

He felt something cold against his lips, and he forced them open. Ice chips. Where was the water?

Clint tried opening his eyes again, but it didn't work. He still couldn't see the doctor. He tried again. Finally, there was something. A little bit of light.

"How is he?" a man's voice asked.

Mason?

How can I hurt this badly when I feel like I've been rolled in bubble wrap?

"Careful," someone shouted.

Was that Mason?

"I'm trying. It's the wind. We've almost got him to the airplane."

"Try harder, airman. This man is a hero."

Who's Mason talking about?

He felt wind on his cheeks. Wind and rain. He was moving.

"You with me, Clint?" Mason asked. "We're loading you up on a plane to get you home."

He felt Mason gripping his hand.

At least I can feel something!

"Mase?"

"I saw your lips move, but this storm's too wild, I can't hear you. Wait 'til we're on the transport."

His face wasn't cold. Someone was wiping it off. Oh, it was covered with rain. Got it. He felt movement as his bubble-wrapped body was belted down. Clint strained and was able to open his eyes. The light was dim, but it felt natural being on a military airplane. He rolled his head just a little.

Fuck!

Pain!

Who is that groaning?

"Connect his IV, so we can push pain meds," someone said.

Clint didn't notice anything, the evil dragon of pain had him clamped in its jaws. Rain was running down his face again. He couldn't breathe with the dragon's fire engulfing his head. Clint tried to shut down, to escape, but he was stuck in the moment, unable to leave the wrath of the teeth and fire that was intent on consuming him.

Years went by, then he was released. A calming mist chased away the dragon, leaving peace behind.

"Clint, can you hear me? It's me, Mason."

"Did you kill the dragon?"

"What?"

"My head doesn't hurt." Clint knew instinctively not to

move it. Then he realized the dragon wasn't real. "They gave me drugs, didn't they?"

"They had to, your pain level was too high. We're going to get you to Walter Reed in Bethesda Maryland. Best damn hospital in the world."

"What happened to me?"

"What's the last thing you remember?"

Clint thought long and hard. Hard enough that he began to feel a headache coming on. He knew that he'd been in the briefing room at Coronado. He remembered being in the room. The lights were out, and he was looking at something on the screen, but he couldn't see what it was.

"Coronado. You going over the mission. Can't remember what." Clint heard himself slur. He sounded drunk.

I never get drunk.

"How bad?"

"The explosion really did a number on your head. That's why all the bad headaches. We need to get you there to do some more tests."

"How long?"

It seemed like it took forever for Mason to answer, but it could be the drugs. "Four weeks. They had to put you into a drug-induced coma until the swelling in your brain could go down."

"Lydia?"

"She's been here. I sent her home yesterday. She'll meet you at Walter Reed Hospital."

How come I can't remember Lydia being here? How fucked-up am I?

He felt the water coming up over his head again. It was like he was floating, drifting down to the bottom of the pool.

"Mase?"

"Yeah?"

He couldn't hear anything more. Who could hear things when they were resting on the bottom of the pool?

LYDIA LOOKED DOWN at Clint's face. It had been five weeks since he'd almost lost his life somewhere she wasn't allowed to know, and his face was still a little swollen. His left arm was in a cast and he still hadn't regained consciousness since he'd arrived two nights ago. She didn't want to admit it, but she was scared spitless.

It had been easier when she'd been in San Diego for the few days between leaving Germany and then coming to Maryland. There she'd had her support group—they'd prayed with her when she got the news of Clint's injury, they'd held her when she'd sobbed after visiting Clint in Germany, and they never ever let her believe anything other than that he would make a full recovery.

Visiting hours were almost over at Walter Reed, and she still hadn't gotten any movement from him. Mason had assured her before he left that Clint had been talking to him in Germany. He'd even squeezed his hand. One of the men, through the SEAL team network, had reached out to her. She'd known him because he was a computer geek as well. Clint had gotten help from him on two different occasions and Lydia had been involved, so she'd gotten to know Kane McNamara. He and his team were on a mission right now, but before he'd left, he'd said that he would be in touch. They were based out of Virginia. She hated it, because Clint's team had turned right around and left on another mission, so she didn't have their support either.

Lydia pushed out of the chair she'd been sitting in beside Clint's bed. For the thirtieth time, she stroked her fingers down his jaw, down to his throat. The nurse said that Lydia could feed him ice chips. If he didn't wake up soon, they might have to put him on a feeding tube.

She got a small spoonful of ice chips and placed them against his lips for the fourth time since the nurse had brought in a fresh batch.

"Clint!" she damn near shouted, when his mouth opened like a baby bird's to sip from the spoon. She felt tears welling up, stinging the backs of her eyes, but she refused to let them fall. This time she was going to be the strong one. *He* needed *her*, and by God, she was going to be *his* soft landing.

Spoonful after spoonful she lovingly made sure her fiancé, her lover, the man who was the center of her world, got some of what he needed. Finally, he turned his head and coughed. Then groaned.

Lightly, Lydia touched his bearded jaw; it was one of the few places on his face that didn't look swollen. He'd been injured five weeks ago, and he still looked like a prizefighter who'd just left the ring.

"Baby?"

He didn't respond.

"Clint, it's me, Lydia. Do you want a little bit of soup? I know it's hospital food, but some of it isn't half bad. I've tried it all, so I won't force you to suffer through the bad shit."

He coughed again. Not a loud one, it was a pitiful cough, a sound a child would make. It broke her heart.

"Clint? Can you hear me?" she asked softly.

She saw his eyelids flutter.

Oh God, was she going to finally see the beautiful hazel eyes of the man she loved? She waited. Then waited some more.

"Come on, Baby, you can do it."

His eyes opened just a slight bit, not enough for her to see his eye color, but enough to see the red where white should be. It looked so painful, but she'd been prepared for it. The doctors in Germany had prepared her for many things, then there had been all the research she had done on traumatic brain injuries. With all the research, she went way past frightened into the terror realm three weeks ago.

Then there was the moment her resolve hit. In no way shape or form was she scared for herself, or what this meant for her relationship with Clint—no she was scared for what it would mean to *him*. He was the smartest man she knew. He was strength, calm, and caring all rolled into one. The idea that this injury was affecting his brain, the core of who he was intellectually and emotionally, made her ache for him. But she knew, deep in her heart, he could pull through to the other side, whatever that was meant to be for him.

His eyes opened a little bit more and she let out a breath she hadn't even known she'd been holding. He slammed them shut.

"Hurts. Lyd?"

"Right here." She stroked his beard.

"Light hurts."

Shit, she should have thought of that. She went and turned out the lights, including the one over his bed. She left the one on in the bathroom but left the door open only slightly. When she went back to his side, his eyes were open.

"Better," he smiled.

An actual smile!

She could finally take a deep breath again.

6

NOT BETTER.

Hospital.

What the fuck?

The only good thing was Lydia. She looked beautiful, but too damned worried. She was trying to hide it, but they'd been together for five years now, and trying to hide something from him was useless. He'd known every...every...?

"Dammit!"

"What is it?"

"Nothing." Her hand holding his felt good.

"You can tell me anything," she coaxed.

"Birthday present," he spit out. Why had it taken so long for him to remember that?

Birthday and Christmas present.

"Your birthday was three months ago. I got you the Nintendo Switch so I could beat you at Pac Man, old man."

He tried to smile, but it was a half-hearted effort. How come he couldn't remember that? How come he couldn't even call up the word 'present'?"

"I'm so glad you woke up. The doctors were talking about a feeding tube, but I told them to wait. I knew you couldn't resist the idea of hospital food."

"Feeding tube?" Even with the dim light, his head was pounding. Every word that he said hurt like a son-of-a-bitch, but he needed answers.

"Yeah, you've been out of it for a while."

"How long is a while?"

"Five weeks," she admitted slowly.

Clint struggled to sit up, then realized one of his arms was in a cast. As soon as he moved, he groaned. His head felt like Quasimodo was inside, ringing a church bell. At least he'd let out a manly groan and held back the little girl whimper that was close to the surface.

"Jesus, Lydia, I hurt."

"Well then don't move your head," she said tartly.

"Is there something wrong with my head?"

He watched as she bit her lip.

Okay, there's something wrong with my head, hence the reason I can't come up with the word 'present'. At least I just thought the word, 'hence'.

Fuck. Even that small internal grin of satisfaction hurt.

"I'm calling the nurse for pain meds."

"Is that why I haven't been awake? Drugs?"

She bit her lip again.

"Dammit, don't be coy, tell me!"

Whoa, calm down, Sailor. Your head might split open.

Lydia looked at him with wide eyes. She looked hurt.

"I'm sorry."

"Nothing to be sorry for. I know you're impatient. I would be too in your shoes."

"Doesn't allow me to be an..."

Fuck, what was the word?

"...asshole."

"Anyway," she said briskly. "You've been out because of a brain injury. It was bad. They had to put you into a drug-induced coma."

That triggered some memory that he couldn't access. There were reasons to do that, but he couldn't remember why.

Why can't I remember?

"Why did they do that?"

"Honey, they needed to stop your brain from swelling."

Clint shut his eyes, finally putting it all together. "Traumatic brain injury? How bad? How long have I been ousht? When did it happen? What daysh is it?"

Why are my words slurred?

He watched as Lydia, his beautiful woman, paled. She took a deep breath. "Yes. TBI. They don't know how bad. You were injured five weeks ago. You were out of the country when it happened, and you know I don't know anything about that. Today is my best birthday ever."

Clint involuntarily squeezed Lydia's hand...hard. He didn't notice until he saw her wince. He let go fast.

"Sorry."

"It's all right. Any kind of touch from you is a blessing."

He smiled. "You're full of shit, my Dork Queen."

"Look here, Nerd King, I know what's important, and that's holding hands with you." She gave him a steely glare. "Got it?"

"Yes, ma'am."

"Now tell me the truth, how bad is your head hurting?"

"Not bad."

"On a scale of one to ten."

Ten.

"About a threes."

"Okay, I'll get the nurse."

Clint frowned. "They don't admin...admin...give drugs for a three."

"You're at a ten. Maybe you forgot with your brain injury and all, but you lost the ability to lie to me a year into our relationship."

Clint felt his chest ease. Having Lydia tease about his injury made it less traumatic.

Traumatic. Good play on words, Archer.

He laughed.

"What are you laughing about?"

"You make me happy, Lydia. But no more lashing. It hurts my head."

She leaned in and cupped his face. He looked into her brown eyes. Up close she was blurry but still gorgeous. Her thumb stroked along his lower lip. It felt so good. He parted his lips in anticipation. As she came closer, he could taste her cinnamon-flavored breath just before she touched her lips to his. Pain floated away as he was lost in the sensation of Lydia's heated mouth and intimate caress. He felt loved and cherished. Safe.

When her tongue traced his lower lip, then pushed forward to tangle with his, he lifted his hands to hold her closer and was hampered by his cast. He tried lifting his head instead, and a shard of glass lodged into his temple. He gasped in pain.

Goddammit!

"Shhhh, shhhh, shhhh. It's all right, Baby."

Don't call me baby!

Clint sighed. "My head's really hurting. It might be up to a six now. Maybe you should ask for some pain meds," he admitted reluctantly.

"Got it, it's a twenty. I'll be right back."

She caressed the back of his hand and was gone. Clint squeezed his eyes tight and gritted his teeth. Even that hurt. He didn't care. What hurt more was that kissing Lydia seemed beyond his ability. What the hell was wrong with him?

Clint stared at the darkened ceiling. The blinds were shut tight. Was it day, or was it night?

Fuck me! I didn't say Happy Birthday to Lydia. What kind of lame-ass am I?

He huffed out an angry sigh.

Seriously, how bad is this goddamn TBI?

The door opened. A woman in a white coat entered. Intern? Doctor?

"Welcome back, Chief. It's good to see you with your eyes open," she smiled. She had long dark hair pulled into a braid. She spoke with a slight Indian accent.

"Are you my doctor?"

"One of them," she answered.

"How many do I need?"

"We weren't really sure. My name is Dr. Varma. My specialty is Neurotrauma and Brain Injury Rehabilitation."

"Who were the others?"

"Well, now that you're awake and cognitive, you won't need Dr. Fitzgerald. He specializes in Disorders of Consciousness, but you'll see."

Clint thought on that a minute and couldn't make head or tails of it. "I'm conscious, why wouldn't I need Fitzgerald?"

Dr. Varma came over and picked up the blood pressure cuff off the wall and applied it to his arm as she answered. "Dr. Fitzgerald works with patients who are in vegetative or minimally conscious states."

She frowned as she put down the cuff. "I think that wasn't my smartest moment."

"Hmm?"

Shit, I'm confused a lot.

"Taking your blood pressure while discussing minimally conscious states."

"It was the term vegetable, Doc."

She gave him a half-smile. "The good news is that we're having this conversation. You're doing well, Chief."

"You keep calling me Chief. I'm in a military hospital?"

"Walter Reed," she nodded.

The door opened and a nurse came in followed closely by Lydia. Dr. Varma turned with a smile. "You're just in time. I need you to increase his pain medication this evening. We'll reevaluate in the morning."

The nurse smiled at Clint. "Good to see you awake." He smiled as he plunged medicine into Clint's IV tube.

"Can he have some soup from the cafeteria?" Lydia asked.

Clint's stomach rolled over at the thought of food. He shook his head. "Not now, Honey. Maybe later."

"Actually, we need you to get down something. Maybe some jello?" Dr. Varma suggested.

"We've got a really light smoothie," the nurse suggested.

Clint thought he would gag. He shook his head, which made the pounding worse and his stomach want to heave all the more.

"I just can't stand the thought of any kind of food. I'd throw up."

"Nurse, I'm prescribing him some anti-nausea meds for tonight. I'm putting in his chart that if the nausea persists, he can continue with the medicine, but I want to be informed if it lasts longer than forty-eight hours."

The man nodded and left the room.

"Lydia, Clint is probably going to be feeling pretty tired soon. You need your rest too. You've been here for thirty-six hours. I think it's time for you to head to your hotel room."

Lydia nodded. "But I'm going to stay until he goes to sleep."

"It'll be soon," the doctor warned.

"That's fine. I'm just happy to see his eyes opened."

Dr. Varma nodded and squeezed Lydia's arm as she left Clint's room.

"I'm so sorry, Honey. I didn't say Happy Birthday."

"Sure, you did, you woke up. What better present could I have?" He heard tears in her voice, and it killed him.

"Lydyya," he slurred. "Lydyya," he tried again.

"I'm here. You need to rest."

"Love ya."

He felt himself falling into darkness. *Was she crying? Why was she crying?*

7

LYDIA WAITED UNTIL SHE GOT INTO THE UBER BEFORE SHE looked at her phone. Her voicemail was full, and she had more calls than she could count. The only outgoing calls she had made had been to her sister and Clint's parents and sister. They were currently snowed in, in Colorado. She had talked them out of trying to drive to Maryland. Lydia's sister, Beth, meanwhile, was keeping her husband updated on Clint's progress the two times he had called her from overseas. He was a member of Clint's SEAL team, and Lydia was sure he was relaying the info to the rest of the men Clint served with. Lydia hadn't had the mental or emotional strength to talk to anyone else.

When they pulled up to the Residence Inn, she paid the driver and got out. She wondered if she'd be able to make it to her room, she was so exhausted.

"Lydia. It's about time you showed up!"

It took a moment for her to register who was talking to her. The petite little blonde looked unfamiliar, then the woman grinned.

"Rylie!"

The waterworks started and Rylie ran over to her, her arms wide. That was her Oklahoma sister, all heart.

"Oh God, what happened?" Rylie's voice was drenched with worry.

"It's all good," Lydia rushed to assure her. "Clint woke up tonight. He's in a lot of pain. But he was talking to me and everything."

"That's great news," a woman's Texas twang spoke up behind Rylie. Lydia looked over Rylie's shoulder and saw Finn's wife, Angie. It was like old home week with some of the SEAL wives here to lean on. She'd been doing that the week before when she'd come back from Germany. A lot of time had been spent at Mason Gault's house with his wife Sophia, who was on bedrest for a risky pregnancy. She had miscarried twice before. All of the team wives had been staying with her on and off when Mason wasn't available. Mason's parents had flown down from Portland for two weeks to spend time with her, and her father-in-law had even let her win at gin rummy.

Sophia and she had really won in the in-law stakes—too bad Lydia had such shitty luck in the father lottery.

"Lydia, are you with me?" Rylie asked.

"Huh?"

"I asked, 'what did the doctors say'?"

"When I spoke to his doctor out in the hallway, she was cautiously optimistic. Her words, not mine." Lydia sagged.

"Let's get you to your room," Angie said. "You look like you need about twenty-four hours-worth of sleep."

"No, I have to be back when Clint wakes up."

Rylie raised her eyebrow and asked, "What, so you can sleep in the chair beside him?"

"Trust me, after waiting so long for him to wake up, there isn't a chance in hell that I'll sleep if he's awake."

"You look wasted. You're no good for him like this. Just sleep in as long as you need," Rylie responded tartly.

"Look, Rylie—"

"Peace, ladies." Angie wrapped her arms around both of their shoulders. "Peace." She hugged them both gently. "Lydia, Rylie just wants what is best for you. Rylie, back off a bit, Lydia has been scared spitless for too long. She knows what she needs to do."

Lydia looked at Angie gratefully.

"What room are you in?" Angie asked.

"I don't remember." Lydia went into the side pocket in her purse where she kept her car keys and things like room keys and found the key card still in the paper holder with the number.

Rylie pulled it out of her hand. "This is not a secure way of traveling. Anybody could break into your room with you keeping it with your key and room number together."

Lydia snatched it back. "I know what I'm doing." She tried to glare at her friend but her attempt failed as she yawned. "Anyway, it worked out since I don't know my room number. Quit the overprotective schtick. I can't handle it right now. Anyway, I'm a cop. At least for now." Lydia heard her voice crack. So did Rylie. She put her arms around Lydia and squeezed hard. When she pulled back, tears were in the petite woman's eyes.

"I'm sorry. I've been so worried about Clint and you. I just want to help."

"I know. I know." Lydia rushed to assure her.

"Let's get you up to your room," Angie said.

"What about you two, where are you staying? How long are you staying?"

"We're staying here," Angie answered. "I'm sure Finn will fly out too, after he's back from wherever."

"Same here. There's no way Darius won't be coming here to visit Clint."

Lydia felt tears coming on again. She loved these people. *These* people were family. Fuck her father. And there was always her sister, Beth. *Always* Beth. And her mother, she supposed.

"I don't know what I would do without you."

"You know you'd do the same thing," Rylie said.

Lydia didn't know how to respond, she was just too tired. Angie saw it and started moving their little party toward the elevators. "Lydia, don't bother setting your alarm. I'll call the hospital and have them alert me when Clint wakes up. I'll call you on the hotel phone when that happens and drive you over. I saw you took an Uber, so I assume you didn't rent a car, right?"

"I did," Lydia answered Angie. "I left it at the hospital. I was so tired, I didn't think it was smart for me to drive to the hotel."

"Good girl," Angie approved.

"Are you sure you don't mind about driving me? I don't mind having the hospital..." Lydia lost her train of thought for a moment when the elevator door opened.

"Trust us, we don't mind at all," Rylie chimed in. "We'll take care of it. Hell, we'll even get you food and coffee in the morning."

Lydia felt tears threatening again. It was all too much. Too much.

When they got into the elevator, she didn't know which number to press.

"You're on seven. We're on nine," Rylie prompted. "We'll walk you to your room to show you how a key card works," Rylie smirked at her.

Lydia's tears dried up. "You're a smartass, do you know that Mrs. Stanton?"

"Yep, I do. I have the official club badge and everything."

By the time they escorted her to her room and Lydia got inside, Rylie had somehow even gotten her to laugh, it was amazing. Only her.

"Get some sleep, Sweetie. We'll see you in the morning, no matter how early," Angie assured her. Both women gave her a hug. Angie went into her room and did a quick check. You could take the private investigator out of Texas, but you couldn't take the over-the-top over-protective Texan out of the girl.

"All clear," Angie assured her as she put her gun back in her holster.

"You do realize I can take care of myself, right?" Lydia asked.

"You don't know if you're coming or going," Angie patted her on her shoulder. "I'm in charge right now.

Rylie grinned.

"Hey, better safe than sorry," Angie shrugged. "I'll call you on the hotel phone in the morning. Now get some rest."

Lydia's eyes gleamed as she saw the fluffy, white duvet cover. She looked over at her one lonely suitcase that she hadn't bothered to open and didn't now. Instead, she just stripped and walked into the bathroom, grabbed the little bottles off the counter, and took them into the shower with her. As soon as her hair was washed and her body was clean, she put her hair up in a towel and then climbed naked into the bed.

She didn't even notice the tears that hit her pillow as she fell into a restless sleep.

CLINT WAS ALL OUT of sorts the third time—or was it the fifth time—he woke up. His head was still hammering, but he was damned if he would ask for any more pain meds, they just made him more stupid. He squinted at the blinds. Was it morning yet? He thought he saw light, but maybe it was just streetlights or lights from the parking lot. Why wasn't there a clock in the damn room? Were they trying to keep him in the dark?

Clint thought about grinning at the stupid joke. Yeah, dark was good for the headaches, but not for enlightenment. This was bullshit.

I need to know what's really going on. Not with Lydia here, she's keeping stuff from me too.

Clint swiped across the sheet and blanket with his good hand, trying to find some kind of button to push to get somebody to come in with answers. He wanted them now. What was that pretty Indian doctor's name? Parma?

I can't even hold a name in my head? What the fuck! What is wrong with me?

He finally found the button. Pressed it. He waited for an eternity with no one showing up. Fuck that noise. He pressed it again but kept his thumb down on the button. Let it annoy the shit out of them, he didn't care. He wanted answers.

A woman in nurse's scrubs came in. She was smiling, but even in the dim light, Clint could tell she was annoyed.

Join the fucking club.

"Chief, what can I do for you? Are you hungry? Are you in pain?"

"I need to talk to my doctor."

"Dr. Varma isn't on the floor yet. I don't expect her for another hour."

"Fine, get me another doctor who can explain my condition to me. Or can you?"

He saw her fidget. "Really, it's Dr. Varma you need to talk to."

"How long have I been here? I'm at Walter Reed, right?"

"Yes," she nodded slowly.

"How long have I been here?" His words came out slowly and concisely. He liked that, he sounded normal. A bit of an asshole, but normal. No slurring like whenever Lydia had been here. Was that yesterday?

"You've been here three days."

"When was I injured?"

"I don't have that information, Chief."

"Then let me speak to someone who does have that information."

"That would be Dr. Varma, and she won't be available until ten o'clock this morning. If you let me get you something to eat, she should be here by then."

"I don't want something to eat! I want to talk to my doctor!"

"It's fine," the nurse soothed. She didn't seem at all upset by his outburst. "Let me go and see if I can page her."

She left his room.

"Jesus."

Did I just yell at a nurse? Yell? Where had that come from?

Clint rubbed a trembling hand over his sweaty face. He didn't yell. That was not him. And the nurse didn't seem troubled by his raised voice in the slightest. It was almost like she'd expected it. What the hell was wrong with him?

What was wrong with him?

Am I going crazy?

8

———

Lydia was jarred awake by the ringing of a phone. She didn't recognize the room she was in, and she was sleeping naked instead of in one of Clint's Navy shirts. Everything was wrong. She squeezed her eyes shut tight, trying to kick her brain into gear.

Clint.

Hospital.

Maryland.

She struggled to reach the phone before it stopped ringing.

"Angie?"

"No, it's me, Rylie. We just got word that Clint is awake. He's snarly, demanding to see his doctor."

Lydia's heart clenched. Clint wasn't snarly. Unless he was protecting someone, Clint was the calm in the storm.

"I can be ready to go in five minutes," she said to her friend. "Make that three."

"Don't you want to shower first?" Rylie asked.

It was at that moment that Lydia realized there was a

towel on the pillow and her hair was still damp. "Make it ten minutes, I have to dry my hair."

"Okay, meet us in the lobby. We'll have some food and coffee ready for you."

Lydia felt herself breathe just a little easier. "You know you might not be able to visit him, don't you?"

"Honey, it doesn't matter. As long as we're supporting you, we know we're supporting Clint."

Lydia bit her lip. "Okay, okay. Nine minutes."

She hung up the phone and rushed to the bathroom. She had her hair dried in minutes and was then scrambling through her suitcase. At least she had been smart enough to pack warm clothes.

She dressed in a Henley shirt and a heavy sweater over it, with skinny jeans and boots. She put on an opal necklace that Beth's mother-in-law had given to her. She said it would give her strength in her life. She thought it was hooey, since she'd told Beth something totally different, but she'd been wearing it ever since she'd been told Clint had been injured. She'd take all the strength and support she could get.

When she got down to the lobby, Rylie was holding out a take-out cup of coffee, and Angie was holding out a breakfast burrito.

"Which do you want first, like I don't know?" Rylie asked smugly.

"Give me that," Lydia said, reaching for the coffee.

"No make-up, but you put on some hot jeans for your man," Angie grinned.

"I have lipstick in my purse. Let's go."

By the time they got to the hospital, Lydia had drunk the coffee, eaten the burrito, and applied the scarlet lipstick that Clint was so fond of. All three of them rushed to the nurse's station. There seemed to be a bit of a commotion going on.

"Excuse me." Lydia tried to wade through and get someone's attention. It didn't look promising.

"Hey! We need permission to go to Clint Archer's room. This is Lydia Hildalgo, his fiancée."

One of the nurses turned around with a wary expression on her face. "Now might not be a good time, Honey. Maybe you should come back in an hour."

"What are you talking about. He's awake, isn't he?" Lydia asked.

"Yes. But he's...distressed. His doctor is in with him, and I really suggest you give him an hour to get himself together."

What in the hell is this woman talking about?

"No, I want to see him, right now."

"That's not advisable," the nurse said firmly.

Rylie and Angie stepped up beside her. "Lady, you need to listen to her. If anyone can get Clint to calm down, it's this woman right here," Angie said in her slow Texas drawl.

The nurse reassessed Lydia. "Maybe you're right. Follow me."

She came out from behind the nurse's station and Lydia followed closely behind her. As soon as she got close to the room, Lydia could hear Clint's voice. He was pissed.

"What do you mean you can't tell me what my prognosis is? What kind of half-assed hospital are you running here?"

Lydia winced. "Who is he talking to?" she asked the nurse.

"You mean yelling at? That'd be Dr. Varma and Dr. Ivanhoe."

Shit, this wasn't good. Dr. Varma was really calm and nice. How could Clint be going off on her of all people? Lydia sped past the nurse and went into the room.

Clint looked up. "Lydia, I don't need you here."

"I think your wife should be here," the new doctor said.

"She's not my wife," Clint growled. "And I sure as hell don't need her for this conversation."

Lydia sucked in air. It was like he'd punched her—not in the gut, but in the heart.

Dr. Varma saw her stricken expression and turned back to Clint. "Mr. Archer, you need to take it down a few notches and realize we're all on your side."

"How do you figure?"

"Why would we be against you?" Dr. Varma asked logically.

"Because you don't know your ass from a hole in the ground?"

Lydia stepped forward, she'd had enough. This was not the man she loved, this was not Clint. She'd read up on TBIs and she knew that people who suffered from them usually had trouble with their emotions. Clint sure was having trouble controlling his anger.

"Clint, do we need to bring in Drake so he can fight you on this? Or Mason so he can boss you around? What's it going to take for you to listen to the doctors, because I realize it isn't me."

"It's going to take someone who has a reasonable answer. Something definitive. If I hear, '*I don't know*' again, I'm going to strangle someone."

"Good luck with that. You're so weak you can't even stand up."

Clint tried to push himself up from the bed and then flopped back against the pillows. He glared at Lydia.

She shoved her fists on her hips. "Yeah, you got something to say, Sailor?"

They continued to lock eyes, and Lydia finally saw his

lips twitch. She watched the start of a grin develop. Then a smile. Clint started to laugh, then it was full-blown.

When he finally stopped laughing, he turned to the two doctors. He shook his head in defeat. "I'm sorry. I don't know what got into me. I'm not usu...usu... I'm not like that. I'm okay to listen to what you have to say now."

The other doctor cleared his throat. "Actually, Chief, what you just experienced is quite normal with your kind of injury."

Lydia watched Clint carefully as Dr. Ivanhoe spoke. He was listening intently.

"Your brain suffered a traumatic injury."

"A TBI," Clint interrupted.

"Exactly," Dr. Varma said. "And everyone responds differently with a TBI. We won't know what to expect with you until you begin your recovery process. To tell you the truth, I'm amazed at how quickly your language and cognitive skills have come back after being unconscious for five weeks."

Even though he was trying to remain stone-faced, Lydia could see Clint's relief at the doctor's words.

"So, what are the milestones you expect for someone with a traumatic brain injury?" Clint asked. He said the words slowly. Lydia could tell he was trying to ensure he remembered and said each word correctly.

"Before we can set milestones, first we need to determine where you are today. We need to check out what you're capable of doing physically. We also need to check your cognitive skills, as well as your memory. You need to realize that some of your memory will probably be lost forever. That's to be expected, but other parts can be regained."

"I am the communications and computer spe...spe...go-to guy for my team. I think we should also check out my, what do you call it? My ab...ab... good work with equipment," he shot out the last words with frustration. "Why could I talk when I was angry? I remembered words just fine then. This is ridiculous," he said angrily.

Dr. Varma suppressed a chuckle. "That's understandable. Your brain is on auto-pilot then and isn't thinking, it's just reacting. The fact you can do that bodes well for a full recovery."

"As for your idea to work with computer equipment, I think that's a very good idea," Dr. Ivanhoe agreed.

"Why do I keep popping off?" he asked quietly. Lydia knew he was mad at himself and probably ashamed of his behavior.

"Chief, you've got to understand, and prepare yourself for, swings in your moods. We're also going to assign you a psychologist to help you better monitor your emotions and deal with the mood swings. If he or she thinks it is necessary, we will prescribe some medication to help with this."

"I don't want drugs," Clint said adamantly.

"I'm not surprised," Dr. Varma's smile was kind. "But I think you're going to find the medicine more tolerable to a loss of control."

"We'll see."

"Tomorrow we'll send in a physical therapist to start some gentle exercises here in bed. You should be walking around the ward by the end of the week."

"Sooner than that," Clint smiled grimly.

"We don't want you to push yourself. If you do, that could push back your progress."

"Lady, I'm a SEAL. If you think it is going to take a...a...

physical ther...doctor and a week to get me walking the hallways, you're out of your mind."

"He's right about that," Lydia chimed in, choosing to ignore the fact that he'd been having trouble remembering words. "You've practically thrown down the gauntlet."

It felt good to be on more familiar territory with Clint. She was just going to shove his earlier words down deep and try to forget he'd ever said them. If she could.

"See, Lydia knows." Clint smiled at her.

"Yep, I know him."

"Yes, you know your man." He held out his hand to her. She grasped it in relief. Yes, maybe he hadn't known what he'd been saying. Maybe it was his head just going wonky.

"Well, we are sending in a physical therapist tomorrow as well as a psychologist. They will be the ones who will get base lines for us to determine what we're working with, and determine where you are, and then we can start talking about milestones." Dr. Ivanhoe was all business.

Clint squeezed her hand tighter. He was worried.

"Chief, remember, you are already an amazing case. I can't think of one other TBI case where the patient has been in a coma for basically five weeks and then the next day is having clear conversations." Dr. Varma had a kind smile on her face.

"Not clear." He said slowly. "I can't remember words."

"Trust me, you're doing incredibly well. Having trouble finding words here and there is nothing, believe me. But let's let the therapist and psychologist in here hopefully tomorrow so we can get started." She walked over to the computer in the corner of the room and typed in some notes, then she turned back to Clint. "Dr. Ivanhoe and I will be back here daily to check on you. We'll also be getting updates from the other two people involved with your case as they come aboard."

"And the milestones? When will we set those up?"

Dr. Varma turned to Lydia. "Is he always this determined?"

"This is mild," Lydia answered with a smile.

"Chief, as far as I'm concerned, I plan for you to be my star patient that I write papers on." Dr. Varma said with a smile. "But you're going to also have to follow directions and know this is not going to be an easy trail, even if you are the best recovery from a TBI known to mankind. You were put into a medical coma for three weeks while you were in Germany to allow your brain to rest so the swelling could come down. Then you stayed in a coma for two weeks afterwards. That alone would cause anyone to have some cognitive issues, let alone someone who had the kind of trauma to the brain that you did."

Lydia felt Clint's grip on her hand tighten, even as his palm felt clammy. Her heart ached for him.

"Five weeks? I didn't know I was in a coma for five weeks."

Shit, I've told him that twice, haven't I?

"Yes, five weeks," Dr. Varma nodded. "Since you're into computers, think of this as needing some time to reboot."

"Alright," Clint said slowly. "I guess that makes sense."

He was now crushing her hand. She knew the others couldn't tell what was going on in his head, but she could.

He looked apprehensive.

He looked exhausted.

He looked scared...and that scared the hell out of her.

9

His cast hit the railing on his bed, his head was pounding, and he was dripping in sweat. He tried to see around the room, but it was like everything was underwater. No, he was in a tornado, it was spinning him around, tunneling him through the vortex.

Clint clutched at the rail, but it was with his hurt arm, and pain rocketed up to the top of his spine, sending lightning bolts of agony into his brainstem. He leaned over the bed and heaved up the little bit of food he'd eaten onto the floor.

What was happening?

He'd never felt so helpless in his life.

He felt tears at his temples.

Now a roaring freight train was tunneling through his brain and he needed it to stop.

"Chief."

The sound got louder.

He heard someone shouting.

"Chief Petty Officer Archer, you're safe. You need to calm down." It was a soothing female voice. Clint couldn't see her.

She seemed far away, like she was at the other end of the tunnel.

"No!" he roared when the train came at him with its bright lights.

"Does your head hurt?" a new voice asked. He was so dizzy and nauseous, he thought he'd puke if he answered.

"Get a basin."

Something touched his head, and it felt like a glove covered in tacks as it moved his head to the right. He puked again, but he heard it hit plastic, not the floor.

"Get an orderly, he's detached his hand IV. We're going to need to hold him down to reinsert it so I can administer medication."

Nobody is going to hold me down!

Clint swung with his cast. He didn't have the satisfaction of hitting anything.

"I need you to calm down, Clint. We need to give you some medication. It will help with the pain."

"No drugs."

Was that my voice? Why am I yelling?

"What do you need, ma'am?" a man's voice asked.

"I need help getting his IV back in. Can you hold his arm down?"

Clint swung again with his cast, happy when he heard the man grunt.

"Chief, you almost hit a woman. Is that who you are?" the man growled.

The tornado stopped. The roaring in his head went quiet for a blessed moment. He stopped moving.

I couldn't have done that. I don't hit women.

He tried to open his eyes, but the light was like sandpaper on his eyeballs. He couldn't stop the groan that turned into a gag.

"Oliver, he didn't almost hit me, you didn't need to say that."

Clint turned his head and kept his eyes open. He was seeing double. Two Dr. Varmas. Two brunette women. Two Olivers. The man was pissed.

I'm pissed too, and sick. What's wrong with me?

He gagged again, but there was nothing left to throw up.

He felt the slightest prick in the back of his hand as the needle slid in.

"Clint," the woman, Dr. Varma, spoke softly. "Tell me how you feel."

"Head. It hurts."

"On a scale of one to ten, how badly does it hurt?"

Clint gritted his teeth and gasped at the pain. "Eleven, nineteen. Don't know, bad."

"I'm going to give you something to relieve the pain."

"Need to work through the pain," Clint bit out.

"You won't get well that way. Your body needs to rest. These bad headaches will not help you get well. It will hamper your progress."

"My pogess...pogess..." Clint tried again. "You said I was getting bedder," he slurred. "Shit, you gabe me drugs," he accused her.

"How is your head now?" Dr. Varma asked.

"I'm dizzy again, but it's not a torn...torn...whirlwindy." Clint laughed.

"I'm taping this button to the rail, within easy reach. The first sign of pain, nausea, or anxiety, press it."

"Nopers," he smiled easily. "No drugs."

He saw two Dr. Varmas roll their eyes. "Nurse, I'm writing in his chart that he needs to be checked every half hour for the next day."

Clint rolled his head and saw a pretty brunette. "Hiya. You look like Lydia. Where is she?"

"It's after visiting hours. Her friends took her back to the hotel. She's been here too long, she needs some rest."

Clint squinted at her. "But I've only been hee a day, right?"

"Eight days. She's been by your side the entire time."

Clint yawned. "Love her. Hopes she came back." His eyes shut.

THERE WAS something so lonely about this hotel bar. She and five other people were in it. Lydia had done her best not to make eye contact with the guy who'd been sitting in the corner and had offered to buy her a drink an hour ago. There were two other couples. One flirtatious, obviously a new couple, the other an old and tired couple.

Riley and Angie were upstairs. They thought she was in bed, which she had been—for thirty seconds. Why had she reserved a king-size bed when she should have asked for two double beds? She ached in such a big bed without Clint beside her. She'd been in pain since the moment Mason Gault had called her to tell her to get to Germany. But back then the pain had been overridden by terror. Now she was buffeted by waves of pain and confusion.

Lydia felt Clint's frustration with the medical staff's non-answers, but she understood them. She was frustrated too, but not nearly to the level he was. He was over-the-top. Then there were his headaches and the way they took over his entire body. She wanted to be like that character on Star Trek who could absorb his pain and make it her own. She would do anything to change places with Clint. She had no idea how to help him. The professionals she had talked to all had said the same thing. You need to just *'be there for him'*. What a load of shit. She wanted to *do* something. Clint would definitely find a way to *do* something if he were in her shoes.

She thought back to when he had carried her through the Mexican jungle for five days, in the rain. He had saved her life. Without him, there were hundreds of times she would have given up and let death take her. He wouldn't let her go. The stubborn bastard.

She gave a rueful grin. That was good, wasn't it? Her lips had smiled, kind of. Lydia gave a watery sigh. She wanted Clint to get better and she didn't know how to make that happen.

What am I supposed to do, God? What am I supposed to do? Give me something tangible to fucking do!

God, why hadn't she gotten a degree in medicine? No, she had to get a degree in criminology and computer science. Fat lot of good that was doing her now. She didn't even have anyone in her family who could help her unless she tapped her sister's husband to throw money at the situation, and he'd already offered.

Nope, she was stuck in a holding pattern, and Clint was stuck in hell. She needed to be able to help him, *she did*! It was like everything she had accomplished the last three years since she'd become an American citizen didn't matter. Sure, she'd put her education to use and ended up in the San Diego Police Department's Cyber Crimes Unit. She might feel good about it, but it never allowed her to do what she wanted, which was hunt down more of the kind of animals who had traumatized and almost killed her sister. Beth's tormenters might be dead, but many others needed to be banished to hell.

But not right now. All of that took a back seat to Clint Archer. Hell, Even SDPD was making a lot of noise that she couldn't have indefinite leave and she couldn't care less, but her immediate boss was fighting the good fight.

Fuck 'em.

How could she make this better? She looked down at her phone again and stared at the website that detailed the myriad of symptoms of TBIs. Apparently lashing out at people you loved was normal. It didn't feel normal, it felt like a personal hit. Had Clint guessed what she'd been hiding? Did he know?

She felt someone behind her. She looked up and couldn't see Romeo where he'd been watching her. Oh God, please say he hadn't snuck up behind her.

"Are you okay?" Angie asked as she slipped into the seat across from her. Then she looked at Lydia, "stupid question. Sorry."

Lydia gave her friend a half-smile. "I've been researching TBIs. No two are alike, that's what they all say." She swirled the little bit of watered-down scotch that was left in her glass. "They also say that he's going to have to go through the stages of grief. I get that. I really do."

Angie nodded, but didn't say anything, she just listened.

"But he's in the anger stage, and he's lashing out. He's not himself. I try to help, but it doesn't seem to matter."

She took a big gulp of air, ensuring she didn't cry.

"That doesn't really matter though," Lydia said as she straightened her shoulders. "What matters is ensuring his recovery. Whatever that's going to look like."

Angie reached out and grabbed Lydia's hand.

"I get it," Angie said. "I really do."

It took a few heartbeats for Lydia to remember why Angie could say that with such authority. She had met her husband, Finn Crandall, when he was breaking under the stress of PTSD. He'd basically gone AWOL, but Mason had covered for him.

It had been scary for the whole team. Lydia truly believed that had it not been for Angie there was no way that Finn would have made it out of his own personal hell. Of course, the cherry on top had been attending sniper school and ranking first place. According to Clint that was the toughest training any of them could go through. It took intense mental and physical fortitude, and Finn had aced it, to the point that they tried to recruit him as an instructor. His team had been in awe.

"What did you do? How did you cope?" Lydia asked.

"It was damned hard, and don't let anyone tell you any differently. I just wish you had family around right now, that would make a difference. I had my granddad."

Lydia grunted. Like having her parents around would help. Her mother would cry, and her dad was still resentful that he had to take help from Clint. It was a clusterfuck. Beth, her husband Jack, and their two beautiful children were the only bright spots in her family. Angie didn't know about her parents, and there was no need to tell her now.

"I know Clint's family are beside themselves that there's that damn snowstorm in Colorado that's kept them away so far. Clint adores his parents. His sister is so big she's going to pop at any minute, so she can't come. But she's FaceTimed me every day so far. Still..."

"What?" Angie asked.

"Clint's emotions are all over the board. I don't want him to say something to them that will hurt them. Something that he'll never be able to take back."

"They're adults, they can handle it."

"That's not the problem. It's the amount of guilt that Clint will feel afterward that I'm worried about."

Angie sighed. "I sure do remember that. Finn carried a lot of guilt around. Declan and Drake both helped him let it go."

"Drake? I can believe Dec helped. But Drake?"

"Oh, don't think he was Mr. Sensitive or anything, but in his in-your-face manner, he got through to Finn and really helped."

Lydia considered what Angie was saying. "I can see that," she murmured with a smile.

"Declan and Finn grew up together, right?"

"Yep. He knew Dec, long before the man started up the Shadow Alliance. When it looked like Finn wasn't going to be able to go back to the teams, Dec was all about recruiting him. Mason was not happy."

"No, he wouldn't have been. That's one of my biggest concerns for Clint. This is going to be a long recovery process. I mean long. Months, maybe years. With no guaranteed outcome. It would kill him not to be able to rejoin Midnight Delta."

"Finn didn't return for seven months," Angie reminded her.

"But Angie, Finn's was more psychological. Clint's is actual brain damage, there is a big difference."

"But the men are the same. They have that same strength. That same willpower. You don't know what his prognosis is, you said it yourself."

Lydia looked down at her empty glass. It was like her life. Angie caught on.

"Where's the woman I know whose glass is normally half-full?"

"She's not here right now. Clint usually helps me keep

my glass half-full. I do the same for him. It's tough to do when he keeps knocking the glass out of my hand and shattering it."

Angie got out of the booth and sat down beside Lydia and hugged her. Lydia rested her head on her shoulder. "Maybe I can sleep now. Thank you."

"No problem. Let me walk you to your room."

10

CLINT COULD FEEL SOMEONE IN THE ROOM WITH HIM, HE JUST wasn't sure who it was. He was still feeling a little loopy from the drugs. He hated them, but remembering the state he had been in, he'd needed them. He'd never felt so out of control. At least when he was in the middle of a mission, he felt like he had power, he had an opportunity to impact the situation. But not now.

"Clint?"

He felt Lydia cupping his raspy jaw. He leaned into the caress. He took her comfort like a man stranded in the desert gulped water. Only Lydia would sustain him during this nightmare. He opened his eyes and stared into the most beautiful face in the world.

"Lydia," he smiled.

"There's my Nerd-King." She brushed a butterfly kiss against his lips. He wanted more. He needed more, but she stood up straight.

"Can you get me a glass of water? My mouth is as dry as the Sahara."

Clint struggled to sit up in bed, finally finding the button that raised the bed into a sitting position. He felt much more human after that. He watched as she poured him a glass from a pitcher. He could see the condensation on the glass, and he couldn't wait to taste the water.

"Careful, it's slippery."

He arched his eyebrow and she laughed.

"What was I thinking? Of course, my Big Bad SEAL can handle it." She handed it to him.

He downed the glass full of water in damn near one swallow.

"Want more?"

"That should do me for now."

Lydia put the glass back on the nightstand and shuddered out a long breath. "What is it?" he asked.

"You've scared me." She grabbed his bicep above his cast then traced his collar bone, all the time continuing to look at him.

"I never meant to scare you, Baby." His voice was husky with emotion.

"I know. I've always known the possibility of you getting injured, or worse, was part of the job, and I wouldn't change a thing." But her eyes welled with tears just the same.

"Come here." He reached out and sifted his fingers through her dark silky hair and brought her closer so he could kiss her.

A real kiss.

A carnal kiss.

A loving kiss.

He brushed his lips against hers, and sparks flew. He savored the feeling, luxuriating in her plump lips as they softened against his. Slowly, oh so slowly, he teased her to gain entry into her mouth, then flames ignited. He rubbed his tongue against hers. More electricity, more fire, as their tongues slid against one another, as if this was their first kiss.

Lydia whimpered.

Clint remembered.

He clenched his hand a little tighter in her hair and she sighed her pleasure as he angled her head for an even deeper kiss. A kiss where he could control every move, every taste. Sometimes, his woman reveled in his dominance, she said it made her feel safe. More than anything in the world, he wanted her to feel protected.

He reached down and hit the lever that lowered the damn bed rail, then he pulled Lydia in even closer. She pulled away.

"I don't want to hurt you," she protested.

"It's my head, not my body. And trust me, this is making both of my heads feel a hell of a lot better."

Lydia laughed out loud.

"There's the Clint I know and love."

She let him draw her closer and put her arms around his shoulders. He hated the fact that he'd lost so much weight. She must feel it too.

"What?" Her lips hovered over his. "What are you thinking?"

"Nothing important."

He put his hand on her back and pulled her down so that her breasts rested on his chest, and his other hand awkwardly kneaded her scalp even with the cast, as he feasted greedily on her luscious mouth. He was in heaven, he could feel her nipples pebble through her thin cashmere sweater, and that added to his arousal. He bit at her lower lip, and she opened wider, so he could thrust deeper, a mating of mouths. He had been dreaming of making love to Lydia, for the last two weeks that he'd been in the hospital. Lydia was gorgeous, inside and out. She was his everything.

He heard the nurse a moment before the door opened. He broke the kiss and lowered Lydia's head down to his chest, just holding her. But there was no 'just' to it. He gloried in it.

"Looks like I came at a bad time," Sharon laughed.

"Could you come back in five?" Clint smiled over Lydia's head.

"You got it, Chief."

The door closed, and they were alone again.

He coaxed Lydia to lift her head, a blush went from the V of her sweater up to her brows. "We were almost caught." Her eyes were wide.

"They would have just saw us kissing."

"You were about to put your hand up my sweater, Sailor, don't lie to me."

Clint laughed. She was right. He rubbed his nose against hers.

"You know me well. On a serious note, where is Dr. Varma, I want to talk about my discharge."

Lydia's gaze skittered away from his.

"Do you know something I don't?"

She shook her head.

"Lydia," he warned.

"I hear the exact same things you do, Clint. We just hear the information differently. You think because you're doing well with Sal, that means you're good. Have you slept through the night once?"

"I sure as hell have. I was sleeping eighteen hours a day for a week, and you know it."

"But what about this week?"

"I get an hour in, here and there."

"And your headaches?"

"They're not too bad."

"Bullshit. You know it. I know it. And the doctor knows it. Until that is under control, they're not letting you the hell out of here."

Clint tried pushing himself upright and swinging his legs out of bed. The room began to swim.

Fuck me.

Lydia immediately saw what was wrong.

"You're supposed to take it slowly. Treat this like a concussion squared." She helped to ease him back down onto the bed.

"Honey, you can't want to hang around for this. Don't you have to be back to work by now?"

"No, I'm good."

"Lydia, you do realize that you have a 'tell' when you lie, don't you?"

"What is it?"

"I'm not going to say, you'll try to correct it. What did the police department say? Are they extending your leave?"

She bit her bottom lip, the same one he had just been nibbling on.

"Goddammit, Lydia. Tell me you did not give up your job to come play nursemaid to me!" Clint thought his head might explode, both literally and figuratively.

"Honey, you need to calm down, your psychologist said that getting upset is one of the worst things you can do, it brings on the headaches."

Clint remembered what Dr. Emily Murphy said. He took a deep breath. Then another. And another again. It helped a little. He still wanted to dump Lydia's boss's boss into a live volcano, but the breathing exercise his psychologist had taught him helped.

He looked down to where Lydia was stroking his arm. "Come kiss me. That will help a lot," he grinned.

The door opened.

Clint let out a loud groan. "Foiled again."

Lydia laughed.

11

THE DOOR OPENED, AND LYDIA STOOD THERE HOLDING A plant. "I thought this would liven up your room."

"Why haven't Mom and Dad come and visited?" Clint stared at Lydia. She'd been keeping secrets from him again.

"They did," she sighed.

"What do you mean? I've been here for three weeks, and they haven't even bothered to come. Give me my phone. I want to call them."

"Four weeks," she corrected. "Your phone was destroyed in the blast. You can use mine." Lydia put down the plant, then reached into her purse so she could hand over her phone. She looked so defeated. It was an act. He knew it. She was on the doctor's side. Especially Emily Murphy. He hated her. He didn't need a goddamn psychologist.

He looked down at the phone and pressed in the area code for Colorado. His thumb hovered over the number four. But was the next number four or five? He couldn't remember. How could he not remember the telephone number to his parents' house? It was the home he grew up in.

"Clint, they're number six on my speed dial," she said quietly.

He wanted to ask her why he couldn't remember their number, but she would just report back to Emily, and it would be one more black mark against him. That's all they did, every one of them; spent hours figuring out ways to trip him up, to prove that he wasn't good enough.

Clint erased the area code, then scrolled down to his parents' name and called them. It went to voicemail.

"Hi, Mom. Hi, Dad. It's Clint. I was hoping to see you. When are you going to come visit me?"

Lydia's wince did not go unnoticed. Served her right, trying to lie to him. His parents would straighten things out. *They* would be on his side.

"Maybe this was a bad time to visit. Your physical therapist is due to arrive any minute now. Sometimes you don't like it when I'm here to see your PT sessions."

What is she talking about?

The door opened and a middle-aged man backed in with a walker.

"Ready for the gym, Chief?"

"You seem pretty chipper," Clint commented. What was his name? Clint recognized his face.

But what is his fucking name?

"I'm Sal. Short for Salvador. I'm here to make your life miserable." He winked at Clint.

"What day is it?" Clint glared at Lydia.

"Tuesday."

"No! What's the date?"

"December third." Now she was pretending to be hurt. *Yeah sure.* Like anything he did could hurt her. She didn't care anymore—that is, if she ever had.

Clint scanned his memory. He remembered it being late

summer. He looked toward the window, but the shades were closed. That window looked wrong.

"You're lying to me. Why are you lying?" he spat out.

"Hey, Man, go easy on the little lady. She's telling you the truth."

He looked over at Lydia again. Now her expression was shut down. She looked like she was made of marble. Wait a minute, was he wrong? Everything was so damned confusing. It had been since he'd woken up a half-hour ago. Then Lydia had walked in, and it seemed like he was looking at things through a funhouse mirror.

Sal's right, I'm out of line. I'm behaving like a horse's ass.

"I'm sorry, Lyd," he reached out his hand for her to hold it, but she didn't. His heart clenched. "I don't know what got into me. But seriously, how can it be December? How long have I been in the hospital? Have I been unconscious this entire time?"

Her jaw unclenched and he saw her relax just a little. "No, you've been conscious for the last four weeks."

"Huh?"

She can't be serious.

"You had one of your worst migraines ever, last night. Dr. Varma warned me that you would wake up disoriented. Just wait for another half-hour, and everything will come into focus." Her voice had softened just a little bit.

"Yep, then you'll remember me and hate me," Sal piped up.

He looked at the muscular man and something struck his memory chord. "Squats. I remember squats. And sit-ups. Lots and lots of sit-ups."

"There you go." Sal grinned.

"Then why in the hell did you bring in a walker?" Clint demanded to know. "If I'm doing squats, I sure as hell don't need a walker." Clint sat up in bed. He wanted to get out, but there were rails and he was hooked up to an IV.

"What the hell, Lydia? An IV? If I've been awake for four weeks, why would I need an IV?"

She came forward and tentatively touched his right hand before backing away again. He had a flash that it had been in a cast.

"Honey, don't push too hard, it'll come back. It always does."

"What do you mean by that? What's wrong with me?"

"You were injured overseas. It was bad. You were in a coma for five weeks. Now you're recovering here at Walter Reed."

Clint searched his jumbled brain and found the answer.

"Traumatic brain injury."

Lydia nodded.

Fuck.

"How bad?" he asked.

"It's not as bad as they first thought; you're doing amazingly well," Lydia gave a half-smile.

If I'm doing so great, why am I only getting half a smile?

"Define amazing? How can amnesia be amazing?" He couldn't help the sarcasm, or the frustration.

Sal laughed. "Kid, I always like your fighting spirit, no wonder you were a SEAL."

Clint froze. His skin turned to ice.

Were a SEAL?

Was?

His head turned so fast he thought he might break his neck as he glared at Lydia. "Tell me what the fuck is going on," his voice came out like cracking glass.

"He didn't mean anything by that," Lydia rushed to

assure him. "As a matter of fact, the team arrived stateside yesterday. Some of them are flying this way as we speak."

Clint sucked in a breath. The last time he could remember them on a mission was...was... When the fuck was it?

"I was injured overseas, wasn't I?"

Lydia nodded.

"Do you have any details?"

She shook her head.

Of course, she wouldn't, it would be classified.

I am losing my damned mind.

Clint looked over at Sal. Shit, he remembered him now. Good man. Marine Corps medic, served in the first Gulf War.

"I don't get it, why can I now remember you served in Desert Shield, Sal?"

"Yep, 2nd Marine Division," the older man said proudly. "Hell, Chief, you got your head unscrambled pretty darned quickly today. Probably because you want to stay sharp for your buddies."

Clint looked over at Lydia for reassurance.

She nodded.

"Sal, can I take a pass today? I need to talk to my Lady."

Sal looked at Clint, then over at Lydia. He got it.

Yep, he's a good man.

"Sure, sure. I'll see if you're up for it later this afternoon." He vacated the room taking the hated walker with him.

Clint held out his hand. Lydia walked over to him but didn't take it.

"You're mad at me. It's no fair holding it against me when my brain is swiss cheese and I don't know what asshole thing I've done."

Her eyes watered up.

"That was almost verbatim to what you said four days ago. I'm getting sick of that tired old line, Clint."

God, I must have really fucked up.

"Lydia, you know I love you and would never hurt you. Don't you? Please at least hold my hand."

He didn't know what he was going to do if she rejected him. He felt like she was his only life-line to reality at the moment. She was it, and he had done something to cut that cord.

Her hand trembled as she put it in his. He grabbed it; not *too* tight, but tight, nonetheless.

He took a deep breath. Trying to think. Trying to come up with anything that might bridge the gap, even though he was a few bricks short of a load.

"We've got to do better than this, Lydia. We're smarter than this. You're my Dork Queen, and once upon a time, before my brain turned into scrambled eggs, I was your Nerd King. So, a scrambled nerd and a shiny dork should be able to overcome a little brain injury. We can overcome whatever asshole move I made, because by the looks of things it was a hell of a lot more than miscommunication, right?"

She shrugged.

"Can't we come up with our own code, so we don't end up hurting one another day after day, week after week?"

A tear dripped down her cheek, but she didn't shake her head. She didn't nod. She didn't say a word.

"Give me something, Baby. I have to know how I'm fucking up. Maybe you make me tattoo it on my arm after I do it, then make me apologize on my knees, then I have to read it when I wake up again? How does that sound?" he cajoled.

Still nothing.

"Come on, Honey, what's going on?"

"It's a lot of little things," she said quietly. "I'm finding out you have a whole hell of a lot of pent-up bitterness and resentment built up against me. Knowing that, how can I help but think that deep down, deep *deep* down, you don't like or trust me." Her words were merely a whisper in the end.

Oh God.

"Is this true, or is this part of the injury? Because right here, right now, I've got to tell you I like and trust you more than my parents and my teammates."

Lydia barked out a laugh and pulled her hand out of his. "Yeah sure, that's why you were just saying you wanted to talk to your mom and dad so you could find out the truth."

Clint didn't know how to respond.

Lydia stood there with her arms crossed over her stomach, obviously trying to protect herself from harm. "Help me out here, Lydia. Let's start from the beginning. First, it's been about a half-hour now. I remember Mom and Dad coming. I even remember them telling me that I'm an uncle, which is way cool, by the way. So, I know you're not keeping anything from me."

Lydia shrugged her left shoulder. "Hmm, mmm."

"Next, I remember Dr. Varma, Sal, and the evil Emily Murphy who is my psychologist. How could something so mean be wrapped up in such a pretty package?" He rolled his eyes.

Lydia let out a little laugh. "You really have something against psychologists, don't you? I can't wait to hear you tell Finn about your aversion," she smirked, then it turned into a sad sigh.

Shit, I had her for a second.

Something pinged for Clint and he remembered his

teammate Finn needing not only a psychologist but a psychiatrist to help him with his post-traumatic stress disorder a few years ago. The man had not been thrilled to begin with, but in the end, he said they had helped him a lot. Oh, Christ, Finn had even needed meds. Clint had to stop himself from groaning out loud.

Okay, okay, at least I'm remembering shit. This is good.

Clint looked at the dark-haired beauty in front of him and wanted to weep. How could he have ever made Lydia Hildalgo, the woman he desperately wanted to make his wife, ever feel less than completely loved by him?

"Sweetheart, can you sit down next to me so we can get straight? From everything Dr. Murphy and Dr. Varma have had to say, this is a long road. I want to know how you feel about this."

Clint practically gagged on the words. As much as he needed to say those words. Ask those words, he wanted to scream and beg for Lydia to never leave him. He loved her down to his bones and not having her in his life would kill him. But, loving her down to his bones meant that he had to do what was right for this woman. Obviously, he had been hurting her. It was bad enough that he was literally fucked in the head, but if he was being an abusive asshole as well, then she was right to run.

She shook her head sadly. "You know how I feel about this, Clint. I've told you."

He patted the space beside him on the bed. "Sit down and tell me again."

He braced himself.

She sat and released her arms. One hand hovered over his chest until it landed as lightly as a butterfly. Then she stretched out her fingers, caressing him. Clint shut his eyes, savoring her touch, loving this feeling. Would it be his last?

"You are my heart. You have been for five years. But half the time you don't believe me. I can handle the TBI, I can. I understand there is going to be anger and paranoia. I have read all the literature, I've talked to Varma, Ivanhoe, and Murphy. I've talked to other spouses of men and women with traumatic brain injuries, and they've told me what I can expect. But what you're saying is different."

"How?" Clint asked as he softly pressed his hand on top of hers, holding her even closer as he looked into the brown depths of her eyes. She turned away, but with his other hand, he tilted her jaw back toward him. "What am I saying that's different? How am I pushing you away, Lydia?"

"You don't trust me. It's like you don't believe in our relationship. You keep bringing up that we're not married."

Clint picked up her hand from his chest and looked at her dainty fingertips. She was petite. She looked fragile, but her strength was unimaginable. He flashed back five years ago to when she was fighting for her life in the jungle. Like she was fighting for her life right now. His Lydia would always take the bull by the horns.

"And?" he asked.

"What do you mean?"

"That can't be all, not for how upset you are. What else is there?"

"It's everything."

He bit out a laugh. "Well, we've always known that there are times I've needed a personality transplant, maybe this is a good thing. Instead of being the class clown, I can be more serious like Darius. Or I can start doing more handyman types of things. I can learn from Mason's dad. Maybe I can become Finn's assistant coach at lacrosse. Can't you see me wrangling a bunch of twelve-year-olds?"

Lydia tried to extract her hand, but Clint wouldn't let her.

"What? If that's not it, what is it, Lydia? I'm flying blind here, ya gotta help me."

She stifled back a sob but let him keep her hand. "Clint, it's been more than that. If you were angry at everybody, that would be one thing." Then she hiccupped. "Okay, you're angry a lot, I grant you, but with me, you seem both angry and disappointed. I just don't get it, it's like I'm trying to bail out a sinking ship with my cupped hands. It's not working. I never knew we had such deep underlying problems."

"We don't, Babe. We don't."

Clint felt the panic skittering along every one of his nerve endings. What the fuck had he been saying? Doing? How could Lydia ever have been a disappointment to him? She was his own personal miracle. He'd come close to losing her to death too often for him to ever be disappointed in her.

"Clint?" She pulled back and cupped his face. He leaned forward.

"What? Tell me?"

"Honey, this is what I want you to tattoo on your arm. I want you to think long and hard about this. You need to figure out why you are angry and disappointed with me. I buy into the fact that we have your brain injury to deal with. I'm here for you. I'm not leaving 'til you're one hundred percent. But if after that this isn't working...I'm going to give you the freedom you seem to want."

He gripped her wrists, thankful that even in his state of raw terror, he was still careful with this precious woman. "Lydia, there's nothing. I swear it to you."

She leaned forward and pressed a kiss to his lips. "Honey, I truly believe that this is a good thing. Not that I would ever in my wildest dreams want you hurt, but I think there is something going on in your heart that is finally coming to the surface that you've only been able to speak about freely now."

"That makes no sense."

His head pounded. His vision was beginning to blur. If he had any sense it would be tears, but instead, he felt the edges of a migraine begin to scrape his eyeballs. He deserved as much pain as the world could throw at him for having hurt Lydia.

"Let me call for a nurse."

"I don't need one, we need to talk."

This time the kiss that she gave him wasn't placating, it was a smoldering temptation that reminded him of all that he needed to fight for. She was pleasure, laughter, and all that was good in the world. She slid one of her hands from his jaw to the back of his head to spear it through the short hair at the back of his neck. He winced and she felt it. She drew back.

"I'm calling a nurse," she said as she got up and left the room.

This time when his vision blurred, he was pretty sure it was tears.

12

DRAKE AVERY AND FINN CRANDALL WALKED INTO HIS ROOM as the second round of drugs was taking hold.

"Damn, guys. You're a sight for sore eyes." He laughed. His eyes were sore, so it was funny.

"Ah God, Finn. He's stoned." Drake dragged a chair close to Clint's bedside and sat next to his head. "For Fuck's sake, Archer, you were supposed to be better than this by now, what the hell? You've been here at Walter Reed almost five weeks.""

Clint laughed. That was Drake; he couldn't be tactful even if somebody paid him a million dollars and duct-taped his mouth. He laughed again.

"He's really stoned." Drake rolled his eyes.

"Just imagining you wish your moush duct-taped." Clint grinned.

"Doesn't sound stoned to me," Finn said drolly. "He actually sounds pretty with it. I wish your mouth was duct-taped shut on a regular basis." Drake shot a glare over his shoulder at Finn.

"So, what's been going on now that you're in the land of the living? Been getting any hospital nooky?"

"Jesus, Avery, just shut the hell up." Finn pushed forward and looked at Clint. Thank God he had received meds, otherwise, it would be disconcerting. Lydia had left hours ago, but the pain from the conversation still lingered.

"Thanks, Finn, I knew I could count on you."

"You look like shit. Happy and loopy because of good drugs, but I'd say life is not going your way."

Clint frowned. "Sures, my brain is mushy, Finn. My career is in the shitter. What the hell did you expects?" Hot damn, he hadn't slurred his words. He found the button beside his bed and pushed it so his head was lifted.

"I expected my friend, who is a freaking medical miracle, to be doing a little bit better," Finn said gently.

Two sets of eyes examined him, and it was ten times worse than whenever Emily looked at him. She might have the degree in psychology, but she didn't have the senses of a SEAL, and she'd never been in combat with him. These guys knew him down to the grit under his toenails. Nope, couldn't fool them, but he was damn well going to try.

"Half the time I can't remember what day it is. Then, I was asking Lydia why my parents hadn't visited when I woke up this morning. Of coursh, they'd already been here for a while before my lovely personality chased them back to Colorado."

"You taking a page out of my book?" Drake asked.

Finn gave Clint a long look.

"I thought you liked your parents. I mean if they were anything like mine, I could understand being a touch surly," Drake winked.

Like a shining beacon, Clint remembered everything that had happened with Drake's dysfunctional family from the eighth circle of hell. "You know, Avery, I always thought you were a little rough around the edges, but knowing where you come from, you're the freaking miracle, and those sisters of yours are angels."

Drake preened.

Finn continued to watch their byplay.

"Finn, you can stop staring at me anytime you'd like," Clint invited.

"I'm just standing here being entertained."

"Like hell," Clint said bitterly. Oops, he was talking too slow.

"Guess they didn't give you enough happy sauce. I thought you'd be glad to see the men who saved your ass."

Clint stared at them blankly. "Tell me what happened."

Both of their expressions turned serious. "It was a shitshow," Drake started. "We were in Syria and you got caught in a bomb explosion rescuing all of us. I really thought you'd bought the farm."

"Drake caught you, though," Finn chimed in.

Clint looked over at Drake who didn't change expression.

"Thank you," Clint said solemnly.

"You would have done the same thing. Only difference is, I would have had the decency to remember," Drake grinned.

"Fuck yous, Avery."

"So how bad is it, do you know yet, or are they telling you all the same crap they told me, way back when?" Finn stuck out his fingers and made quotes in the air, "It depends on how you progress, then we'll know." Finn grimaced. "Are you getting that kind of happy horseshit?"

"God, I wish they hadn't topped the tank with meds before you came, then I could talk about this with my whole half a brain I have left. But yeah, thash pretty much what they're saying."

Drake reached into his jacket pocket and pulled out some papers. From what Clint could see it looked like printed-out e-mails. "Not for nothing, but we pulled some strings with Dex over at Black Dawn. He got some of the real scoopage, if you're interested."

Clint struggled to sit up even straighter.

"Hell yeah, I wantz that." But he realized that as he had sat up straighter, he got woozier. "Ah shit, these meds are going to put me out for the count, realz soon. Can you come back? I want to hear about Mason and Sophia too. I figure that's why he's not here, right?"

Finn and Drake nodded at the same time. Clint let his head drop back down onto the pillows and instantly regretted it as he let out a moan.

"Does any of Dex's info tell you what I have to accomplish to get the fuck out of here?"

"Yep, it's spelled out. We can get your ass back to California if you can hit certain benchmarks. According to what Dex has found you're not excelling at the ADLs, you're not always oriented. Apparently, when you are conscious, you're pushing too hard, and that's probably causing you setbacks. What a surprise, you're your own worst enemy."

Clint tried to take in what they were saying, but it was too much.

"Then there's Lydia. I've got to figure her out."

He couldn't stop the yawn that overtook him. He wasn't going to last. He really wanted to hear more.

"What?" Finn asked. "What about Lydia?"

"She's broken. Or I'm broken. I don't know. I need to fix it."

"That can't be right, Clint. You guys are solid," Drake said emphatically.

Clint tried to shake his head, but it wouldn't move.

"Need to unbreak us."

He closed his eyes so he could remember his train of thought, but it never came back to him.

———

"I'LL SEE you in the morning, Sweetheart. Right now, I'm going to go FaceTime with Karen and the kids," Drake said as he left the booth. He threw down far too much cash. Lydia would have objected, but she'd just be wasting her breath.

"You are such a softie," Lydia teased as she reached up to kiss Drake's cheek.

"Don't tell anyone, it'll ruin my rep."

"Bullshit. As soon as we saw you with your younger sisters, excluding Evie, we all knew you had a heart of gold."

Lydia watched as he blushed. Rylie would have loved it if she had still been here, but she'd gone back to California early. There'd been an issue with her young charge Georgie that she needed to handle.

"If you two need to go on up too, that's fine. I'll just stay here and do a catch-up on my laptop," Lydia smiled at Finn and Angie.

Finn draped his arm around the back of the booth behind Angie and sat back. "Nope, I'm enjoying myself. It's nice to spend time in the normal world."

Lydia gave an inward sigh of relief. Truth be told, she didn't want to be alone. She'd talked to Beth a little bit, but her sister had her hands full right now. Maybe she'd tell her more now that Jack had come home to the ranch. Then there was Sophia, another good friend who she would normally lean on, but she was struggling with her pregnancy. If anything, Lydia was always calling her trying to keep her spirits up.

Who the hell was she kidding, the person she relied on the most in this world, was Clint. They were the Nerd King and the Dork Queen. They'd been solid for five years. He was her best friend. She didn't just love the man, he was her soulmate. But finding out she wasn't his, was killing her.

But let's get real, I did this to myself. I'm so sick of being alone with my own pitiful thoughts. Thank God Angie and Finn are here to keep me occupied tonight.

"So, Clint was teasing me about possibly being your assistant lacrosse coach, what do you think?" Lydia asked.

Finn laughed. So did Angie. Their response was so immediate that even though Lydia agreed with them, she kind of took offense. "Why couldn't he be? He's good with kids. Look how he was with Billy when he was growing up. Let's not forget how he is with Rylie and Dare's kids."

Finn took a sip of his lemonade. "There's no question that the kids would think he was the man. He'd do great with them."

"So why the laughter?"

"He's too competitive," Finn's grin was rueful. "You have to be willing to let the kids lose. Don't get me wrong—he would never come down hard on the kids, but he'd try every angle possible to make sure the team won, and it would suck a lot of the fun out of it for the kids. What's more, they have to learn how to lose, and lose well. It's part of what this is all about."

Lydia frowned. It was a dog-eat-dog world out there; personally, she felt it was important for kids to learn how to come out on top.

Finn chuckled.

"She's doing it too, you can see her thinking of ways to win," Angie said to Finn. "That's why you and Clint are perfect for one another. You can't handle the thought of losing either, can you?"

"Not really," Lydia admitted.

"That's what makes you such a damn good cop," Angie said.

"So, you're a private investigator, are you telling me you ever set out to lose?" Lydia asked.

"Absolutely not." Angie agreed. "I go for the win every single time. I'm still pissed about some things that happened years ago. But, because of my dad, and Pops especially, they taught me how to get past that. I couldn't have stayed in business if I hadn't learned to let things go. Anyway, I thought you were getting into yoga and meditation?"

"That was to help me calm down and focus. In Cyber Crimes I would get hit with so many cases, and so much data coming in on a daily basis that I needed a way to relax and give my lizard brain a chance to process some of it. Yoga and meditation were key."

"So, you didn't get into any of the spirituality aspects?" Finn asked.

"I was raised Catholic. My parents go to Mass on Sundays and Wednesdays. Beth and I were raised in a very strict household, but then to find out he was working for a drug cartel, it really disillusioned me. How could a man who preached such devotion do something like that? How could he think to betray us like that? How could he use us like that?"

Finn stilled.

"Use you?" he asked quietly.

Lydia realized she'd said too much. "I mean allowing us to get caught up in his crimes," Lydia covered.

"I knew he was money laundering for the cartel, but he ended up testifying against them, didn't he?" Angie asked.

Lydia nodded.

"Are you talking about being targeted and left in the jungle? Are you talking about Berto coming after Beth when he came across her at your father's office?" Finn asked.

She nodded mutely.

"You don't blame him for that, do you?" Angie asked.

Lydia gave the slightest shake of her head, lying to her friends.

She had to leave it at that.

But she'd heard the words her father had said at the trial. He'd said: "The men who worked for Guzman had to do whatever he said. If they didn't, they would be tortured and killed. Their family would be tortured and killed. It didn't matter what they demanded. You did it."

Those words had stuck with her, and she suspected the worst. No, she'd *known*. She was sure that he had offered up Beth to be sexually abused at sixteen to save his own life. His perfidy knew no bounds. But Lydia had never confronted him, sticking her head in the sand. Because then she'd have to act, then it would become a family matter. And her mother would be involved. Lydia would die if her mother forgave her father, or worse yet, stood by him. So, she tamped down these thoughts into the smallest compartment of her soul, and she could go months without thinking about it. But having this secret would sometimes eat at her in the middle of the night, like a beetle boring into her ear with its sharp mandibles nipping and snapping, going so deep she could never get it out. She'd wake up in a cold sweat, praying that

Clint wouldn't notice. If she told him, he would know just what a coward she was. How deeply she had betrayed her oath as an officer of the law, her sister, and their relationship.

"Lydia, you're so pale. Are you all right?" Angie asked with concern.

Lydia looked down and grabbed at the empty straw wrapper and nodded quickly. She tilted her head so she could rub her ear against her shoulder.

The waitress came to the table. "Would you like your bill, or would you like to look at the dessert menu?" she asked.

"Dessert." Finn smiled easily as he took the proffered menu.

"I'll be back in a bit."

Lydia took that time to smile. She wasn't going to go down that road with Finn and Angie. She'd stick to the easy stuff, like lacrosse, yoga, Finn's PTSD. Hell, she'd even be happy to talk about spirituality. Anything but why she knew her father was destined for hell. She put on a false smile and put down her dessert menu.

"I'm going for the berry pie. I know it won't be as good as anything that Sophia would make, but it'll remind me of home."

"I'll second that," Finn said as he put his menu down.

"I'm all about the chocolate decadent cake," Angie grinned. "I can't resist chocolate."

"Finn, Clint told me you did a lot of things to cope when you were on leave. I'm wondering if you'd mind sharing some of those things with me. I think Clint's in for a longer haul than he realizes." Lydia tore at the paper straw wrapper.

"Sure, I'll tell you anything you want to know. Angie told

me that she's been explaining things from her point of view, which I think is great."

That was a relief.

"Rationally I get that Clint is subject to mood swings, emotional outbursts, a whole gamut of emotions. Hell, I'd really be screwed if he went the blank-slash-apathy route. I can't imagine a life with Clint stonewalling me. But he's angry, intolerant, depressed, and anxious."

"Is he verbally abusive?" Finn asked gently.

"I wouldn't go that far." Lydia tore some more of the wrapper.

"How far would you go? I'm not taking sides. I just want to get a clear picture."

Something was soothing about Finn's voice, it made you want to listen and respond. Emily Murphy could learn a thing or two from him.

"He doesn't yell." Lydia stopped. "At least not at me."

"Does it scare you when he yells?"

"Hell no. A man raising his voice is no big deal. That happens all the time at the precinct," Lydia scoffed.

"I'm sure they do, but Lydia, I don't remember Clint ever being a yeller."

Her shoulders fell. He was right. Sure, Clint would bark out commands when the situation warranted it, but yell for no reason? Nope, that wasn't him.

"No," she said slowly, "he was never a yeller. Even when I was in danger and he was worried, he would keep it together."

"So, it doesn't bother you that he's yelling now?"

Lydia looked up at Finn under her lashes.

"Fine, it does. It bothers me. Even when it isn't directed at me."

As soon as the words were out of her mouth, she knew

she'd fucked up. But Finn didn't make it a gotcha moment; he let her sit with her words. Lydia was thankful when the desserts arrived. It gave her even more time to think.

"Finn. Angie. I don't want you to think badly of Clint. Please don't. He's still the best man I know." She pointed her fork at Finn, "Except for you. You're tied with Clint."

Finn nodded solemnly.

"His moods are all over the place. But it isn't the yelling, which has only happened a couple of times to me. He saves most of it for his docs. No, it's the killer remarks. He knows how to cut me up with just one sentence. I try to grin and bear it and put it down to his injury, but it's getting to the point that I can't anymore."

Again, Finn didn't ask anything further. He understood that if she wanted to divulge more, she would have.

"See, this is why I wanted you to talk to Finn," Angie chimed in. "He couldn't pull that with me, because as he was dealing with his issues, we were just meeting. So, we didn't have a history where he knew all my pressure points."

"But I did resent her at times, because I found myself relying on her." Finn rubbed the back of Angie's neck and she arched into his touch. Lydia felt envious. "But Lydia, nine times out of ten, she was my touchstone. Clint's in early days."

"It seems like forever." She put down her fork, her stomach too upset to eat anymore.

"Are you seeing anyone?" Angie asked gently. "You need some moral support. Not that we won't be here for you. We will, always. But right now, you could benefit from a counselor who supports spouses of TBI victims, or a support group."

Lydia leaned back in the booth and rested her head. She'd really been hoping for a magic bullet from Finn, since he had gone through so much, and come out the other side. And she wanted to go to a psychologist as much as Clint did. Which was *not*! She'd had to do it after the trauma of her beating at the hands of the cartel, but she'd found Clint's words, his arms, his support had been what *truly* healed her. Now *he* was the problem.

"We've done some snooping," Finn said as he pulled a sheaf of papers out of his jacket pocket. "A lot of this is just bullshit, but this page has the meat." He handed her the page he had indicated.

Lydia began to read this over. Someone had hacked Clint's medical records and the doctor and psychologist's notes. If she had been on her game, she would have done that herself. Where the hell had her brain been? She had been relying on the little bit they had been telling her, instead of going directly into their files. That's what she always did. When had she become that trusting?

Her eyes widened when she got to the part that Clint was basically fouling up his own recovering by pushing too hard. She laughed.

"What?" Angie asked.

"Trust my man to be pushing too hard, and fucking himself over," Lydia said as she shook her head in disbelief. "Why the hell hasn't Murphy just been upfront with him? Just how sensitive does she think he is?"

"I still don't understand," Angie said.

"A lot of the reasons for his setbacks and migraines are because he will force himself to stay awake and work so hard to remember. If I know Clint, he's probably sweet-talked someone to give him some electronics, which is a big ole no-no." She shoved the paper back at Finn. "I'm going to kill him. And Emily Murphy. If Clint knew—"

"He does," Finn interrupted her. "Drake showed him

this today. We got the report from Dex from the Black Dawn SEAL team when we arrived stateside. He didn't know you well enough to give it to you."

"Well, he better get to know me, because if he keeps another goddamn thing from me, I'll rip off parts that he would hate to part with."

Angie snorted. "You can say dick, it won't offend me."

Lydia rolled her eyes. "Seriously, Finn, I've been an ass not doing this kind of hacking myself."

"Cut yourself some slack, Lydia," Finn said gently. "You've been in the thick of things. What's more, your major support system, Beth and Sophia, have had their hands full. If I had to guess, you're still trying to be there for *them.* Am I right?"

Lydia rubbed the back of her neck.

"Not going to answer that, huh?" he smiled.

"It has been a lot. I just want him to get better." She looked up at the stained ceiling of the restaurant. "I want to take him home to California."

Finn reached out and touched her hand that was resting on the table. "You do realize that's not going to happen, right? Home's still a stretch. Darius is checking out good rehabilitation centers in Southern California. They're mostly for people with real physical and cognitive issues. I'm not sure there is something for Clint's situation. He's looking for centers that will allow for spouses, but those are few and far between."

Lydia shuddered at that word. "I'm not his spouse," Lydia said emphatically. Clint had made it perfectly clear that she wasn't his wife.

"Finn meant to say loved ones. It won't matter if you're his fiancée or wife," Angie chimed in.

"I'm not sure he's going to want me there," Lydia admitted in a whisper.

Finn looked shocked. "Of course, he is. I know that I'd be lost without Angie, and Clint's the same way about you. You have to know that, Lydia."

"Not lately." She couldn't look at the couple across from her.

Finn squeezed her hand tighter.

"All the more reason for you to be there with him."

"Unless..." Angie started. "Unless *you* don't want to be there."

Lydia shut her eyes.

Do I? Shut up, of course I do. And the big baby will just have to put up with me.

"Clint has been a royal ass, hasn't he?" Finn growled.

"No, he hasn't. It's the injury," Lydia protested.

"Yeah, I get that. But I know my friend. With enough time, with the right tools, medicine, and patience on his part, he has a big shot of pulling himself together. It'll take time and concentration, but he can do it. I talked to him today. He's willing to put in the work. He needs to focus."

"The doctors say not to expect too much," Lydia cautioned Finn. "He's never going to be the man I fell in love with. This is my new Clint."

"He is never going to be a man who emotionally hurts you. This is an anomaly, I know it. Just wait and see."

13

CLINT HAD WOKEN UP TIRED, AND THIS TIME HE DIDN'T PUSH through. He rolled over and went back to sleep. When he woke up again, he felt more rested than he had since being in this ugly-assed room. He pulled the cell phone out from his pillowcase and realized it was ten fifty in the morning. He was so going to owe the janitor big-time when he was released.

The wireless internet connection was crap, but he still could catch some of the current news. Lots going on overseas, but even more going on in Washington. There was a senator who was trying to make a name for himself who kept catching his eye. He gave Clint the creeps.

The screen began to swim in front of him, and he felt the beginning of a headache. He powered off the phone and shoved it back in hiding. Any minute the nurse would be in for her hourly vitals check. She'd also want to know if he was oriented, and with the couple of hours of extra rest, he'd nail it today!

The door opened.

"Good morning, Chief. You slept later than normal, but I

see you're upright and bright-eyed. This is a nice change. You ready for the barrage of questions?"

"Hit me."

"What is today's date?"

"December thirteenth."

"That's one," the nurse smiled. "Let's see if you can do another. Where are you?"

"Bethesda, Maryland, which was always where I wanted to vacation, right after Fiji. Specifically, Walter Reed Medical Center."

"That's two," she held up two fingers. Can you tell me who some of your visitors were in the last couple of days, and who your doctors are?"

"My fiancée, Lydia Hildalgo. Two teammates of mine, Finn Crandall, and somebody who probably flirted with you, a big guy by the name of Drake Avery."

"Yes, he did indeed," she grinned. "And your doctors?"

"Ivanhoe, Varma, and Murphy."

"You just passed with flying colors. If it weren't for the strain around your eyes, I would say everything was perfect. How bad is your pain?"

"What pain?" Clint asked innocently.

"Don't bullshit a bullshitter, Chief. How long have you been up? Were you practicing your answers before I came in?"

"Nope, not me. I was sleeping."

What eye strain? Did the phone do that?

She came closer to the monitors. "Well, your blood pressure looks good, so does your pulse. How's your pain?"

"I'm not in pain," he lied.

"On a scale of one to ten?"

"Zero."

"Want to try that again?"

"Three."

She stared at him. He stared back. Finally, he lifted his pinky. "This has been hurting. Don't know why. Maybe this is at a four."

"God save me from Special Forces. I'm going to call your fiancée; she wanted to know when you're awake. I don't know if she's coming or she's going to send Handsome over. It's a win either way."

She gave a cheeky grin as she left the room.

Clint pulled out the cell phone, pulled up the internet, and started doing some real research on TBIs, something he should have been doing a week ago, ever since his vision had improved.

I'm an idiot.

Yep. Blue light and screen time totally contributed to migraines. Small screens were extremely detrimental. Clint sighed. As per his usual, he made a quick decision; he'd use the phone up until he felt just a niggle of a headache coming on, then he'd stop. He needed to keep up with the outside world. He needed to find out as much as he could about his kind of brain injuries so he could be more participatory in his recovery. He'd be damned if he would continue to have these goddamn mood swings that would hurt Lydia.

It was probably twenty minutes later that he heard Drake outside yakking it up with one of the nurses. Finn would be coming in first. The door swung open. There he was, Mr. Calm Cool and Collected.

Anger hit.

The bastard. That used to be me!

Finn laughed. "And here I had heard you were in a good mood."

"What are you talking about? I'm in a great mood!"

Finn pulled up a chair as he chuckled. "Yeah, I'll let Drake know when he comes in. So, what has your tail in a twist?"

"Nothing. I'm fine. As a matter of fact, I'm pretty damned happy to see you again. I'll even be happy to see Drake's ass," Clint bit out.

"Yeah, your voice sounds like it. Why in the hell are you trying to hide it from me of all people? I've been in your shoes."

"No, you haven't! Yours was all psychological, mine's actual brain damage. I've read about it. We don't know just how much trauma my brain has sustained, and whether I'll ever be able to control my mood swings. Yours was just you pulling up your big girl panties and sucking it up!"

"You're a real asshole, you know that?" Drake shook his head in disgust as he walked in the door. "Maybe your memory of four years ago is gone too, huh, man? Finn had to drag himself back from hell. It was guts and determination. You were one of the guys on his side who helped him fight back those devils. And here you are making light of it. I take it back—you're not an asshole, you're a prick."

Drake turned to Finn. "Let's get the hell out of here."

Finn sighed. "You're so easy, Avery. Now get in here, shut the door, and let's have a reasonable conversation."

"Not with this dick, no way."

"Did you not read any of the info that Dex put together? And for that matter, how about you, Archer?" Finn turned to Clint. "Did you? Because Drake's right, you are being kind of dickish."

Did the man have to smile? Or sound reasonable? Or sound actually nice? Bastard.

"So, what set you off when I walked in?" Finn's question

was reasonable, but Clint didn't want to answer, because if he did, he'd sound pretty fucking petty.

"You did. You were so smooth, and I remembered being the calm one. It pissed me off that I'm not anymore, so I got mad at you."

"Reasonable," Finn nodded.

"What the fuck are you talking about?" Drake demanded to know. "He was wiping the floor with you. That was not reasonable. He was a dick of epic proportions."

"No, I *have* a dick of epic proportions, get it right," Clint smirked.

Finn laughed. "At least you still have a sense of humor. That's good. You're going to need it. Now, do you want to blow this chicken coop, or not?"

Clint leaned forward. "You bet I do."

"Then come clean. What are you doing to aggravate your headaches and your moods? How did you go from chipper to an asshole in the space of a half-hour? According to the nurse you slept in, and you weren't in too much pain. You also passed your orientation questions. So, give."

Clint thought about it and made a decision. He reached behind him into his pillowcase and pulled out the cheap phone.

Finn raised his eyebrow.

Drake shook his head. "Dumb as a fucking rock. Like Dex said, you're your own worst enemy. Now give that to me," Drake said as he swiped it out of Clint's hand.

"No wonder you're hurting Lydia's feelings." Finn's voice was soft.

"Leave Lydia out of this. I know what I'm doing."

"Sure you do," Drake derided. "Just like I knew what I was doing with Karen. I'm damn lucky she agreed to marry me."

"Truth," Clint and Finn said simultaneously.

"Again, they don't think this is a debilitating brain injury based on how cognitively aware you were when you woke up. They did an MRI in Germany. There were some organic issues, but they want to compare the MRI they plan to take four months from then. They want to see if there is more deterioration, that will tell the big picture," Finn explained.

"Hell, of course there are some organic issues. You were always kind of a health nut who ate organic food. Add that to the blast that blew you sideways and there you go," Drake piped up. "What can you remember of the mission?"

"Nothing. Not a damn thing. You said Syria, right?"

Both men nodded.

"So, are you going to fill me in or not?"

"It was just another clusterfuck with wings," Drake said. "Some senator had a bug up his ass to interview a Kurdish rebel, and even more, try to broker some kind of peace deal with al Assad."

"Are you shitting me?" Clint couldn't believe the stupidity.

"Exactly."

"The senator's name wouldn't be, Leonard, would it?" Clint asked.

"Is the mission coming back to you?" Drake asked excitedly. "They never thought that would be a possibility."

"No." Clint tipped his head toward the phone that Drake was still holding. "I read something about the ass, and for some reason, his name tripped a switch with me."

"Well, your instincts were spot on, that's the guy, all right." Drake pulled out his own phone and started a search.

Clint turned to Finn. "So, what else happened? Give me deets."

"It was just supposed to be a normal extraction. Six

civilians. Like you surmised, Senator Leonard was one of them. Three of his aides and two reporters. Unfortunately, al Assad had just done a major push against the Kurds in Idlib, which is where they were, so we had a shit-ton of Kurds looking to get to Turkey. It was a mess. Meanwhile, these six were embedded like a tick on a hound. The senator wasn't leaving until he had a meet with Kurdish rebels, preferably higher-ups."

"Yeah, that should have been easy," Clint said sarcastically.

"He fell into it with an aide and a reporter. Meanwhile, the other two aides and reporter were separated. We had to babysit them while finding the senator."

"Lovely."

"You were in charge of communications and found out we had a Syrian terrorist group headed our way." Finn continued.

"Just what we needed," Drake said grimly. "They were armed with anti-aircraft guns on their trucks."

"We needed to round up everybody and get the hell out of there," Finn explained.

"Yeah, and I got stuck babysitting the demon-spawn aide from hell. I've never met a bigger douche-bag. Anyway, Mason, Darius, and you ended up finding where the senator was meeting with the rebels just when he had a gun to his head. The three of you managed to get him the hell out of there, by magic."

Clint snorted at Drake's description.

"You hightailed it back to Drake when you realized how close the trucks were. You wanted to help him. God knows why," Finn winked.

"Don't tell me—it was that stupid move that got me in this hospital bed."

Drake held up his hands. "Whoa, whoa, whoa. I would have done the same thing to save your sorry ass," he grumbled.

"So, what happened?"

"You decided to do the hero bit. You faked out the anti-aircraft guns, had them pointing to one building that you were on, so Drake and the civilians could make their escape from the building next to it. Hotshot that you are, you figured you could jump from that building to the one Drake was on, but they fired. Somehow, because you have the luck of all the Norse Gods on your side, you got one foot onto the roof, and Drake was able to drag you all the way onto it."

"Seems to me, Drake's the hero."

"Hell, I wouldn't have been alive to save your ass if it hadn't been for you. Nope, you won the sweepstakes. Could have done without saving Deadwood, though." Drake held out his phone and handed it to Clint. At least it had a larger screen than the one he'd been using. He saw a picture of some balding, squinty-eyed guy who seemed full of himself. There was something about his eyes.

"He's shifty. I wouldn't trust him," Clint said as he passed back the phone. "Should he mean something to me?"

Drake sighed. "I was hoping he would. He's the aide that caused so many problems for us. He was shifty, all right. He'd sell out his grandmother for an interview on any network. He was taking video of us, and here he is a member of a senator's staff. He knows the rules—no filming a SEAL. But he was trying to film us anyway."

"Did he get away with it?"

"Nah, we stopped him. We destroyed both of his phones."

Clint nodded in appreciation. Having their faces

recognized almost had all of them killed not so long ago. He rubbed his temple.

"Good one, Drake," Finn glared at the big guy.

"What?"

"You just confiscated Clint's phone, but you had him looking at yours. Look at him, you can tell a headache is brewing."

"Fine, he'll be an asshole, we can cope," Drake grinned. "Bring your worst, Clint."

"Lydia's going to show up; you want him taking out his mood swing on her?" Finn chastised.

"Quit talking about me like I'm not in the room. I'm not going to turn into Mr. Hyde."

"Maybe. Maybe not. You still don't know what's going to happen. That's the problem. Take it from somebody who knows." Finn smiled kindly.

"I'm. Not. Going. To. Turn. Into. The. Hulk." Clint ground out. He was getting really pissed.

"Look at him, do you see him turning green?" Drake laughed. "Any minute his hospital jammies will split open."

"Shut the fuck up, Drake. I really don't need your shit right now, feel free to leave!" Clint grabbed the rail of the bed so hard it shook as he pointed at the door.

"See what he's doing, Finn?" Drake shook his head in pity.

Clint grappled with the mechanism that would lower the rails.

"Clint," Finn said softly. "Take a deep breath."

"Fuck you, Crandall."

The bed rail lowered. His hand slipped as he tried to get out of bed. Drake caught him and struggled to lie him back against the pillows as Clint raged.

Finn stood to the side of Drake. "Do you want the nurses

to see this? It'll put back your chances of discharge." Again, Finn's tone was calm and reasonable as he touched the middle of Clint's chest. "Take a deep breath. You don't want to be angry."

Clint looked from Finn to Drake and back again. He was confused and pissed off.

"It's going to be all right, man." Drake's voice was solemn. "One easy breath. You can do it."

Clint's mouth was as dry as a desert, but he took a shallow breath and held it.

"Good. Now, exhale slowly," Finn urged.

He tried, he really did, but it came out as one big gasp.

"Try again, but inhale through your nose."

Clint did what Finn said, inhaling through his nose, then slowly exhaling through his mouth. He kept focusing on Finn's calm tone of voice as he had him do it again and again and again.

"Better now?" Finn asked.

"What do you mean?" Clint asked.

"Are you angry?"

"About what?"

"Dude, you were about ready to go ten rounds with me." Drake looked at him bewildered.

"Shut the hell up, Drake," Finn said in the same calm voice he'd been using as he told Clint to breathe in and out. "How do you feel, Clint?"

Clint racked his brain. "Disoriented." He looked down at his jumbled sheets and the bed rail. Then it came back to him. But he wasn't angry. Instead, he was remembering what was said dispassionately. "Sorry, guys, I was out of line."

"Happens," Drake said as he sat back down.

Clint closed his eyes, then looked upwards. "But for

pity's sake. It took two of you to get me under control. What happens when it's just Lydia?"

"That's where you come in," Finn said. "You're going to have to become more aware of what is going on and come up with some safe words that people can say to you that will stop you in your tracks. It's going to take training and a lot of time and patience."

"I can't do this to Lydia. I can't."

"She's going to be the most important person in your recovery," Finn disagreed.

"She's going to be the biggest victim," Clint said wearily. "She needs to stay away. How am I going to tell her?"

14

"Finn said to wait for him here."

Lydia was frustrated. It seemed like everybody was telling her what she should and shouldn't do. She didn't have control of anything in her life. She was currently suspended from her job, or on leave, it was totally up in the air. Her mother was a basket case. The only two things going right were that Mason was home to support Sophia, and Jack was home with Beth. She hated to admit it, but that took some of the heat off her because she'd been trying to encourage them from afar when her life was going down the toilet.

"Honey? Did you hear me?" Angie gently touched her shoulder.

It took everything Lydia had not to shrug it away. "I'm sorry, I was in my own little world, what did you say?"

"Finn has some ideas that he wants to run by you before you go and visit Clint this afternoon."

"Angie, I already feel bad enough, not having been there this morning."

She'd stayed up 'til four in the morning, so that's why she got up so late. Even though she was on suspension, that didn't mean she was leaving all the victims to fend for themselves. There was one woman who was being cyberstalked by her stepfather and it was escalating. Nobody but Lydia was taking it seriously, so even with just her laptop, she was doing her best to stay on the trail. She needed to get home to her real computer set-up where she could really dig in.

There was one other case that was giving her the heebie-jeebies. It was a family that had all of their social media accounts hacked and taken over by someone calling themselves Satan. Then this person had taken over their phones and last she'd checked, they had been streaming satanic videos on-line on their TV. Lydia was close to finding out where the breach had started. Now that was something the Cyber Crimes Unit was working on, but they hadn't gotten as far as Lydia had. She had to bring in some of her hacker friends, STAT.

"Lydia. I'm glad you're still here," Finn said as he walked through the sliding glass doors of the hotel lobby.

"Would someone please tell me what is going on?" She was tired, and one cup of coffee had not gotten the job done. She couldn't understand why people were trying to keep her away from Clint. She saw Drake over Finn's shoulder. He tipped his chin in her direction.

"Why don't we go sit down," Finn suggested, pointing to a secluded section of chairs near a fireplace.

"I'll get you another cup of coffee," Angie offered. "How about you two, want one?"

"I'd kill for one," Drake said.

"Tea for me, Honey." Finn gave her a loving smile.

As soon as they sat down, Lydia spoke. "Will somebody please tell me what in the Sam Hill is going on, before I have Angie bust a cap in your knee?"

Drake chuckled. "I suppose that's directed at me, since Angie probably won't shoot her husband."

"I don't care who talks, as long as someone does, and that it makes sense." She could hear the waver in her voice, and she didn't like it. But there was nothing she could do to stop it.

Finn leaned forward and rested his forearms on his knees. "Lydia, Drake, and I just got back from the hospital," he began.

"Tell me something I don't know."

"Clint is becoming more consciously aware of his mood swings."

"What does that mean?" she asked.

"Well, when he turns into a raging asshole, and I hold him down and Finn tells him to take deep breaths, he gets his head back into the game pretty fast."

"Was that your attempt at being funny, Drake? Because if so, it failed." Lydia glared at the man who was as big as her brother-in-law, Jack Preston, without the tact.

"Unfortunately, that's pretty much how it came down, Lydia," Finn said calmly.

She turned to him and wanted to cry. They couldn't be talking about her man. Clint wouldn't be in such a rage that he needed to be held down. She'd seen him cutting and abusive, but not getting physical.

Liar.

Lydia shook her head. She didn't want to dwell on facts. She wanted to live in an alternate universe. She was good at that. Right now, she wanted things the way they used to be.

If not that, she wanted things the way they should and would be in four months. She didn't like this reality.

She sucked in a deep gasp.

"Just tell me, Finn."

"Drake and I kept him calm before the hospital staff could get involved. I'm not sure that was the best thing, though. They might release him to a rehabilitation center before he's ready, and then he'll end up failing."

"He wants out of the hospital, and I want him out of the hospital. Jack's already lined up a rehab place in Palm Desert that sounds perfect for him that would work on his physical and mental issues. They would determine if he needs inpatient or outpatient treatment. It's outside of the Navy Insurance benefits, and Lord knows my bennies are precarious. But Jack is footing the bill. From what I've read on-line this place sounds perfect for Clint."

Drake pulled out his phone. "What's the name of it?"

"Desert Vista Renewal."

"Sounds like some girly spa, where you get your nails done," Drake protested.

"Shut up and Google it," Finn gave Drake a dark look.

"If it's outpatient, there's a place nearby where we would stay. It's perfect, because we would each get individual counseling as well as shared counseling. He would get all the therapy he needs. Even if it's inpatient, I would still get the counseling."

"But you would be alone with him at night, right, if it's outpatient?" Drake winced.

"What's wrong with that?" Lydia demanded to know.

"That's what we wanted to share with you. His rage was out of line. He was like Jekyll and Hyde. If it took the two of us to get him calmed down, how are you going to manage it?" Drake wanted to know.

"It didn't take two of us," Finn protested. "You kept pressing his buttons. You could have helped calm the situation down so that it didn't escalate, Drake."

"So, what you're saying is that Drake fucked with him, and as long as I handle things right there won't be any problem?" Lydia glared at Drake.

Both men looked uncomfortable.

"What?" she asked as she looked between the two of them. They were silent.

"Just spit it out. I don't have time for this. I want to get to the hospital and see Clint."

"Lydia," Finn started. "When I was in the real throws of a PTSD episode, I didn't know where I was, or what was reality. I'm not saying it's the same thing for Clint, but he's feeling totally out of control. He's been trained to fight or fight. There is very little flight in his repertoire. So, his normal mode is aggression, not tears. That's the normal way his moods are going to manifest. Unfortunately, that aggression is going to be pointed at whoever is around at the moment. If you're with him all the time, that's going to be you."

"I'm a cop. I can handle it." There was no way she was going to show either of them anything but a strong front.

Finn looked up and stood. Lydia looked over her shoulder. Finn helped Angie pass out the hot beverages, and then settled her into another chair.

"So, what'd I miss," she asked in a cheery voice. She was totally faking it. Lydia knew her friend could feel the tension in the air.

"All we're saying, Lydia, is that he's a keg of dynamite, and he might continue to be so for more than a minute. You staying at this posh place in Palm Desert together might not be the best thing ever." Drake's eyes were kind.

Lydia blinked fast. When even Drake's words were soft and compassionate, she had to be worried.

"I told you I can handle it. I just need some ideas. Some tools and direction. Everything I've read said that he'd do better with his support system there with him. I am *not* going to let him down."

"The docs aren't being real upfront about when they intend to let him go, right?" Finn asked.

She nodded.

"Well, Dex's been doing some more snooping. Here's the deal. If he can spend another week acing his ADLs, having his pain levels handled by just prescribed meds, and no more *episodes*." Finn put air quotes around the last word. "Then he can be released as early as the end of next week."

Lydia thought her face would split in two with how wide her smile was. "That's great news!" All of her concerns went out the window with the thought of Clint coming home to California. "I just know that he'll do better when he's out of the hospital. I know it."

"It's still a big *if*, Lydia," Drake warned. "I think number one and two will be easy as long as he gets enough rest. But number three is going to be tough."

"What set him off today?" Lydia wanted to know.

"Basically nothing. It was Finn's attitude. Clint said he didn't like how calm he was. Said that used to be him."

She tried to assimilate that. Everyone was quiet as she processed Drake's words. "I know I'm supposed to be expecting illogical behavior from him. But that takes the cake. I don't know what to say."

"It's nuts. That's the word you're looking for." Drake took another sip of his coffee and studied her over the rim of his cup. "Now do you see what you're going to be dealing with?"

"They will have people at the facility to help me."

"But you're not going to be at the facility, you're going to be spending nights together at the hotel nearby," Finn reminded her.

"Clint would never hurt me."

"My gut says he wouldn't either," Finn said. "But I want more than my gut. I'd say he's two months away from being ready to spend days and nights with you, Lydia, no matter what the program suggests."

Lydia sat up straight and glared at the two men. "That's horseshit. I am not staying away from him for two months." She set down her cup of coffee. "Now if you'll excuse me, I'm going to go visit my fiancé."

She stood up and left the lobby.

Behind her, she heard Drake say, "Well, that went well."

CLINT WAS asleep when she got there. She liked it when he was; he seemed like the same Clint she'd been sleeping beside for the last five years. She hated this for him. She couldn't give a shit how it was impacting her, she ached for him. She knew that every single time he didn't behave the way he normally would, and he came to realize it, he blew it gargantuanly out of proportion and agonized over it. That was no way to live your life. He needed to be patient with himself. Who the hell cared if this was his new normal? She didn't.

"Blow up as much as you want to, I don't care. I just want to be part of your life," she whispered close to his temple.

"Lydia?"

His beautiful hazel eyes opened. They were clear and bright, but then they dimmed.

"Stop that," she admonished softly.

"Stop what?" he asked as he looked at the wall behind her.

"Stop feeling guilty about whatever petty nonsense you're feeling guilty about. Enough is enough already." She ghosted her hand down under the sheet and blanket and found the one special spot beneath his ribs and tickled him.

He gasped.

She did it again.

He jerked.

She did it one more time.

He laughed.

"You are not tickling the brain-damaged man, that's so not right," Clint protested.

"I'm tickling the man who is taking himself far too seriously. What has your dick in a wringer today? It has to be big, because Drake and Finn were bent over too when they came to the hotel."

Clint laughed some more. "My, you have a way with words. I think you've been hanging around with Evie because I damn well know that English is your second language."

"Evie might have taught me some of the colloquialisms," Lydia grinned. "I only use them when they're appropriate. So, tell me what's wrong." She stood up beside the bed and leaned her hip against it, happy that she'd put down the rail so she could be closer to Clint.

"Lydia, I ended up going off on Finn for no good goddamn reason. Drake had to hold me down. I was a mess this morning."

"I could understand you going off on Drake, but Finn?" she teased.

"My point exactly." He looked at her with eyes filled with sorrow.

"I don't get it, what is your point exactly?" Lydia wasn't going to let him get out of not stating exactly what his worry was about.

"If I can blow up at Finn Crandall, how in the hell can I be trusted around you?"

"Well, first of all, let's not forget all the training I had to do to become a cop. You're not exactly dealing with the average woman. I'm armed and dangerous most of the time. And those times I'm not armed, I'm still dangerous."

Clint gave her a long stare.

She sighed and her shoulders dropped. "Fine, when it comes down to it, you're going to win every single time. I get that. But I don't think it would ever come to that."

Clint slid his palm against hers, then twined their fingers together. "I want to believe that, I really do, but how can I? From the moment I carried you out of that jungle, I swore to keep you safe. I'm not going to break that promise now."

Her fingers tightened in his. How could she make this better? What could she do or say?

"So how do we solve this? I'm not letting you go. That isn't an option. You're the Nerd King. You're the smartest man I know. I'm the Dork Queen. Come on Clint, we have to be able to solve this."

She stopped.

"Did I just whine?"

He gave a ghost of a smile. "Sure did. It was kind of cute."

"Fuck you."

"Hey, I said you were cute." This time she got a real smile. She lived for his smiles. But...

"We've got to figure this out."

"I think I have, but you're not going to like it." He stroked back her hair.

She closed her eyes and waited, sure he was right.

"I read over more of Dex's notes. That man is good. He's Lydia-good. Seriously, between the three of us, we could rule the world."

"I'm glad to see you included me with the two of you SEAL computer geniuses," Lydia said wryly.

"I always include you, Baby. Now stay on track. I read through Dex's info. Couple that with Jack's place to rehab, and I gather I'll be an outpatient."

"That's my assessment too," Lydia leaned into his stroking hand. "I've already found a great place for us to stay that's twenty minutes from the facility.

He kissed the top of her head. "Here's the part you won't like."

She gently grabbed his wrist and moved so she could look him square in the eye. "If you think I'm not going to like it, then I won't. So spit it out, Archer."

"I want to do this alone for a while. I think it's best that for at least the first month or two. I need to work to get control of these mood swings before I'm spending the nights with you."

She blinked back tears. She didn't know if they were tears of sorrow or anger. Maybe both.

"Ah, Baby, don't look at me that way, it breaks my heart. Or scares the shit out of me, I'm not sure which."

She dropped her head on his chest and listened to his heartbeat. "I can't stand this, Clint, I need you so bad. At least come home for a day or two. I don't know how, maybe Drake or Finn can stay at our house and just monitor the situation. But before you abandon me, I need some time with you."

"Lydia, that's not a good idea."

She shifted and once again looked into his eyes.

"Do I have to beg?" she whispered.

Now his eyes filled up with tears. "Never. Never that."

15

JESUS, I'M WALKING LIKE AN OLD MAN. AND IF DRAKE LOOKS AT me like I'm going to tip over one more time, I'm going to take a swing at him.

Clint gratefully grabbed the handrail of the stairs leading up to his townhome. He needed to get to the gym at the base. This was ridiculous.

"If you even *think* about more strenuous exercise than what they've recommended over the next three days, I'm driving your ass straight to your girly spa early. Got that?" Drake's voice rumbled. "Anyway, you have other activities you want to save your strength for."

Clint perked up at those words. Damn right he did.

Thank God his townhome was rather large, so the master bedroom had some privacy from where Drake would be sleeping.

The door opened and Lydia's smile felt like the sun beaming down on him. She was even wearing a yellow sundress. He made it up the last four steps even faster so he could take her into his arms. It was the first time he had hugged her standing up. She'd left Walter Reed a week before he was discharged so she could deal with the San Diego Police Department and put in for a six-month leave of absence, which she got.

God, she felt wonderful. But soon he felt himself flagging, and he didn't want Lydia forced to take his weight, so he stepped back. He cupped her cheeks and kissed her. It didn't last nearly as long as he would have wished, but he needed to sit down. Damn, seven weeks at the hospital and he was still this weak, how pathetic!

"I have cake." She smiled. "Why don't the two of you come in and sit down, and I'll cut you each a piece."

She was a sharp cookie, his fiancée.

He got inside and looked around the living room. He breathed a sigh of relief that everything looked so familiar. There was even that crazy vase that Lydia had gotten at a farmer's market, the one he really hated, but he'd never said a word. God, just looking at all the vibrant colors was giving him a headache. He looked back at Lydia—now *she* was a sight for sore eyes.

Drake sat in the armchair beside the couch so that Lydia and Clint could eventually sit together. Since it was an open floor plan, they both watched from the couch as she cut huge slices of chocolate cake for both of them. This was right up there with sex, but sex was definitely first on his list, and with Lydia in that sundress, that was about all he could think about.

He watched her unconscious sway as she brought over the plates and put them down on the coffee table. Drake better not be eyeing her cleavage. He gave him a sideways glance and Drake winked. The bastard, once again he knew exactly what Clint was thinking.

"What would you both like to drink?"

Clint was struck by her slight Spanish accent. How come he hadn't noticed that all the time he'd been in the hospital? It had always turned him on. Then again, everything about Lydia Hildalgo turned him on. Her nose. Her imagination. Her curves. Her heart. Her soft skin. Her compassion.

Stop!

He put the plate on his lap to cover his erection.

Get it together, Archer.

"What?" he asked.

"I asked what you would like to drink."

Drake smirked at him.

"Milk," Clint answered.

"Good choice," Drake smiled. "It was my choice too."

"I should have known that you growing boys needed calcium to keep your bones strong."

If my bone gets any stronger, it will lift the plate.

Lydia went back to the kitchen and Drake snickered.

"Go to hell, Avery. Don't you have to be with Karen and the kids?"

"Her mom came to help for the week I was in Maryland with you. I've got a reprieve."

God help me.

"I was hoping it was Finn who was going to babysit us."

"If wishes were horses, beggars would ride," Drake said solemnly.

"Huh?"

"Here's your milk." Lydia leaned over as she placed the glasses in front of them. Clint tried not to ogle her breasts. It was a losing proposition.

"Aren't you going to eat any cake?" Clint asked as Lydia sat down close beside him.

"I licked the icing bowl, so I'm good." She smiled. "Oh yeah, I also licked the batter off the beaters, so I'm really covered."

My dick is going to explode if she says the word lick one more time.

"Clint, is something wrong? Don't you like the cake? I know it's not up to Sophia's standards, but I used her recipe." She looked worried.

"This is great, Lydia. Ignore him." Drake grinned. He'd already eaten most of his piece. "I'm going to want another slice."

"I think it was the flight and the excitement to get home. I'm sorry, I'm exhausted, Baby." He kept his plate on his lap as he reached out and caressed her cheek, his thumb teasing her lower lip.

"That's right, it's ten o'clock East Coast time. No wonder you're tired."

"I have to check in with Karen. I want to talk to Andrew before he goes to bed," Drake grinned. "Maybe I'll have a chance to tell him a bedtime story. He loves the ones about dinosaurs, soldiers, and angels all fighting against the evil troll named Derwood. It's still not finished yet."

Clint chuckled. "How does it end?"

"Damned if I know." Drake shook his head. "I'm just playing it out as long as I can. Mind cutting me another slice and showing me to my room?" Drake asked Lydia.

"I have some chili mac simmering on the stove, and cornbread. I just thought you might want a treat before dinner," she protested.

"I can help myself to dinner when the sugar rush evaporates," Drake assured her. "But I've got to tell you, I think I'm done for the night. I'm exhausted. You can put that in the fridge, and I'll have it for breakfast."

Lydia got up and Drake picked up his duffel and followed her down the hallway. Clint put down the plate and looked at his lap.

"Behave," he admonished his penis.

He got up slowly, something he had learned at the hospital, so he didn't have a head rush. He went over to the mantel and frowned. He picked up a picture of him and Lydia at their engagement party. There should be a wedding photo by now. He set it down.

"I've always loved that picture," Lydia said as she put her arms around his waist and laid her cheek against his back. He turned around and pulled her in for a real hug.

"Did you get him settled?"

"Yep, he was talking to Andrew. He put it on speakerphone for me a little bit. That kid is really something. He was talking so fast, and he has a little bit of his father's Southern accent. He was already trying to figure out the ending of the story and was peppering Drake with questions."

"Sounds like Drake, always wanting to be one step ahead."

Lydia walked her fingers up his chest, then clasped her hands at the back of his neck. "What about you? Can I interest you in some chili mac and cornbread?"

He shook his head slowly.

"More cake?"

Another shake of the head.

"Milk?"

"You're kidding, right?"

"Do you remember the way to the bedroom?" Lydia teased.

"Not only that, I remember making love to you, but I think this is going to feel completely new, and I can't wait."

He just hoped he had the stamina to give her the pleasure he had in the past. The pleasure she deserved.

LYDIA SAW trepidation in Clint's eyes, and for the life of her she couldn't figure out what it was for. Maybe she was confused. That was it. Because now she saw heat and need —now *that* made sense.

"I can't carry you tonight," he whispered into her ear.

"Can I tell you a secret?" she asked quietly.

"Absolutely."

"After being carried five days in the Mexican jungle, I'm okay that you don't always carry me."

Clint laughed. Just as she'd hoped.

"Then walk with me." He held out his hand and she took it, and everything clicked into place. She hadn't lit candles or anything hokey like that, just made the bed and kept only one bedside light on so his head wouldn't hurt. She'd turned down the covers. She had done *one* thing, however.

When he reached for her, she demurred. "Let me go change."

"Honey, the only way I want you to change is by letting me take off your clothes."

"But I bought something you'll like."

His eyebrows raised as he pulled her into his arms. "Baby, I appreciate the effort, I truly do, but there's no need for props tonight. It's finally just you and me. Do you hear me? You and me, stripped down to our very souls. I need to reaffirm our connection." He began to unbutton her dress and she shivered.

It took a moment for her to clear her throat. "I need that

too. I need you, just you. I love you so much. My life would be nothing without you in it."

He stopped where he was and took her by her shoulders. "Don't say that, Lydia. Don't ever say that. You're too important. Too beautiful and good. You've got to promise me if something happens to me, you'd go on. You'd live a wonderful life."

What was he talking about? "No, I promise no such thing."

"Lydia, you have to promise." He sounded desperate.

Her fingers scraped through the scruff on his cheeks, pulling so she had his attention.

"Would you promise me such an idiotic thing?"

He stared at her as if he were made of stone. His expression flat.

"Exactly. Never, ever ask that of me again, Clint. It's a non-starter." She jerked at the front of her sundress, buttons flying as she worked it off her body. She watched his hazel eyes gleam as she stood there in front of him in a yellow thong and pretty yellow lace bra. Yeah, she'd had a gorgeous negligee planned, but she liked to have all of her bases covered, just in case.

Clint reached out and touched the top curve of her breast. She shuddered. It had been too long. Too damned long. She waited, wanting, wanting so much, wanting everything. His other arm stretched around her waist and pulled her close.

She closed her eyes and smiled. He still knew how much it turned her on to have him clothed and her naked against him. She loved him taking power in the bedroom, it felt so good to her. His hand stroked up and down her back, and she felt her bra loosen. Stinker had unlatched her bra and she hadn't even noticed.

She gasped when his big hand cupped her butt cheek and then his fingers trailed along the lace of the thong. Her entire body became one shivering mass as she focused on his fingers as they trailed up and down.

His other hand plowed into her hair and pulled her backwards. His hazel eyes didn't just gleam, they were ingots of fire as they demanded her surrender.

"Clint," she whispered, right before he claimed her mouth. There was no other word for it. He was taking her over, demanding she give herself to him. Claiming. Demanding. Willing a response, she was only too happy to give.

His tongue thrust into her mouth and she moaned with pleasure. She needed this. Her hands hovered over his head for just a moment, before remembering that he'd had surgery there, so she rested her palms on his shoulders and dug in. Two could play this game. She could be just as dictatorial as he was. But as soon as she pressed her nails into his heavy muscles, he pulled her closer, his grip was tighter in her hair and she groaned at the exquisite pleasure that he was bringing her. She needed to feel Clint's possession, like she needed to breathe.

He walked her backwards until the back of her knees hit the mattress, then he slowly lowered her onto the bed, and he came down on top of her. His weight was like a balm to her battered soul. She'd almost lost him, having his weight on her, having him surround her, was like getting her heart to beat again. Her hands moved down to the middle of his back, trying to pull him down even more so she could feel his every heartbeat, but he resisted.

"I'm too heavy for you, Baby."

He kissed the corner of her lips.

Her jaw.

Her neck.

Ah, God, he was kissing her behind her ear. She wouldn't survive if he kept doing that. Now he was licking and sucking.

Lydia heard herself whimper.

"You like that, don't you?" His voice was the most expensive chocolate and brandy ever made, all intent on seducing her.

Lydia shrugged, trying to break free, trying to loosen the straps of her bra so that he would be tempted to lick and suck her other places. She needed. She needed so much.

Clint chuckled. Drat the man, he knew what she was doing.

"I want you naked!" It was the only way to make this fair. It was the only way to gain some semblance of control.

"No, you don't," his voice a knowing, husky whisper.

"Yes, I do," she wailed.

"Liar." Clint lifted up so he could divest her of her bra, then he shifted, and his lips enclosed one nipple and Lydia felt herself flying heavenward. When he scraped his teeth against her pebbled flesh, she bit her lip so hard it was a wonder she didn't taste blood. But one tiny portion of her brain remembered they had company in the house.

Then he sucked hard.

Fuck it.

Her moan was loud, even to her ears.

Drake better have music on.

Clint chuckled and looked straight into her eyes. Reading her mind, he laughed harder.

"Quit laughing and get to work. It's been too long."

ONLY LYDIA COULD DEMAND and plead in one sentence. His woman, his life. Clint stroked back her hair and dove in for another kiss that soon shot into flames. Clint licked inside her mouth, tasting chocolate and Lydia, one flavor so much more extravagant than the other. His tongue dueled with hers, and his body hummed with delight. He moved his elbows so that they took his weight as he pressed his denim-covered erection against the frothy lace that was supposed to act as panties.

She squirmed against him, lifting up her knees, squeezing his thighs. It was either his head or his cock that was going to explode. He got up from the bed and toed off his shoes and socks, then yanked off his clothes in record speed. He knelt down in front of the bed, caught Lydia's ankles, and began to pull her toward him so they dropped on either side of his body.

"No! That's not what I need." She sounded so sure of herself. Silly woman.

"It's what I need." He'd dreamed of this and so many other things while he'd been in the hospital. As soon as he had her positioned as he wanted, he lightly traced the yellow lace along her hipbones. Lydia arched. She was so sensitive there. He did it again, and again and inhaled her arousal. Now he knew, it was his cock that was going to explode, and he hadn't even tasted her.

Slowly, ever so slowly, he brushed back the gusset of her panties and was greeted with her glistening sex. So ready for him, so gorgeous. She parted her legs even more. He grinned. Five years, and they knew how to give and take pleasure from one another, was it any wonder he was crazy for this woman?

He traced the lips of her sex, then parted her so he could dip his tongue deep and taste the arousal that called to him.

For a moment he looked up and saw the crook of her arm covering her eyes. He smiled as he licked and pleasured the woman who was made especially for him. He found her engorged clit and traced around the bud until she was writhing up and down, begging for more. He sucked the sensitive nub deep and lashed it with his tongue, reveling in her low cries of pleasure.

He sped up his ministrations, then lightly grazed her with his teeth and she let out a loud cry of satisfaction.

"Now, Clint."

Cloth rent as he ripped off her panties. He moved her body so that she was positioned comfortably up on the bed before he allowed the engorged tip of his cock to slide through her wet sex.

"No teasing."

"I need this Lydia," he moaned. Gently he moved forward. Her tight muscles clasped his erection in welcome. He stopped and savored.

"More. Deeper."

He stayed still as he looked into brown eyes that had gone black with desire.

Clint pressed deeper until he was home. He relished every moment of this soul-deep connection, but he couldn't stop the urge to move. He needed so much more. He felt her tremble beneath him. The beginning of her orgasm started and he needed to be with her. He pulled back and pushed back in, deeper and harder. The intensity blew his mind. Lydia's nails dug deep into his naked back and he basked in the feel, knowing she was leaving marks.

Over and over, he pushed them up higher. His lower back tingled.

He brushed back tendrils of her damp black hair then tenderly kissed her temple.

"More, I need you," she whispered.

"Deeper, I want you," she gasped.

"Please, make me yours," she moaned.

"God, I love you," they said in unison.

With those words, they both shot to the stars.

16

CLINT WALKED DOWN THE STAIRS BETTER THAN HE HAD walked up the stairs three days ago, but that didn't make her happy. Lydia felt as if her heart were breaking once again. He had said he would be back, but she just couldn't wrap her head around it. It felt like he was walking out on their life together. She'd seen him looking at their engagement photo with an expression of sorrow. Something wasn't right in their relationship, and no matter how many times he professed his love, she felt like she was losing him. Add that to the fact that he thought it was necessary to be on his own for one to two months, it was more than she could take.

She smiled and waved as Drake and Clint drove away in the monster truck, then she shut the door and gave in to tears. The only saving grace was that her parents were in San Antonio with Beth and she didn't have to deal with their presence in the duplex next door. Their presence would have been catastrophic.

Maybe Clint finally sensed her failure. How was she ever going to face him when he found out?

She went over to the mantle and picked up the engagement picture that was the happiest moment of her life and hugged it to her breast.

"Is that it?" She asked Clint. "Is that what's wrong?"

She looked down at the photo again and traced the lines of his face, remembering the party in Mason's backyard. Tears welled before she sucked them down.

"Nope, not going to do it. I'm finally going to face this head-on. But when he's better. Not now."

She put down the photo and lifted her chin. It was time to get back into the saddle and call Ed Sherman. Her boss was going to kill her. First, she asked for time off, now she was going to ask to be put back on the payroll for two months, at least until Clint came back home. Or maybe even past then.

She shook her head. What the hell did she know about the future? She just knew she needed to do something and do it now.

When she got Ed's voicemail, she strode over to the command center that she and Clint had used hundreds of times. It had five monitors, two laptops, and a state-of-the-art tower that she'd dare anybody to hack. She stretched her fingers, then fired things up. As soon as she was up and running, she got two pings.

Rylie and Melvin. She answered Rylie first.

How's Georgie? Lydia typed.

Asleep next to Dare. *They both had a rough night. Rylie answered.*

. . .

LYDIA HATED HEARING THAT. Georgie was on the far end of the autism spectrum; he had his good days and his bad days. Since Rylie and Dare had been together, his days were now mostly good. He was even somewhat verbal, and he was attending a special school—nobody could have expected that three years ago.

His older sister Charlotte also worked wonders with him. That and the new school he was attending were the only reasons that Rylie had felt comfortable leaving him for five days to come to Maryland.

WHY THE ROUGH NIGHT? Lydia typed.

PROBLEMS AT SCHOOL. New teacher. We can't figure out why he doesn't like him. He says he doesn't understand him, and he comes home mad and frustrated ever since this teacher started substituting.

WHAT ARE you going to do? Lydia asked.

DARE'S GOING to go to the school tomorrow, he's already talked to the principal and the teacher, this time he's going to take Georgie with him.

SOUNDS LIKE A GOOD PLAN. Lydia agreed.

· · ·

So, why are you online? I'd thought you'd be playing footsie with Clint.

LYDIA HATED to type the next sentence. *He's already left.*

WHAT?!!! But he just got there!
Lydia could almost hear Rylie speaking through the computer.

YOU KNOW HE'S WORRIED. It was for the best.
Lydia waited long moments for a reply.

ARE YOU OKAY?

YES, she lied.

WHY'D YOU GET ONLINE?

THERE'S a case I'm working on. I've been working it in my spare time and would have continued even if they'd let me go. I wanted more eyes on it.

I'VE GOT TIME. You going to bring Melvin into it? Rylie asked.
Lydia could picture Rylie rubbing her hands together.

.   .   .

YEP. The more the merrier. My gut's telling me this family is really in trouble.

STALKER? Rylie wanted to know.

THIS IS NOT your average stalker. Whoever this is, is terrorizing an entire household. It's Amityville horror, only with technology. This is some creepy stuff. I don't think a writer could even make this stuff up. Lydia explained.

I'M IN. I love Freddie Kruger movies. I know some others who would love to sink their teeth into this too.

OKAY, I'll shoot you some details. Lydia promised.

TELL me when you've brought Melvin into the loop so we can all chat.

Yep, Rylie was definitely rubbing her hands together.

RYLIE POPPED off and Lydia pinged Melvin. When he didn't respond, she told him to get in touch with her. In the olden days, she would have promised a Skype chat and her wearing an angora sweater, but since she got engaged to a Navy SEAL that all ended. Clint had insisted and Melvin valued his life, so it was an easy agreement. However, Clint had ended up asking her to wear the sweater for *him*.

Lydia got up and went to the kitchen. It was time to check in with Sophia and Beth. Sophia she would be able to bullshit...maybe. But she really didn't look forward to the Beth call. Her sister *knew* her. She'd be all over her like white on rice. She started to dial Sophia's number, then thought better of it. She'd go over there; it was a fifteen-minute drive at most.

Baskin and Robbins had three quarts of Pralines and Cream when she stopped on the way to the Gault's house, so obviously it was destined that she visit. By the time she got to the door, it was already opened. Billy grabbed the bag out of her hands.

"Whoa, don't eat it all; one of those quarts is for your sister and me."

She still couldn't believe how far up she had to gaze to look Billy Anderson in the eye. There was a big difference between fourteen and nineteen. He gave her a hug.

"How are you doing, Lydia? How's Clint?" he asked as he ushered her into the house and down the hall to the living room. Mason and Sophia were sitting beside one another on the couch. Sophia had her feet up on Mason's lap. That was one way to keep her off her feet, offer her a foot rub. *Sly... The man is sly...*

"Do I see a pink-and-white bag? Is that ice cream?" Sophia cooed.

Billy looked inside. "Pralines and cream. You only get one dish."

"What are you talking about?" Sophia glared at her younger brother. Lydia could no longer consider Billy the 'little' brother.

"The doctor's worried about your sugar levels, you know that Sweetheart," Mason whispered. But Lydia caught it.

Sophia's frown turned upside down. She reached out her hand and Mason took it and brought it to his lips.

"I think with all that sweetness, you wouldn't need ice cream," Lydia teased.

"Lydia, you know better than that. There is always room for ice cream. Billy, scoop us two big bowls, then anyone with a penis, leave the room."

Mason lifted an eyebrow and Billy snorted. Lydia was startled. This was not Sophia's normal way of behaving. When she saw her friend blush, she knew she hadn't been taken over by the pod people.

"Sweets, I gotta say, these pregnancy hormones are a hoot and a half," Mason said as he bent over and gave her a long kiss before getting off the couch. He walked up to Lydia and gave her a big hug.

"So how were Clint and Drake doing today?"

"You just came over yesterday," Lydia laughed. "They're the same."

"Clint's walking even better and Drake's obsessed with his phone. He can't get enough of his family."

"Hmmm," Mason said.

"What?" Lydia asked.

"It's good that Clint is doing better. I hate to see you two apart though. Are you going to be reinstated?"

"I got the six months' leave of absence, but now that Clint is going to be gone for a while, I'm asking to come back for a couple of months. I'm sure my supervisor's head will explode."

"Here's your ice cream," Billy said. "Lydia, do you want to eat on the couch with Sophia?"

"Absolutely," she smiled as she tried to take her bowl. Billy wasn't having any of it. He held them over his head and brought the bowls and napkins over to the coffee table, then moved it so it was easy for Sophia to reach. God, that kid had grown up to be an amazing man.

"How's school going?" Lydia asked him.

"Slow."

Mason and Sophia laughed.

"Just one more year, and you'll have your associate's degree. Then you can join the Navy *if* that's still what you want to do."

"No, I'll want to be a seaplane pilot," Billy said sarcastically. "Sawyer and I will move to Alaska and start our own little business."

Sophia rolled her eyes at Lydia. Mason rubbed the back of his neck.

"Sorry," Billy said. "Right now, the classes are near the end, and the tests are easy. It's frustrating. I should have signed up for something more challenging."

"What did you sign up for?" Lydia asked.

"Engineering. They're letting me take a calculus class on the side. I would have done Computer and Information Sciences, but that's Sawyer's gig."

"So that's too easy, huh?"

"He read all the assigned texts last summer before starting class. So did Sawyer. It was what Kenna's son, Austin had suggested. He did it his sophomore year and he aced everything," Sophia explained.

"Yeah, that poor sucker ended up having to go to a four-year university before he gets to sign up," Billy smirked.

"God help the Navy, the three of them are joining at the same time," Mason shook his head wearily. "I just pray they don't end up anywhere near my team."

"Ah come on, that's not nice. We'll be excellent students," Billy grinned.

Lydia looked over at Sophia who was beginning to look pale.

"Okay, you penises, time for you to leave, our ice cream is melting." Lydia made a shooing motion. Mason looked over at Sophia and got the picture fast.

"You got it. Come on Billy, time for us to vamoose."

"Yeah, I have plans with Rebecca tonight, so I have to get ready," Lydia heard Billy say as he left the room with Mason. She hurried over to the couch and gave Sophia a tight hug.

"You okay?"

"I don't know what worries me more. Thinking of him one day going on missions or thinking of him one day married and a dad."

"Ah, Honey." Lydia looked down at Sophia's distended stomach with envy. She jerked back in surprise. Where had that come from? Sure, she and Clint had talked about a family, but that was way off in the future. Right now, they were focused on their careers. He went on deployments and she worked crazy hours with the police department. She winced. Then there was the gnat under the carpet that she'd let grow to the size of an elephant. She was so screwed.

"What?" she hadn't heard a word of what Sophia had said.

"I asked how Clint is doing? How you're coping? For real this time, not what you pawned off on Mason."

"He's doing really well. Really well," Lydia blushed.

"I know that face. All is well in the Clint and Lydia lovemaking department. But..." Sophia put down her ice cream and maneuvered awkwardly to hug her friend again. Lydia accepted the hug gratefully.

"Tell me, Honey."

Lydia thought about what she could tell. "There's something wrong, and I can't figure it out."

"What makes you think that?"

Lydia paused. She knew the truth. What she told Sophia would go to Mason, sure as the sun would rise. But would that be a bad thing? Wouldn't it be good to get Clint's best friend's perspective?

"You know about the mood swings, I told you about those on the phone, right?"

"They sound awful."

"They are." Lydia bit her lip. "In all the years we've been together he's never been as hurtful as he was when I went into the hospital room. He about killed me." At Sophia's shocked expression, Lydia immediately clarified. "Nothing physical. It was the killer statement. He told me he didn't want me in the room because I wasn't his wife."

"No! You must have misheard him."

Lydia stared at her friend. "Do you really think I could have made a mistake about something like that?"

Sophia sadly shook her head.

"I always thought you two were just waiting until your careers settled down and then you'd surprise us all and say come to Hawaii. I know you don't want your father to give you away, so that's why I thought you'd spring it on us."

"It's like you can read my mind. Beth is the peacemaker, so she had our father walk her down the aisle. Clint told me that Jack was less than pleased. He thought he wasn't worthy of the duty, considering how he had let Beth down," Lydia's voice trailed off.

"Families are complicated. You know I was never going to have my dad walk me down the aisle. I held more love in my heart for his second wife than I did for him. God knows I adore my little sister, Louisa."

"Have you seen her much?"

"No. I asked Ashley to keep her away in case this pregnancy doesn't work out."

Lydia squeezed Sophia's hand. "It's going to work, you're at thirty-one weeks. You're following all the doctor's orders."

"I pray, Lydia. I pray every day." Sophia's eyes glistened.

"Ice cream will help. Just a little." Lydia smiled and picked up the half-melted bowl of Pralines and Cream.

"Perfect, I love it when it's melty."

17

IT WAS THE THIRD TIME THAT DRAKE PICKED UP HIS CELL phone that put Clint's Spidey senses on red alert. He knew that everything was okay with Karen and the kids, they'd already had a half-hour conversation with them when they passed Escondido. Nope, this was something different.

"Fess up."

Drake gave him a distracted look. "What?"

"What has your tail in a twist?"

"Nothing." Drake's tone and answer tried to totally shut Clint out. Unlucky for Drake, Clint wasn't having one of his paranoid hours.

"I call bullshit. You're even driving like a little old lady. Normally we'd be in Palm Desert by now. There is a serious stick up your ass. Should I have had someone else drive me?"

"No, now can it, Archer." Drake picked up his phone again and grimaced. When he put it down, Clint immediately picked it up before it had a chance to shut down.

"Goddammit, you give that back, you asshole!" He couldn't lean over the console and reach Clint, so he was stymied.

"Na-uh," Clint said as he checked the messages. There was something from a D.C. number. The last message had come in last night.

BE AVAILABLE TOMORROW, you won't like the consequences if you aren't.

CLINT QUICKLY SCROLLED through the past texts—they went back three weeks. Whoever was texting Drake had told him to set-up a WhatsApp account and communicate that way. Drake had refused until a dropbox was downloaded to his phone. Then Drake had acquiesced. Of course, the dropbox was now empty.

Clint looked up. They were now pulled over to the side of the freeway. He'd never seen Drake so angry before.

"Who's blackmailing you? What do they have on you? Why are you putting up with this shit?" Clint asked quietly.

"Give me my phone and don't ever bring this up again."

"No." It was the principle of the thing. There was no reason to keep it. He knew there was nothing else of value. He'd memorized the D.C. number. At least he'd retained that ability. Clint knew that anything substantial had been said on WhatsApp and was in the now-empty dropbox, so he was flying blind.

"Drake, I can help."

"No, you can't. I've got this covered."

"Yeah, sure you do. That's why you're on pins and needles and acting like you're going to have a heart attack.

This is not you. You're forgetting the first rule of being a SEAL—trust your teammates."

"This is my fuck-up, I'll take care of it. I refuse to involve the rest of the team." Drake looked defeated, angry, and anguished as he held out his hand for the phone. Clint was stunned. This was not the man he knew. The one and only other time he had seen him like that was when he realized his own mother had wanted him dead.

Clint didn't hand him his phone. The truck was still idling. He pushed in Mason's number.

"What the fuck!"

"We're a team."

"What's up, Drake? Did you drop Clint off?"

"It's me, Mase. We're on the side of the road on the way to Palm Desert. Drake's being blackmailed. He isn't talking."

There was a long pause.

Softly Mason asked. "Drake, talk to me. It's got something to do with Syria, doesn't it?"

Drake slammed his hand against the steering wheel. "How the fuck do you do that?" he demanded to know. "How in the fuck did you manage to pull that out of your ass? That's fucking impossible."

Clint laughed. "You're right, Mase, the text on his phone came from a D.C. number. This has to have something to do with the senator."

"Dammit, Drake, you fucked up not telling me," Mason's voice was lethal. "When we get this over and done with, I'm going to find some piddly-assed formality to write you up for, like tardiness or out of uniform, but it's really for not bringing me in on this. Got it?" Mason's voice was as deadly as Drake's had been fifteen minutes ago. Clint approved. "Now spill your guts."

Drake didn't say a word.

"Answer me," Mason commanded.

"Fine, I'll talk. The little fucker's going to say how we, mostly me, tried to murder him when we were saving his punk ass. It's all because of my big fucking mouth, but the whole team will be implicated."

"So, it's that Devon shit-heel guy, huh?" Mason asked.

"Got it in one," Drake acknowledged.

"Is that the guy you showed me a picture of? The aide to the Senator that I said was shifty?" Clint asked. "What does he have on you? What does he want from you?"

"He showed me a video that he altered. It shows me sounding like an out-of-control bastard threatening to turn him over to the enemy."

Clint and Mason both laughed. Clint could easily see Drake threatening that. Based on the little he had been told of the mission, it sounded like this Devon freak had been a pain in the ass from the get-go. If he had been as out of line as they say he was, Drake would have done anything possible to get him to cooperate, including threatening him.

"So, we can explain it," Clint said.

"I agree," Mason said.

"Guys, you don't know how damning it is. I don't care about me—well not much—I care about Karen and the kids. But I really care how it will reflect on all of you."

"So, we gut him," Clint said. He was starting to get angry, really angry, that somebody would try to do this to his friend and teammate.

"Whoa there, Archer," Mason said calmly. "We need to put on our thinking caps. Drake, he wants something from you, right?"

"Yes. But I don't know what it is yet. It's not money. He says he has a job he wants me to do."

"That's not good," Mason stated evenly.

Clint shook his head. Devon needing a Navy SEAL did not bode well at all.

"I've been trying to think of a way to get the video and all copies away from him. I just don't know how," Drake said as he dropped his head against the back of his seat.

"That's my area of expertise," Clint said.

"Ah hell, I can't ask you to do that for me. You've only just been cleared to watch a little bit of TV." Drake rolled his head to look at Clint. "Not that you did any of that, these last three days," he grinned.

Clint smirked. Damn right he hadn't. Not while he had a chance to make love to Lydia.

"I've also been cleared for one hour a day on electronics if it's a large screen monitor. No phones."

"Then what the hell were you doing looking at my phone?" Drake demanded to know.

"That was need to know. I didn't have a choice."

"Good thing you did," Mason spoke up.

Drake started up the truck again and merged into traffic fast, really fast. Clint sucked in a deep breath as the yucca trees whizzed by, making his stomach heave. He slammed his eyes shut and let Mason and Drake continue to talk. He wished to God that he could remember more about the mission, just one small piece. He was positive if he could, he could be a bigger help than just doing an hour a day of sleuthing. But it was all one big blank. His only reference was the names that Finn had supplied, and the pictures Drake had shown him. He knew everybody they'd rescued.

"I still don't know how he could have had a camera. We patted him down for every recording device and destroyed them," Drake was saying.

Mason didn't reply, which just meant that their lieutenant was saying they'd fucked up. And they must have.

"Is Devon really this stupid? I don't think so," Clint said with his eyes still closed. "What I read about him shows him as the type who would sell off his own kid if it would further his career or push an old lady into the street in order to get a cab, but he's not dumb. He's one of the up-and-comers on the D.C. circuit, he's not an idiot. Shifty and ruthless, yes, but not dumb."

"You okay, Clint? Why are your eyes closed?" Drake asked.

"I feel a headache coming on," Clint admitted. Might as well tell it like it was.

"Do we need to quit talking, or should I pull over again?" Drake wanted to know.

"Keep talking. Just no more fast maneuvers. Your talking helps keep my mind off the nausea."

"What?" Drake exclaimed. "Don't you dare throw up in my truck, man."

Clint and Mason chuckled.

"Clint, I agree with your assessment of Devon," Mason said. "This is a huge risk for him to make, so there has to be a huge payoff for him. If we could figure out what it was, and then cut it out at the root, we would be in the clear."

"Can't we just kill him for real?" Drake whined. "It'd be doing the world a favor."

"Can it, Avery." Mason was clearly exasperated.

"Guys, that tape has really been altered, I need you to know that. Sure, I said what was on that tape, but there was a hell of a lot more on it that was edited out. If they saw the whole thing it wouldn't be nearly as damning."

"But would it still be damning?" Clint asked as he looked over at Drake.

"I'm really not sure," Drake said as he glanced in his side mirror before passing a car. "I know I threatened the little shit. He wouldn't shut up and get it together. We had to get a move on to get out of there, and he was wasting time. I told him if he didn't shut up and get moving, I'd throw him in front of the tanks."

"Sure, that doesn't sound bad at all," Clint said sarcastically.

"Yeah, but he was telling me to leave his colleague behind because she was slowing us down."

"For real?" Clint asked. "He really is a shit-heel."

"Exactly. That's not on the videotape."

"You know, it could be that he doesn't want Drake to do a job for a pay-off, it could be that he wants Drake to help him out of a big ole jam. Let's say his ass is on the line for something. Something that is life and death? I mean, nobody in their right mind would go up against a Navy SEAL for money, no matter how much, let alone Drake. You're fucking scary."

"Thank you," Drake grinned with satisfaction. "See, you're firing on all cylinders, this brain damage bullshit is bullshit," Drake grinned over at him.

Clint gave a wan smile. If only that were true.

"We need to get our hands on all versions of that tape, then we need to find out who is twisting Devon's tail and eliminate that threat. Then we need Devon to understand we're the scariest motherfuckers on the block," Mason's voice was deadly.

"Clint, this is Midnight Delta only. We're not pulling Dex in, and I'm sorry, Lydia can't know about this. So, they've only cleared you for an hour screen time a day?"

"That's what they said last week. We'll see what these

new folks say at the day spa. I'm a big boy, I know when to push, and when not to."

Drake gave him a sideways glance. "Clint, we can't take the chance. If you fuck up your recovery, you're worthless to me. Do what the docs say."

Clint felt his hands clench into fists. He hated listening to his friend, especially when he was being reasonable.

"Clint, listen to Drake," Mason said. "We need you at the top of your game. Otherwise, I'm forced to bring either Dex from Black Dawn or Kane from Night Storm, and I would prefer to keep this in the family."

"Lydia is part of the family." Clint hated and loved the idea of having Lydia work on this. He worried for her but knew that she would be invaluable.

"She is," Mason agreed. "But she's vulnerable. She might be a cop, but she's not equipped to defend herself. Nope, it's you or the other team's computer experts. Can I count on you to do the right thing?"

"Yes," Clint said. "The chance to be useful after all this inactivity is a Godsend." Then having realized what he'd said, he glanced over at Drake. "Sorry, man."

"I didn't take it wrong," Drake smiled. "I understand."

"I'm going to say this again. If you overdo, you're fucking your recovery over, and you're fucking us over. Remember that," Mason said. "I've got to go. There's somebody else I'm worried about doing too much."

"How is Sophia? Really?"

"She has pre-eclampsia. She's going in every week for tests, we're monitoring her blood pressure here at the house on a daily basis and calling it in. So far, the meds are doing the trick, but she is antsy as hell. She's scared that she'll lose the baby. She refuses to even find out if it's a boy or a girl this time. Won't allow us to buy a single piece of baby clothing for fear of jinxing things. She puts on a good front, but she's a basket case. Having Lydia come over today was great medicine for her."

"That's good to hear," Clint smiled.

18

"KAREN'S MOTHER IS STAYING ANOTHER WEEK. MASON IS going to be here tonight," Drake said as he unloaded the large monitor from its box.

Clint looked around the roomy suite that his brother-in-law had booked for him. Jack never did anything small. There was a full kitchen and an impressive work area. The fact that Drake hadn't oohed and aahed over the size of the TV screen told Clint just how worried he was with everything going on.

"What were you thinking bringing this tablet if you knew you couldn't work on the small screen, Clint? How'd you manage to slip it past Lydia, anyway?"

"Lydia and I were busy most of the time. When we weren't busy, she and I were mostly sleeping, except for the one time I got up and packed while she continued to sleep."

"She's losing her touch. The woman I know would have been all over that."

"She *was* all over that," Clint said with a shit-eating grin.

"Okay, you got me there," Drake grinned back. "But what about rehab and taking this seriously?"

"I was going to do the same thing you're doing, only difference is, *I* was going to pay for the monitor," Clint's grin got even bigger.

Drake gave him the finger.

Clint didn't mind in the slightest.

"I think you're cured, my man."

"Sometimes it feels like it," Clint sighed with satisfaction. "Then there are other times when I feel like there is someone else living inside my body. I fucking hate it. Let's not forget the fact that I can't remember about three months of my life, and my vocabulary ain't worth shit."

"Hold on while I get the world's smallest violin to play for you." Drake plugged in the monitor and Clint attached the cord to his laptop.

"We have lift-off."

"Seriously, I don't want you doing anything on my behalf that'll set you back," Drake said as Clint sat down in front of the monitor.

"In all seriousness, neither do I," Clint glanced at his friend. "The longer I take to recover, the less chance there is of a full recovery. I'm not FUBAR'ing this."

Drake's hand came down on Clint's shoulder and squeezed. "Glad to hear it."

"But at the same time, getting weasel-dick handled is time-critical. Now, I need to see your phone's SIM card, and I need into your WhatsApp account."

Drake took out his phone and handed Clint his SIM card. "I'm going to read your SIM card with this reader, and then do a fun little thing called SIMjacking. I can't copy all of your old SIM data into the phone, but I can arrange it so that new incoming texts and calls will come into the new burner phone at the same time as it does to your phone."

"Please tell me that can't be done," Drake begged.

"Watch and learn," Clint smiled.

Clint used Drake's SIM card, the special program he had on his computer, and the burner phone. He worked for ten minutes, then he gave back Drake's SIM card so he could re-install it into his phone. "Hold on while I call your phone number from *my* phone, Drake."

As soon as Clint dialed, Drake's phone rang and so did the burner phone, Clint answered that at the same time and held the receiver to his chest.

Clint nudged Drake to answer the call on his phone, and he did. "Talk, sing a song, do anything," Clint urged Drake.

Drake started to recite the Pledge of Allegiance. Clint took the burner phone away from his chest and put it on speaker. There in stereo, was Drake reciting the Pledge of Allegiance in person and over the speaker of the burner phone.

Drake stopped speaking and pressed 'end' on his phone. "You're one scary dude."

"That's what the United States Navy pays me for. Unfortunately, WhatsApp is a little more complicated than this, and it will take more than a minute or two."

Clint frowned as he got in front of the big monitor again and typed in Drake's login and password. He hissed through his teeth. The only conversation that could be found was from the last forty-eight hours. Looked like Devon had been smart and deleted the old stuff.

"Drake, how familiar are you with WhatsApp?" Clint asked.

"Hell, my three-year-old Andrew probably knows more than I do. I downloaded the program like he asked and started communicating with him that way. I can communicate on my phone or on my computer."

"Which way do you normally access the application?" Clint asked.

"My phone. But I gotta tell you, I forget about it. I'm so used to checking my messages, it's not until he reminds me to go to WhatsApp that I go over to it."

"This is going to be a tough one to get around. I can eventually install some malware from your phone into his, so we can route his incoming calls to the second burner phone I bought. But the good stuff is going to be on his WhatsApp. I'm going to have to ask around to get the malware that the NSO Group designed. I'm going to need to tap some people who go to the dark, dark, dark web. This is going to cost."

"I don't get it, what is this malware? Why is it so secret, and why does it cost so much?"

"Remember when that reporter was killed? His WhatsApp account was hacked with this malware. So was the head of Amazon—that's how they ended up hacking his phone, through his WhatsApp account using this malware."

"Hasn't WhatsApp fixed this bug so nobody can hack it anymore?"

"They've done some upgrades, but I'm sure so has NSO, despite being sued by WhatsApp. Like that was going to stop this Israeli security company," Clint snorted.

He pressed some keys and immediately called up some code. Now, this was pretty. Very, very pretty. He leaned in closer to look. It wasn't exactly what they had used, but it was a precursor to the eventual code, and it was pretty fricking impressive.

"Do you see this?" he pointed to a particular syntax. "Look at what they did here. It's a thing of beauty."

"Huh? I think you have me confused with your wife."

Clint looked over his shoulder and laughed. Yep, Drake

sure as hell wouldn't appreciate the delicacy of what the programmer had come up with. He went down another page of code and whistled. He called up his messenger and typed up a cryptic message to one of his most secure contacts on the dark web.

"Who was that?" Drake asked.

"Nobody that anybody really knows. But he owes me a favor or two. He might know a guy who knows a guy."

"Well, that clears that up." Drake's sarcasm was clear. "Maybe you ought to slow down."

"Nah, I'm good, it's only a little bit over an hour," Clint said as he looked at his watch. He called up another screen full of code. It was more exciting than the last. God, he wished Lydia were here to see this.

"Holy hell, would you look at this!" He banged his hand on the desk in glee. He paused his cursor over the next line of code that was even better than the last. How had they even thought of this? Unbelievable.

"What in the hell has you wetting your pants?" Drake demanded to know.

"They have figured out a way to attach malware into this encrypted message so that it is damn near undetectable. It would pass through ninety-seven percent of all screening systems. This is gor...gor...beautiful."

"So why is that important?"

"That means that when we get our hands on the actual NSO code today, it will probably be ninety-nine point nine percent unde...undect...not be able to be discovered."

"Are you sure this is right?" Drake asked.

"I told you I had this handled, Drake." Clint bit out the words as he rounded on his friend. "You need to back off now." He rubbed his temple.

"No, you don't understand. I was just asking about

putting malware on his phone, won't that contaminate his WhatsApp?"

Clint couldn't understand what Drake was saying. It was spinning in circles around his head. His vision was fine, so it couldn't be screen time.

"Drake be quiet, I'm trying to think," he roared.

"Ah shit, you're doing it again." Drake touched Clint's shoulder and Clint swiped at him. It felt like bugs were under his skin, and having Drake touch him only aggravated it.

"Go away. Let me think."

Drake crouched down so he was eye level with Clint. "You need to take slow breaths, Man. Just like Finn said."

It took every ounce of strength Clint had not to haul off and hit Drake. Why was he so mad at him? Why wasn't he in focus? Instead, sparks surrounded him. Lots of painful sparks, making it impossible to look at him. He slammed his eyes shut.

Somebody took his hand and pressed it against his chest. "Feel your breaths. In and out. Breathe in through your nose. Hold it. Long slow breath out through your mouth."

Who was talking?

Forever, or for minutes, or for hours, or for seconds, Clint continued to breathe. Finally, he heard Drake.

"Let me get you a towel, you're a sweaty mess."

Where am I?

His eyes shot open. Please say he hadn't hurt Lydia. Please, please, please. He looked frantically around the room and it didn't look familiar.

"I knew I pushed you. This is such a bad idea. Mason better get here soon."

"Drake?"

"I'm here, man. I'm with you. You're in Palm Desert. You checked into Desert Vista Renewal today and met with your team, now you're in your suite here at the Hacienda Palms living the high life thanks to your brother-in-law and teammate, Jack."

It was starting to come back. He was slumped in an office chair in front of a huge computer monitor.

"Fuck, I had an episode, didn't I? What did I do? Did I take a swing at you?"

"Nope, you passed out. You weren't focusing, your eyes rolled up in the top of your head, and out you went."

Fuckity fuck fuck.

Clint sat up straighter in the chair and clasped the edge of the desk. He turned away from the bright light of the monitor. "Turn that off," he waved to Drake. Drake immediately shut down the laptop, and the monitor went dark.

"Do you need the lights dimmed?"

Clint turned his head slowly. "No, those are all right," he sighed with relief. He yawned. "I'm sorry Drake. Apparently, I'm still trying to figure out my limits. I don't think it was the screen time, I think it was looking at the code that did it to me."

Drake just stared at him.

"What?"

"I don't care what it was. You did too much, and we just got done agreeing you weren't going to FUBAR your recovery. Why don't you take the bed in the other room and get some shut-eye? You need extra rest. In the meantime, I'll wait for Dick-Weasel's call."

"You need back-up. I don't want you doing anything without back-up."

Drake raised his eyebrow. "Unlike you, I don't intend to

Fuck This Up Beyond All Recognition, now that I'm waiting on the cavalry."

Clint barked out a short laugh. "Yeah, like you would have brought us in if I hadn't had taken your phone and shoved my way into the situation and then called Mason. Talk about FUBAR. You're such an asshole, Avery," Clint ended on a grin.

"Right back at you, Archer. Now go to bed."

"I've got to call Lydia."

"Bring me your cell phone when you're done."

"Are you telling me you don't trust me to not use my phone's internet when I'm done?" Clint wanted to know.

"That's what I'm telling you."

Clint laughed as he headed to the bedroom.

19

"WELL, YOU SURE ARE MAKING WAVES, HILDALGO," THE OLD man chuckled as he plucked the toothpick out of his mouth and pointed it at her. Lydia knew he could care less, he thrived on causing a commotion in the San Diego Police Department, that was the reason they'd put Eddie Sherman in charge of the Cyber Crimes department way back in the day before anyone knew it would amount to anything, they wanted him out of the way.

"Sorry about that, Boss."

"Either you're pandering to me, or you're lying to me, can't say I appreciate either choice."

"Actually, I was just being polite like I was raised."

He raised one bushy white eyebrow and smiled. "That I can handle. How's Clint?"

She smiled. "A lot better than last week. It was good to have him home this past weekend."

"Do they have a real prognosis yet? It's been five weeks since he woke up, right?"

"Nope, it's been seven and a half weeks. The doctors haven't been up front with us, but he has a chance of making an almost full recovery if he doesn't push himself too hard and follows the doctor's orders."

Eddie scratched the side of his jaw and his piercing blue eyes stared at her. "So, what I'm hearing is that you've got info that the docs haven't shared with you, is that what I'm hearing?"

Lydia nodded.

"Good for you," he cackled.

"Before you start shaking my hand, I wasn't the one who hacked the system, it was one of Clint's SEAL friends. I had my head in my hands, so to speak, as I worried about him. Hell, Boss, I don't know why I didn't think to dig on my own."

Eddie got up from behind his desk and leaned against the front so he could stand next to Lydia. He put his hand on her shoulder. "Hell, kid, cut yourself some slack. Your place was beside Clint, giving him all the support you could. You were not supposed to be the computer genius you are, that wasn't your job."

Lydia pinched the bridge of her nose. In front of Eddie, she could be honest, she'd been working with him day in and day out for almost three years. He was more than just her boss, he was her mentor. "I feel like I fucked up. But I'm trying to make up for it now."

"How?"

"Well, Clint doesn't think we should be together while he's 'healing' in Palm Desert." She used air quotes around the word healing.

"Why doesn't he think you should be there?"

"He has pretty significant mood swings; he thinks he could end up hurting me if he gets too angry. It's ridiculous," she said vehemently.

Eddie leaned back against his desk and folded his hands. "Is it?" He was all boss and business.

"Yes." Again, she was vehement.

"What would I find if I checked his records?"

"They would say I should be worried, but they don't know him like I do," Lydia protested.

"Jesus, Girly, you sound like every other victim I've ever talked to." Eddie shook his head, then started to speak in a high-pitched voice, "He loves me, he'd never hurt me."

"He does love me, and he would never purposely hurt me," Lydia spit out.

Eddie bit down on his toothpick. "I hope you heard what you said, because I sure as hell did."

Lydia felt herself deflate. "Purposely. You mean *that* word?"

"That would be the one." Eddie's voice was kind. Too kind. If she could, Lydia would kick herself.

Her eyes began to sting. She blinked fast because there wasn't a chance in hell she was going to cry here in her boss's office. She was one of the guys. She gripped the arm of her chair tightly and swallowed.

"I don't know what to do."

"You do what the doctors say. You do what Clint says. And in the meantime, you help me solve crimes."

Her fingernails unstuck from the leather arms of the chair. But she still wasn't sold. "Knowing he's out there hurting, and I'm here just living my life, seems wrong."

Eddie walked around his desk and sat back down. "Tell me something—don't you feel like shit?"

Lydia nodded.

"Then you're hurting too. Now that that's solved, can we get your head back in the game here at work? I can only play counselor for so long."

Lydia laughed. She loved working for this cranky old man.

"Okay, what you got?"

"No, the question is, what have you got? My guess is you took a file home with you and you've been working on it. I bet I can even guess which one."

Lydia smirked. He'd been right on one, but he wouldn't guess the second one.

"You took Satanic Voices, right?"

She nodded.

"How far did you get on it?"

"Far. I figured out how he's gotten into all of their devices. The TV took me a little bit longer since it wasn't hooked up to Bluetooth, but I figured that out as well."

"Shit, none of our guys have figured that out. Richards will be pissed that you nailed that while you were on leave."

"When *isn't* Richards pissed?"

Eddie shrugged. "But that means he'll be gunning for you even harder. You sure you want that? I could say I figured it out."

"Richards is a gnit on a gnat in my world. Let him come after me, I'll make mincemeat out of him. Wanna guess what the second file was?"

"McKenna?"

She shook her head. "Pearson."

Eddie looked puzzled. "Give me the details, I don't remember the name."

"That's where the mid-twenties woman is saying that her step-father is stalking her."

"That's bullshit. We put that to the back of the cabinet. She's some kind of celebrity wanna-be. She's looking for one more way to get publicity."

"Nope, I feel it in my gut, this is real. I want to interview her."

"I've got seven more cases I'm giving you." Eddie gestured to a pile of folders on his desk. Lydia huffed out a laugh. Cybercrimes was supposed to be a paperless environment, but with Eddie running the show, this department probably had more paper than any of the other departments in the SDPD.

"I thought the rule was four cases per officer?"

"You would have been in here bitching next week that you needed more work, so I'm front-loading you so I don't have to hear it."

Lydia shrugged, the man was right. She took the seven folders.

"Are you still intending to work the Pearson case?"

"Yep."

"You're running a fool's errand."

"I have to trust my hunches."

He pulled out his toothpick. "Good luck. And not just on the cases. But on everything. Be smart and keep electronic tabs on your man. If he needs help, get your ass out to the Palm Desert. But in the meantime, stay put."

"Aye, Aye Captain."

"Cut that shit out, I'm not in the goddamn Navy."

It had been three weeks and Clint didn't know who was getting to him more; Dick-weasel for not contacting Drake and keeping all of them on pins and needles, Lydia calling nightly and always asking how he was, or Drake and Finn assessing his every move. At least Mason had gone back to

San Diego. His lieutenant vibe was seriously getting on his nerves.

Finn was smoother. He still was always assessing Clint, but he did it in such a way that it didn't bug the shit out of him. Drake, however, was another story.

The Desert Vista Renewal van dropped him and Lisa off at the resort.

"You're not even walking with a limp anymore," she noted as they got to the lobby. "They're pretty sure I'm going to need a cane for the rest of my life," she grimaced.

"How long have you been a patient at Renewal?" Clint asked.

"Three weeks. I had my stroke two months ago. I was in the hospital for two weeks, and then in another rehab place in Kentucky that didn't seem to be doing me any good. My father did research, and that's how I ended up here, but I'm not sure it's helping."

"I've been here for about three weeks too, and I think they're damn good," Clint said. "I didn't think I'd like it when I started, but I've seen a difference already. Ask to be changed to my physical therapist, Arnold. He's amazing."

"Okay, I will. Thanks. I'll see you tomorrow morning," she waved as she walked off to the elevators.

Clint sauntered down the hall to the first-floor suite that he and Drake were sharing. He was still pondering the latest idea that the psychologist had come up with. Seemed odd. But he'd popped off at Drake again two days ago. He'd been out of control again, and it was over nothing. Sure, it was Drake, but he wanted to get his shit together. Drake might still be Drake, but he was no longer Clint Archer, and that was unacceptable. He didn't care if his brain had been rattled by the explosion. It was un-fucking-acceptable. And here he'd thought he was getting his shit together. He didn't care if the psychologist said that was the thing that would take the longest. It had been twenty-one days already!

The breath he took rattled. Jesus, he wasn't getting ready to cry, was he? God, he was more messed up than he thought. Then there was the team. Would he ever be good enough to be a SEAL again? They couldn't have someone who wasn't in control one hundred percent of the time. He took another deep breath, only this time it seemed to be bringing on a headache, not the calm he needed.

He used his key card to open up the door. Finn and Drake both jerked, looking guilty as hell.

"What's the deal?" he tried to act casual. For all he knew they were talking about his retirement.

"The weaselly dick just WhatsApp-ed me," Drake looked hunted. "He wants me in Kazakhstan in two days."

"For what?"

"No matter how much I pressed, he wouldn't say."

"Don't go," Finn said emphatically.

"I'm going with you," Clint said.

Finn stood up, furious. "Nobody's going!"

"Finn, this isn't just about the video anymore," Clint said. "There is something really wrong with a senator's aide in the country of Kazakhstan. Do you realize how perilous that is? Do you know what's gone on over there in the last two years?"

Score one for Team Archer, his memory was on-point about miscellaneous trivia again.

"Of course, I do," Finn's eyes flashed.

"Then you know they're now the new Swiss bank for international bad guys, and anyone who wants to hide money. For all we know they're laundering money as well. This is not good, not good at all. This probably leads back to the senator. We've got to cut this cancer out of our government."

"Send someone else, call the CIA. Drake, you're not going to risk your career doing an off-the-books mission like this. If you get caught, you're off the team."

"If that video gets out, I'm off the team. You know there are plenty of places that would pick me up and pay me a damn sight more than Uncle Sam. I'll live. But I want to stop these two pricks from whatever they're doing."

"Same," Clint said.

"Ah hell, Clint, you don't even remember them," Finn shook his head in disgust.

"I might not remember Syria, Dick-Weasel, and the senator, but I know Kazakhstan. You want to go a few rounds? Bet I can beat you in Eurasia Trivial Pursuit."

Drake laughed. "Don't take the bet, Finn. Even at his most brain-damaged, he'll beat your ass."

"Thanks for the vote of confidence," Clint said wryly, as he shot Drake the finger.

Drake held up his hands. "Hey, it was a compliment."

"Anyway, I've caught up on them now, and everything I've read I don't like. Hell, the senator just skated on insider trading charges. He was associated with that absolute bastard who took over that company and then started charging fifty times the amount for that diabetic drug. And everything you've told me about the weasel has made my head hurt."

"Your head is hurting?" Finn pounced on him.

"No, it was a figure of speech."

"Bullshit. You had a headache two days ago after we went around," Drake said and turned to Finn. "You wouldn't know about it, you were out at that barbeque place picking up dinner and having phone sex with Angie."

"Fine, I had a headache," Clint admitted. "Everybody on Earth occasionally suffers from headaches, but it wasn't a debilitating migraine this time. I could still function." Clint turned to Finn. "Drake's right, we've got to go. You know we can't send in one alone unless our back is to the wall. But we have options, so it's a two-man op. We're going to need you on this side of the world to get us updates and Drake and I will check things out over there."

"Clint, nothing personal, man, but you're not one-hundred percent, it should be me that goes," Finn said solemnly.

"No," Drake and Clint said simultaneously.

"You have a career to lose. I'm on the hook," Drake said. "Clint is just playing hooky from the spa for a couple of days. We'll say he went home to San Diego."

"Oh really?" Finn said sarcastically. "You think it's going to be that easy to check Clint out?"

"Sure it will," Clint grinned. "With you arranging it, it will be a breeze. Say it's in celebration of my halfway mark. Seriously, I've been here three weeks, they were thinking one to three months. This *could* be halfway through the program, right? So I went home to see Lydia."

Finn slowly sank down on the loveseat and put his head in his hands. "Fine, it's you two going. But you have to promise me to stay alive. You know that, right?"

"I'm telling you, this will be slicker than snot," Drake said with a grin.

20

"Why is everybody calling this place Astana, when the name is Nur-Sultan?" Drake asked.

"They just changed the name from Astana to Nur-Sultan last year. Not everybody has gotten on board," Clint said off-handedly as he took in the science fiction architecture of Kazakhstan's capital city. "This place is eerie. It's like coming across an ancient city in the middle of the jungle or something."

"Did you not notice that it was nothing but grasslands as we flew in?" Drake asked dryly. "No jungle here, my man, just freezing-cold grasslands and the set of the next Space Odyssey movie."

It was January and ten below zero as they walked along the pristine boulevard, away from their ultra-modern hotel. They were supposed to get more instructions tonight, so they had time to look around. Both men couldn't help themselves. Clint had done some research on this city before they left the US, but pictures hadn't done it justice. He'd known it had been designed by world-renowned architects, and he'd known it would be amazing, but not anything like this.

As he and Drake made the long trek toward the Baiterek Monument, Clint looked for any piece of trash, a cigarette stub, anything that might hint at regular people living here, but found nothing. Soon they were looking one hundred meters up in the air to the majestic yellow orb that sat delicately amidst flared-out poles of highly polished metal that was supposed to resemble poplar branches. This was supposed to be the tree of life, and that was the egg laid by the bird of happiness.

When Clint explained that to Drake, he snorted.

"I bet the people who live here don't believe that happy horseshit, pun intended. There is nothing happy about this sterilized environment. I wouldn't be surprised if you get sent to the gulag if you spit out your gum."

He looked around the almost deserted streets. Very few people were out and about. There were more gardeners and cleaners than there were actual residents of the city.

"How many people go to jail here on a daily basis, Clint? Did you get that statistic, or were you too blown away by the crazy architecture?"

"Nobody who *should* go to jail ever ends up in jail. All of this quirky beauty masks a lot of crime."

"Where is everybody?"

"Inside, where there's heat," Clint grinned. "We're the shmoes out sightseeing."

"I can't wait to work the bird of happiness into my stories to Andrew. Even little Tee likes to listen in. Karen says that it's the sound of my voice that makes her smile."

Clint loved seeing the gooey expression on Drake's face when he talked about his children. He wished to God that he and Lydia had gotten to that point in life.

Drake stamped his feet and put his gloved hands under his arms.

"What's wrong?"

"Huh?" Clint asked.

"The look on your face just turned dark. What gives?"

"I'm cold."

"We've been cold for an hour, but now you look like someone pissed in your Cheerios. Tell me what gives."

Clint's shoulders slumped. "Let's head back to the hotel. It's true, I am cold. As for what's got me down? I'm not married. I don't have kids."

"So, ask your woman to marry you."

"I already did," Clint said darkly. "Remember, you were at the engagement party."

"So, what's the hold-up?"

"Lydia's, the hold-up. I've asked her every six months when we can plan the wedding, all I get from her is 'soon.'"

Drake stared at Clint, dumbfounded. "What the fuck?"

"Exactly. I don't know what's going on with her either."

"Not her, you," Drake exclaimed. "Brother, I know you're not me. But geez, even you can't be that patient. Haven't you gotten in her face and asked her what in the hell is going on?"

"Of course, I have. She told me to trust her, that she's waiting for the right time."

"And?"

"And what?"

"Clint, you let her get away with that? You didn't push more and demand to know what in the hell was making her wait? What the hell was stopping her from going the distance?"

"Drake, you don't understand. Every single time I've pushed her, every damn time, she turned into a different

Lydia. She was this fragile woman who looked like she could shatter in my arms. I was scared to push anymore. I didn't want to lose her."

"Lydia isn't going anywhere, trust me."

Clint shook his head. Those were memories that were seared into his brain. It might only be one percent of their relationship, if even that, but since he had woken up from the hospital, it had taken up tons of his bandwidth. Only those three days of togetherness in their home had started to alleviate his fears. Made him think that they were destined for one another. But since he'd left her back in San Diego the doubts had crept back in. He'd even talked to the psychologist at Desert Vista about it. Dr. Martin said this was common. It hadn't made him feel any better.

Then, as if just thinking about her had conjured her, Lydia's distinctive ring-tone sounded on his phone. He did some quick math and realized that since it was two p.m. in Nur-Sultan, it was midnight in San Diego.

"Hi, Honey, isn't this a bit late for a call?" he yawned.

"Don't bullshit me. You're in Kazakhstan," she bit out. "It's two o'clock in the afternoon."

Drake raised an eyebrow. Clint mouthed 'busted.'

"Keeping tabs on me?"

"Damn right I am."

"Oh, ye of little faith."

"And doesn't this just prove me right? Tell me what in the hell is going on."

"Lydia, I promise to tell you everything when I get back to California." Clint forced a smile into his voice.

"Don't even think you're getting away with this. Let Drake know I'm going to tell Karen if you don't give me the four-one-one on this. Now spill."

Clint knew his phone was secure, but what he didn't

know was if there were any parabolic sound-collecting dishes within hearing distance. After all, this country had been part of the Soviet Union not so long ago. "Lydia, I'm not somewhere where I can talk right now."

"Well, you better get somewhere fast. I have Karen on speed dial."

He couldn't let this get any worse than it was.

"I hear you. Give me forty-five minutes to get back to our room and sweep it."

"Makes sense," she admitted. "I'll give you an hour."

"Good," he said into his phone. But it was dead.

"Trouble?"

"Big fucking trouble. For both of us. She knows we're both here, and if we don't come clean, she's going to tell Karen you're here."

"What?" Drake roared. "She has no business doing that."

"You're just a magnet for blackmail this month." Clint was talking to thin air as Drake started hot-footing it back toward the hotel.

Clint followed, whistling. Lydia had been keeping tabs on him and was pissed as hell. And he felt nothing but amusement and admiration. No rage, no anger—nope, he was happy. Okay, he was going to get his ass handed to him when he told her what was going on, but he was pretty sure he could handle that. Hell, he was looking forward to it. Lydia was at her best when she was riled up. She turned him on. It was a shame that she was halfway around the world and he couldn't do anything about it.

"Speed it up," Drake yelled back at Clint. He hadn't realized that Drake was already a good ten meters in front of him. Letting his mind wander to Lydia could do that to him. This was going to be fun.

CLINT HAD HIDDEN the bug-tracking device in a camera so that when their baggage had been searched they wouldn't be questioned. It had worked like a charm. They'd been wearing suits and heavy woolen coats that they'd purchased in a boutique in Palm Desert, so that had helped expedite their entry into Kazakhstan as well.

"Got two," Clint said. "One was a camera in the drapery rod, the other was a listening device in the desk phone. Sloppy."

"Why're you talking?"

"I've already turned on the blocker, I doubt anyone is monitoring the live video feed. We should have time for Lydia's phone call, then Dick-Weasel's call at seven o'clock tonight." Clint had handled everything in under forty minutes. He didn't want to wait for Lydia's call, so he called her.

"Hello, Beautiful," he started the call on speaker. "Now it really *is* past your bedtime."

"Don't fuck with me, Archer," she growled. "What the hell are you doing out of the clinic? Why are you in Kazakhstan? And make it good, otherwise, I'm calling Karen *and* Mason."

Clint's smile split his face.

"I don't respond well to blackmail, Lydia." Drake's voice menaced.

"Then you shouldn't have recruited Clint into this scheme, whatever it is." Her voice was just as menacing.

Drake's head shot up and he looked even more pissed when he saw Clint's shit-eating grin. "This is not funny, Archer." He pounded his fist on the desk. "Get your woman under control."

Clint threw back his head but somehow managed to stifle his laugh.

"I'm a detective in the SDPD; if you think Clint can get the little woman in control, you're dumber than a box of rocks, you Neanderthal. I'm tempted to call Karen just to tell her you said that."

"Lydia—" Drake started.

"And you, Archer, you damn well shouldn't be laughing, because I know you are."

She knows me well.

"I'm going to cut off your balls and fry them up for breakfast when you come home. Now tell me what the hell is going on!" Clint winced, and it wasn't because of her threat, it was because he heard the nascent fear in her voice. It killed him. He liked it better when she was a ball-buster.

"Lydia, this is a quick, in-and-out mission, I promise," Clint tried to soothe.

"But it's off the books, isn't it? What has Drake gotten himself into?"

"Hey, it could be Clint's gotten himself into trouble, and I'm helping *him*," Drake protested.

Lydia snorted, "Yeah, sure. Now spill it."

Clint rubbed the back of his neck and sighed. "Lyd, how much have *you* pieced together, and don't tell me it's nothing. If you've tracked us down, you've figured out some pieces already."

"I know you're using some of the same sources I do for *my* work. When Diamond couldn't get ahold of you, he called me. I pretended it was one of our joint ops so he gave me info to pass along to you. I know you're trying to break into WhatsApp. I know you two bought last-minute tickets to Kazakhstan that cost the moon and back. That's it so far."

"Wait a minute, have you got the code to break into

someone's WhatsApp account?"

Hot damn!

"Sure do." Clint could hear the satisfaction in Lydia's voice.

"When did you get it? We need it. This is critical."

"I got it five hours ago while you were on the plane. If you want it, you have to spill your story."

"I'm in a jam," Drake started. "On the same mission where Clint was injured, we rescued a senator and one of his aides. The aide was a whiney asshole named Devon, who was hellbent on getting us all killed. I tried to explain to him that he needed to stop it, that he was going to get the other civilians in the party killed. He didn't give a shit." Drake sneered. "He was an asshole squared."

"Okay," Lydia said slowly. "And that relates to Kazakhstan how?"

"Well, I might have threatened to paint a bullseye on his forehead and throw him in front of some tanks."

"Sounds like he deserved it." There was satisfaction in Lydia's voice.

"Somebody caught me on video, I think it was him. They edited it to make me look like a crazy man. He's threatened to release it to the top Navy brass, to begin with, then if they don't oust me, he'll blast it all over social media and I'll be ruined."

"Again, you haven't answered my question—you're in Kazakhstan why?" she prompted.

"He told me to get over here, that there's a job he wants me to do. He'll tell me in three hours what it is. He'll do it over his compromised burner phone, or in WhatsApp, that's why we need to hack his account. It's obvious that these guys have something on Devon and possibly the senator."

"Why not just stay in the states and tell him you're in

Kazakhstan?" Lydia asked.

"Clint, you're up," Drake said.

"Right now Kazakhstan has become a hotbed for laundering money and storing illegal money," Clint explained. "The British are filing cases against some of the biggest offenders on this. So it's possible that Devon and the senator got caught up in one of those cases and are trying to cover up their tracks. Or it's possible that the corrupt bankers in Kazakhstan are holding their money. There's been a lot of instances of that lately, too."

"Fine, that tells me why Devon could have his panties in a twist about Kazakhstan. But what's Drake's part in all of this?"

"Once he tells us Drake's assignment, then we'll know who's squeezing that little weasel and the senator. What we're hoping is that then we can turn it around on Devon and squeeze him," Drake said.

"Mmmm," Lydia said through the phone. Clint could see her in his mind's eye, cocking her head to the side and contemplating what Drake had just said. "Do you think the Kazakhstan people have been talking to him via WhatsApp?"

"Absolutely," Clint said. "It's one of the most secure ways to communicate right now, the end-to-end encryption scrambles messages so only the two people communicating to one another can hear the calls or see the messages. Hopefully, Dick-weasel did a lot of communicating via messaging, because those we should be able to access with the WhatsApp code that the Israelis developed. The phone calls were never stored. So we need it, now."

"By the way, I like the new identity you created. Pretty innocuous. Would have worked too, if you hadn't used the credit card we created for Henry Styles three years ago. Even though money gets pulled straight from your corporation, it still pings me. Once I saw the two tickets to Nur-Sultan, you were busted."

"I didn't use Henry Styles' credit card, I transferred over to Raymond Lloyd," Clint protested.

"Yeah, but you just did it two days ago. Sorry, Buster, if you don't think that's going to ring alarm bells, you have another think coming."

That's my woman, nothing gets by her.

"Otherwise, it was a perfect alias. Without that, I could have been chasing my tail for days."

"Enough sucking-up, Lydia, give us the code that Diamond gave you," Drake said harshly. "The sooner Clint can get into the little prick's WhatsApp account, the sooner we can get the hell out of Kazakhstan."

"And Clint back in rehab," Lydia said with relief in her voice. "How are you doing, Clint?"

"I've been fine so far, in my opinion. Drake, what do you think?"

"He's been on-point on everything, Lydia. I'd definitely choose to have him watching my back any day of the week."

Clint smiled.

"That's really good to hear. Clint, I'll send the code to your new alias using our normal secure channels, then send me the account name of who you're trying to hack. Let's work in conjunction with one another. While you're viewing his account's texts, I will too. We can exchange notes in the morning. Don't burn yourself out—if you end up setting yourself back, I'm going to kill you myself. Got it?"

Clint was grinning again. "Got it."

"And stop grinning. I'm serious."

Clint laughed. "I love you, Lydia. I should be back in two days. This shouldn't take long at all."

21

DERWOOD'S VOICE SOUNDED TINNY OVER THE WHATSAPP program. It came into the burner phone where it had taken Clint three-and-a-half hours to download the code so he could unscramble and record the conversation.

"I've got a mission for you, Avery," Deadwood laughed. "That's what you big bad SEALs call it, right? A mission."

Clint had been right; he didn't like the little shit. He didn't remember him from Syria, though he'd been hoping he would.

"Cut the crap and tell me what you want."

"I need two men killed."

Drake's head jerked up and he stared at Clint. Why hadn't he considered that? Why hadn't Drake for that matter?

"I'm not an assassin."

"Bullshit, all you special operations guys are nothing but trained killers. It was a one-off that you rescued us. Your gig is murder, pure and simple. You don't have a heart. They find men with psychopathic leanings, then they train you. I've read things."

What the hell?

"I'm not going to kill anyone for you," Drake said emphatically.

"That's too bad. Your wife and kids are going to miss you when you end up in jail. Or do you go to jail? Is it a military prison? Didn't look that up. I'll be there testifying about how you tried to throw me under a tank in Syria."

"The woman and cameraman who were with us will vouch for me."

"No, they won't. I have the goods on them too. They won't walk one step out of line."

"What do you mean you—"

"Enough! I'm the one with all the cards. You don't get to ask questions. Now, I'm going to tell you the names of the two bankers I need killed. I don't care how you get it done, as long as it happens within the next three days."

Drake sat back in his chair and crossed his arms. There was a hint of a smile on his face. Mr. Bullshitter was about to take center stage. "Three days, two hits. That doesn't allow me to set it up so I get out of here alive. I'm not up for a suicide mission. I need five days at minimum."

"You get three."

"Seems to me, Deadwood Weasel-Dick, I'm holding the cards on this one. If you need these guys killed, I'm your only game in town. I'll get it done in five," Drake chuckled.

"My name is Devon Cron," the little toad spit out. "You will treat me with respect. I work for a United States senator, and he's going places."

"What are the names of the marks? What information do you have for me?"

"Their names are Amir Omarov and Zangar Boyko. They are vice presidents at the Sultana Asianic Investment

Bank. They are brothers-in-law, so it is possible you will find them out together with their wives."

"Why do you want them dead?" Drake asked easily.

"That's none of your business," Devon said sharply.

"Actually, it is. It will tell me if whatever they did is common, and how many people might be gunning for them, and how many bodyguards they might have."

"Assume a shit-ton, these are slimy motherfuckers. There have to be dozens of people looking to get revenge on them."

"Can you name any?"

"No, I can't name any," Devon said sarcastically. "Just get the job done. I'll check in tomorrow night on your progress."

The line went dead.

Drake rubbed his hands together. "I knew if I called him Deadwood Weasel-Dick he'd be forced to correct me. We got him admitting his name. It's beautiful."

"I'd say so. Now, for making contact with Amir and Zangar, that's going to be tough with all the bodyguards."

"How about an appointment at the bank?" Drake asked. "I like the simple, straight-forward approach."

Clint gave out a pained laugh. "Tell me something I don't know."

"You all right?"

"Fuck, Drake, I overdid," Clint said as he began to rub his temples. "We needed to get the code downloaded onto the phone before the call, but it did me in. I need a pill, a bed, and someplace dark to lie down."

His mouth tasted like bile. *Please God, don't say I'm going to throw up.*

"You look like shit. Can you make it into the bedroom on your own steam?"

Clint rolled his eyes, then stumbled as he tried to get out of the chair that he'd been sitting in for four hours.

"Steady there, little buddy. Let me help."

"I fucked up, Drake." His own voice sounded far away. God, this headache was going to be a doozy.

"You did good, man, you kept it together 'til the end. As far as I'm concerned, you did your job and you came out smelling like a rose." Drake was helping him up off the chair before he slipped out of it. "I'm getting you to bed. Migraine, right?"

Clint nodded, and a burning spear went through his right temple. He couldn't help the groan. "Pill," he damn near whimpered. Fuck, he hated this.

"Bed, lights out, then pill."

"Must be like Syria all over again, you having to damn near carry my ass around," Clint tried to chuckle.

"Nah, this time you have some of your own steam, last time you were dead weight. Big difference."

Clint opened his eyes. Great, there were now two Drake Averys, just what he needed in his life. The room was dim, but even the little bit of light that was coming through the blinds killed his eyes. Drake noticed and pulled down the blackout curtain.

"Better?" he asked.

"Yes," Clint said in a pathetic voice, but it was the best he could do.

"I'm getting you a pill and some water. Where are they?"

"Shaving kit."

Both Drakes disappeared.

Dammit, he needed to dig deeper on Devon's WhatsApp account. He didn't have time for this shit. At least he had sent the decoded account to Lydia before he decided to play the victim. He tried to lift himself up on his elbows, but now it wasn't just a spear, it was a spiked ball and chain, continually wrapping around his head, the spikes digging in. Even closing his eyes, he could see the code, and then the spiked ball would land on his eyeballs.

"God, man, I could hear your groans from the living room." Drake lifted his head, and then Clint could hear himself groan. Drake put the pill on his tongue and lifted the bottle of water to his mouth. Clint knew that soon the pain would be behind him.

"Thanks," he husked out.

"You can't be doing code like that. I should have stopped you." Drake sounded disgusted.

"Necessary."

Drake's sigh said he knew it was, too. "Get some sleep."

CLINT FELT like he had been hit by a Mac truck when he woke up. He staggered to the bathroom and threw up. He picked up his toothbrush and spent four minutes brushing his teeth. While brushing he started replaying last night's events.

Eventually, he began feeling human again. The residual head pounding remained, but he could think again, which was a blessing. He looked at his watch and saw that it was eleven a.m. local time.

"Okay, let's see what trouble Drake's gotten into now."

He opened the door to the suite's adjoining living room. Drake was talking to someone on his phone.

"Can you really pull that off?" Drake asked.

He then had to pull the phone away from his ear.

"Okay, okay, my mistake for doubting your abilities. I'm sorry, my goddess of all things tech."

I knew it.

Clint stormed in, his feet hitting the carpet hard so he could be heard. Not a good idea for his hurting head.

"Give me the phone, Drake."

Drake held it to his chest. "I'm not sure Lydia wants to talk to you if you have a stick up your ass."

"Don't make me fight for it. Or you'll end up on your *ass*." Clint was in the mood to knock Drake into next week.

Where is this coming from?

Drake put the phone back up to his ear. "Do you want to talk to someone named Clint Archer?" he asked. "I wouldn't recommend it, it looks like he got up on the wrong side of the bed." Clint loomed over Drake furiously while he listened to the phone.

"Nope, she doesn't want to talk to you," he grinned up at Clint.

Clint grabbed the phone. "Lydia, what in the hell are you doing talking to Drake and not to me?"

"Drake told me how badly you were hurting yesterday. It sounded like you needed at least twenty-four hours of sleep. Seriously, Clint, why didn't you have me do that coding?"

"Don't you have a real job to do?" he asked sarcastically.

"Half the time I work from home, they don't care when I do my work, just so long as I get it done," Lydia responded patiently. It was like she was talking down to him. He didn't like it.

"Back off, Lydia, if I'd needed your help, I would have asked for it."

He heard her suck in her breath. Good, he'd scored a point. He didn't need her butting in on his shit.

Clint winced when Drake straight-armed him into the chest and yanked the phone out of his hand. "Way to be a dick."

"Just stating the truth," Clint snarled. "I—"

"Shut it." Drake's look was menacing. "Shut your goddamn mouth."

"Lydia," Drake started as he spoke into the phone. He listened for a minute. "No, I don't think it's wise to put it on speaker." Drake was quiet for a bit longer, then he set down the phone on the coffee table and pressed the speaker button.

"Clint, can you hear me?" Lydia asked. This time she didn't sound helpful and accommodating—this time she sounded pissed.

"Yes," he answered succinctly.

"I gave you shit about your op, but when we last talked, you were Dr. Jekyll; aka reasonable, smart, not a halfwit. Today I find out that you did the *exact damn thing* the doctors told you would push back your recovery. And for what? Male pride? I could have done that same damn hack remotely. You're halfway through the program and you're going to fuck things up now?" she demanded incredulously.

Clint sucked in a deep breath through his teeth. He tried to get his thoughts together because they were scattered all over like dropped pennies. Lydia was on his side. She was trying to help. This was part of the TBI, he needed to take his over-the-top emotions out of the equation.

"For real, Lydia, and I'm serious. Which of us can do that kind of hack faster, you or me? Hands down, every time, it's me, and you know it. We were under the gun, I had no choice. We needed that call recorded. The second the call was done and I'd cracked the account, I sent you all the information so you could take it from there. I'm not a fucking idiot!"

Way to keep it cool. I'm a fucking idiot.

"I didn't say you were," she damn near hollered back at him.

"It sounded like it," Clint sighed.

"Take it down a notch, children," Drake said as he put his hand on Clint's shoulder. His immediate instinct was to shove it off, but he held it together and stepped away instead.

"Lydia, would you kindly share with the class what you found when you went through Dick-weasel's WhatsApp chats."

"Well first, he doesn't just use it for business. He uses it for his personal life too. And I just want to say ick. Ick. Ick. And ick with sprinkles on top."

Clint took a deep breath and sat down on the couch and forced a smile. "Sprinkles? No peanuts?"

"Oh hell, yeah, it was a whole banana split. This is where he talks to women after finding them on Tinder. It took me an entire hour to weed through that swamp. Then I got down to business, to find out all the different little endeavors our boy was involved in. He's been busy."

"Doing what?" Drake asked.

"He's not just working for the senator, he's playing footsy with a congressman across party lines. I guess it doesn't matter who he's in bed with as long as the money's good."

"Yeah, but doing what?" Drake asked again.

"He's the go-between," Lydia finally answered. "All of these guys have inside information, and there are a few rotten apples who want to make a little inside cash on this knowledge. Devon is more than happy to facilitate this."

"So what did he and the senator cook up, and how did it relate to Syria?" Clint wanted to know.

"I don't think it had anything to do with Syria. According to Devon, the Syria stunt was just Leonard's way of getting votes back home. Nope, this thing he has going in Kazakhstan is all about making money based on some inside knowledge he has about tariffs."

"So why does he want people in Kazakhstan killed if they're working on a profitable deal?" Drake wanted to know.

"It's not so profitable anymore. The tariffs weren't lifted, so the senator is standing there with his dick in his hand looking like an idiot, unable to deliver. These guys in Kazakhstan want the payoff they were promised. Hence the reason Drake was so subtly recruited."

"Oh, it was subtle all right," Drake agreed sarcastically. "By the way, Lydia, I can tell you've been working with cops a long time, with all that colorful language."

Clint laughed. "It's okay, I've seen her with the other Midnight Delta women. She's all angelic with them."

Lydia snorted.

"So what were you all talking about when I first got up and made an ass out of myself?" Clint pushed his fingers through his hair. Even that still hurt his head a little bit.

"She got info on our targets. Amir Omarov and Zangar Boyko and she confirmed they really are vice presidents at the Sultana Asianic Investment Bank here in Nur-Sultan. They're the real deal, right Lydia?" Drake asked.

"Yeppers. They're the equivalent of Russian oligarchs, on their way to being billionaires. If they could count the money in shadow accounts, they would actually be considered billionaires."

Clint looked over at Drake. "These are not going to be easy men to get close to."

"But your woman has an idea."

Clint grinned naturally this time. "Should have known."

"Lydia says she can have fake profiles made up for us by

tomorrow, so that Amir and Zangar will want to meet with us. We're going to be Americans representing large crude reserves who have a plan of diverting the crude out of the US."

"Lydia?" Clint questioned. "What in the hell idea have you come up with? Because you know big American oil is only allowed to sell within the US or Mexico. They've been pissed about that for years."

"You tell them that after you have some assurances on their end that they would be interested in doing business with you, then you would explain how it could be done. Baby them along, you don't have to have a plan. But this gives you an in to find out what they have on Devon and the senator. See if you can offer your deal in exchange for information or something. What you need is that information so you have the leverage to twist Devon."

Clint sat back farther in his chair, processing what Lydia had just said.

"This is good, it has real possibilities, Lyd," Clint finally said.

"Hey, Lydia, Dr. Jekyll is back with us. Mr. Hyde seems to have taken a powder," Drake grinned.

"Can I talk to her?" Clint asked as he held out his hand for the phone.

"Depends. Are you going to be nice?" There was no teasing in Drake's voice. He was dead serious.

Clint met the man's gaze and gave him a solemn nod.

"LYDIA, I NEED HELP," were the first words out of Clint's mouth when he took the phone into his bedroom.

"Sure, what do you need me to do?" she asked briskly.

"No, not that. It sounds like you have us covered right now. I mean I *need* help. I *need* to be in the Palm Desert, I get that. I won't fuck up again while I'm here, Drake's life is on the line."

"And yours."

He nodded. "And mine."

When she didn't say anything he continued. "Seriously, Lydia, those were extreme circumstances last night, otherwise we could have split the work and I would have stopped well before the headache point. If I'd done that, I wouldn't have been such an asshole this morning."

"We've had this conversation before," her voice was flat. "Now you're going to apologize for being a jackass. Save your breath. I don't want to hear it. Let's concentrate on getting the two of you home safe."

"But I am sorry." The words came from his gut.

"You always are. Like I said, we'll table that for now. Read the bios on the guys I've created for you. They're complicated. The one thing I've done to make it easier is allowing you to keep your real names."

"Got it. We'll memorize these. No problem. Are you acting as our liaison or something?"

"Nope, I'm your personal assistant, Melinda Sharpe. When you give me the ready signal I'll arrange appointments for you."

"Will you be wearing a pencil skirt?"

Lydia gave out a startled laugh.

Yay, I've still got it!

"If I am, you won't be able to see it. You know why? Oh yeah, you're in Kazakhstan!"

Clint winced.

"Me leaving is water under the bridge. Drake couldn't go out alone, and I couldn't allow Finn to put his career on the line. You and I know mine is hanging on by a thread until the final eval of the TBI. Better me than him."

"I got that—"

"But the worst part? The worst part is once again I couldn't control my moods and ended up being a royal prick to you. Drake is fine; he has the hide of a rhinoceros and I'm not in love with him. But you? I want to treat you like the precious lady you are in my life. I don't want you to always have to make excuses for me, otherwise one day I'll find you gone."

"Clint! That wouldn't happen."

"Really, Lydia? Because there is a small little part of me that has grown bigger since the explosion that thinks you already have one foot out the door."

"No," she gasped.

"Yes. Honey, I love you as if my next gulp of air depended on it, but you won't marry me. How else am I supposed to feel?"

"Oh, God."

Is she crying?

"This is the worst goddamn time to be bringing this up, but it's time for all cards to be on the table. I don't want you to have to put up with some guy who's emotionally abusive. I'm too in love with you to want that for your future. My gut is telling me to hang on to you no matter what emotional coercive tactic I need to take, but that's not what's right for you. What's more, I'm thinking this might be the out you've been looking for."

"No, Baby, no. You've got it all wrong." She *was* crying. He was having trouble making out what she was saying.

"Lydia, calm down," he tried to soothe.

"I'm the one with the problems. The issues. There's too much filth that clings to me, and I just don't want you to be a part of it." He heard her blow her nose. Then he thought he heard her say. "I don't want to be a part of it."

"What?"

"I want to be with you all of my life," she sobbed. "You're everything to me. Even when you're a cranky asshole. You're everything."

"Then let's go to Vegas when I get back."

"You don't understand, it's more complicated than that."

"Then make me understand."

She didn't speak for so long, Clint had to look down at his phone to make sure the connection hadn't been broken.

"Lydia? Honey?"

"We need to talk when you get home. But know that I love you with my whole heart."

Something settled inside him. He could get through this. Not the job in Kazakhstan, but his future. With Lydia by his side, he was going to make it.

22

THE BLUE SKY AND SMELL OF THE OCEAN DID NOTHING FOR Lydia as she walked down the stairs from Alice Pearson's small apartment. There didn't seem to be anything good in the world, and this interview just confirmed it.

Part of her was so scared about what Clint would think about her father, and her covering it up for so long. Another part was relieved that it would finally be out there. Had she really just given her dad's sins so much oxygen that they had become a monster of epic proportions, coloring every aspect of her life?

She yawned as she opened the door to Clint's truck. She loved driving it when he wasn't around; it made her feel cuddled in his arms.

I have it bad.

She needed to get back to her townhome and put the finishing touches on the alias she had set up for him and Drake.

"Detective?"

Lydia squinted back over her shoulder to see Alice

jogging up toward her. "I forgot to tell you something. It might not be anything, but I thought I'd bring it up."

Lydia shut her car door and forced a relaxed smile on her face. "What is it, Alice?"

"I thought it was weird that Mom's grave had fresh flowers on it, the last time I was there."

"When was this?"

"Her birthday, January sixteenth."

"So three weeks ago. Did Albert give your mother flowers often?"

"No, he never did. That's why it never occurred to me it could be him, but you asked for anything out of the ordinary. Before Albert, it was just mom and me, so I just can't imagine who would have put flowers on her grave."

"Alice, it's good you told me. Now, take those safety precautions I recommended, and I'll call you in a few days, okay?" Lydia asked as she squeezed her arm. She waited until Alice nodded.

"I'll wait until you go back inside." Lydia smiled kindly. She needed to get home and check with Diamond and Melvin that the aliases she had given Drake and Clint were dug in deep. Then she would start acting as Melinda Sharpe, personal assistant extraordinaire, the woman who could work miracles getting appointments for her very important bosses.

She started the truck and her phone rang. She put it on the speaker as she pulled out of her parking spot.

"Lydia, it's Billy Anderson."

Her gut clenched.

"Is it time?"

"Yep, Sophia's at the hospital."

"Mary Birch?" Lydia questioned, wanting to be sure.

"That's the one. Only Mason is going to be let in the actual room. Which sounds good to me."

"Yeah, I guess it would to you," Lydia laughed.

"So she just started labor?"

Billy sighed. "Nope, she thought it was Braxton-Hicks again and didn't want to bother us. So she'd been having contractions for a while. According to Mason when he came out to tell me, she's close."

"Who else have you called?"

"Nobody. I was hoping you could."

"I'm on it." Lydia assured the soon-to-be-uncle.

"Thanks, see you soon."

Sophia had done it, she'd made it to thirty-six weeks! Lydia called Rylie and told her the news, and Rylie said she'd get ahold of the others since she was home. Lydia headed to the hospital.

———

IN THE WAITING ROOM, she and Rylie called Melvin and started working to get Clint and Drake's backgrounds nailed down tight and then getting them appointments with the Kazakhstanis. Just as they were wrapping it up, Mason walked out.

"I have a daughter, and her mama is doing great," he exclaimed. "Sophia is a miracle worker." Lydia could see the sheen of tears in his eyes. He cleared his throat then said. "We can only have two visitors at a time. Billy and Lydia, do you want to come in?"

They wasted no time following Mason back down the hallway to Sophia's room. There was absolute quiet, as Sophia held a pink blanket cuddled close to her chest. The baby had a dusting of blonde hair, a perfect pink mouth and her eyes were closed.

"She's gorgeous," Lydia breathed as she followed Billy toward the bed.

"I'm your Uncle Billy," he said quietly. His grin was huge.

It wasn't until Lydia tasted salt that she realized she was crying.

"Sophia, you done good, Girlfriend," she whispered.

Mason went to the other side of the bed and sat down so he could wrap his arms around his wife and child.

"You're right, Lydia, Sophia was amazing. I'm truly blessed." He kissed the top of his daughter's head, then gave Sophia a tender kiss filled with love and adoration.

IT HAD BEEN two and a half days since he had done all the coding, and Clint felt totally in control again. Just in time, too, since this was one of his biggest roles to date. Thank God Lydia had let them keep their own names, so they wouldn't fuck that up, but everything else about their backgrounds was fake. It was worse than any final exam he had ever crammed for, making sure he had the background down pat.

Seriously, Dare Stanton was better suited for this James Bond shit. He'd had to do it on a mission, and he'd ended up with a wife out of the deal. But no, here he was with Drake Avery as a partner and possibly going to lose a potential wife.

Nope, I'm not going to let that happen. Whatever is eating at Lydia, I'll solve it. We'll get past this and make it work.

Clint grimaced at his reflection in the elevator's gleaming mirror. They'd agreed that Drake would do the talking this time around. The man could bullshit with the best of them, plus nobody, including Clint, was one-hundred percent sure on how well he'd respond under pressure. Which sucked donkey-balls.

When they finally got to the top floor of the bank building, they were greeted by a gorgeous blonde receptionist with cat-green eyes and legs up to her chin. How did she get real work done during the day in five-inch heels?

"Gentlemen," she purred with a sexy Slavic accent. "The vice presidents are finishing a conference call, if you would please be seated, I will bring you some refreshments. What would you like?"

Oh, this is so 007. Clint grinned internally.

"I'll have mineral water," Drake said with a business-like smile. And since that was the way his friend was going to play it, Clint kept his smile subdued and asked for flat water. She swayed out of the reception area to get their drinks.

With no change of expression, Drake leaned over to whisper in Clint's ear. "I'm thinking that her name should be Kitty Cream? What do you think?"

"Nah, nothing beats Ian Fleming's Pussy Galore. It's a classic." Clint kept a lookout on the office doors and the hall that the receptionist had gone down. He sat straighter when she came back with a silver tray and two tall glasses with ice and a bowl of lemon slices. They were definitely living the good life.

She bent and twisted as she set down the beverages, better than most hostesses in Vegas. Seriously, Amir and Zangar were sure as hell living the high life.

"Thank you," Drake gave her a small smile. "How long do you think Mr. Omarov and Mr. Boyko will be?"

"Not much longer," she assured Drake. "Let me go and check."

She went over to the tall, paneled door and knocked. She went inside and they waited, sipping their drinks.

She came back out smiling brightly. "They will see you now." She opened the door wide and motioned for them to walk into the office. The two men were backlit, so it was difficult to discern what they looked like. Neither of them was seated, they were standing on either side of the large desk that sat in front of a breathtaking view of the futuristic city of Nur-Sultan.

Total power move.

"Quite something, isn't it?" the man on the right said.

Clint and Drake walked just a couple of paces into the room, waiting for the men to come forward and show themselves.

"And you are?" Drake asked smoothly.

"Forgive me," the man moved away from the window so that he could be seen. "My name is Amir Omarov." He held out his hand to Drake, who smiled and shook it.

"I'm Drake Avery, and this is my associate Clint Archer. We're here on behalf of a large consortium back in the United States."

"We know," the other man spoke up.

"Of course you do," Clint said. His voice was just barely polite. "You wouldn't have given us this meeting if you hadn't thoroughly vetted us."

"And the same could be said of you, as well. I'm sure you did a lot of checking before you decided that our bank, and Zangar and I, would be a good fit for whatever it is you have planned."

Drake gave a chin nod. "It's not every day we get to meet with true oligarchs."

Zangar laughed and walked over to the trio. "We are mere vice presidents here at a bank, not oligarchs. But I wouldn't be telling the truth if I didn't say that was our goal, right Amir?"

"Perhaps we can help," Drake smiled.

"I knew I liked you," Amir said. "Yes, money is what makes the world go round, is it not? But before we get down to business, first we must have lunch. It is so much easier to do business with friends, is it not?"

"I could eat," Drake said. "What about you, Clint?"

"Yep."

"Not much of a talker, are you Mr. Archer?" Amir asked.

"Nope," Clint replied.

"Perhaps some vodka can loosen you up," Zangar said with a laugh.

Amir opened the paneled door and said something to Kitty Cream, in what Clint assumed was Kazakh, because it sure as hell wasn't Russian.

"She will make our lunch reservations. Come. Come." Amir ushered them toward the elevators. After they got in, Drake and Clint watched as they passed the lobby floor and continued on to the sub-basement.

When the doors opened they found themselves in a parking garage, with a large limousine waiting for them.

"After you," Amir smiled as a building valet opened the door.

Clint stepped into the dark cavernous backseat that smelled of leather and cognac. It took a moment for his eyes to adjust and when they did he saw two big men sitting in the opposite seats pointing guns at him.

Clint turned to warn Drake, but his teammate was shoved forward and then hit on the back of the head with the butt of thug number one's gun. Drake was out like a light.

"Make a move to escape, and we will kill your friend, Mr. Archer," Zangar said as he delicately stepped over Drake's body to seat himself next to Thug number two. Amir came in last and sat down next to Clint.

Amir said something in Kazakh again and Thug Number One dragged Drake closer to him, then rested his foot on Drake's neck.

"Just in case you were thinking you could possibly harm me." Amir smiled over at Clint. "I am fine with having my employee break your friend's neck if I don't like what I hear. So let's talk business."

Clint's gut clenched. They were in some serious trouble, but he figured they didn't want to bloody up the back of the limo, so they would do the killing away from the offices and the vehicle. That gave Drake and him time.

Now, how should I play this?

"No business talk," Clint said. "I was promised lunch."

Zangar threw back his head and laughed. "I like him, Amir. I like him a lot. Maybe we shouldn't torture him too much before we kill him. We can focus on the big guy."

"I want to know the names of the people within the consortium. We never work with people we don't know; it's bad business practices." Amir gave him the snake oil salesman smile.

Clint thought quickly about what to say and then rolled the dice, praying his gut wouldn't steer him wrong.

"That's not true. You don't always know who you're working with," Clint smirked.

"What are you talking about?" Zangar demanded.

"You worked with Devon Cron and you didn't know all the people he represented."

Clint saw the hit coming.

Amir shot his fist at Clint's jaw and easily connected.

Clint had done nothing to avoid it. It wouldn't be in character, so he took it. But it didn't mean he liked it.

"We know everything—don't underestimate us. We made Devon talk before he left our country. We went into business with him three months ago because he had an interesting proposition. Unfortunately for him, Senator Leonard was not able to convince his colleagues on the tariff bill. Therefore what was supposed to be a lucrative opportunity turned sour. We now want another form of recompense."

"What do you want them to pay you?" Clint asked.

Amir chuckled. It was actually an evil villain laugh; what kind of world had Clint stepped into? "We want two sanctions lifted. Senator Leonard is the leader of the Senate Foreign Relations Committee, he can make that happen."

"How do you figure that?" Clint asked as he felt the limo begin to move. At the same time, he saw Drake make a subtle fist, indicating he was awake.

"He's the majority leader. He can lead the sheep to do his will."

"And us? Why are you targeting us? We're just here to give you a deal of a lifetime."

"This is just a precaution. Your friend gets a small bump on the head, and you give me all of the information about your plan. We don't work in the dark."

Ah, shit, a plan that doesn't exist. I'm so screwed.

"Neither do we. There is one more person besides the weasel Devon and the senator who are in on their scheme," Clint lied. He had to make them spill more info on the senator and the Weasel, and hopefully not have to come up with his consortium's plan.

"What other partner?" Zangar demanded to know.

"They have a silent partner, someone that you don't want to cross."

"Impossible," Amir dismissed with a sniff.

"Okay, don't listen to me," Clint said easily. "You're thinking you're the baddest kids on the block, well there is someone that Devon and the senator are more scared of. Someone that has frightened Devon so badly that he's put a hit out on you two."

This time Zangar let out the evil laugh.

Did they teach this to them as kids?

"I don't believe you," Amir said easily.

"Fine, don't. It's your life. But he's put a hit out on your families as well." Clint was way off script now.

"Who is the silent partner?" Zangar demanded to know. There was no hint of laughter in his voice now.

"The Russian mafia. They've already kidnapped Senator Leonard's staff assistant and cut off her hand and delivered it to the senator. They mean business. The money that they gave him, he wants back, with the profit he was promised when the tariffs were lifted. You weren't the only ones he let down. You're not paying, so Devon's bright idea is to kill you and renegotiate with the president of SA Investment Bank."

"Why do they think that our bank president would negotiate with them?"

"It never hurts to have an American senator on the payroll."

Zangar shrugged. "This is true."

"How do you come by this information?" Amir demanded to know.

"We know who was hired to kill you," Clint said easily. "For enough money, they talked. We will suggest they continue with their mission if you don't do the deal with the people we represent." Clint leaned back and crossed his arms.

"So you are telling us this out of the goodness of your heart?" Zangar asked skeptically.

"No, we want you around because we think you're the ones who can pull off our deal. But at the same time, the fact that you've been played by the Wonder Weasel doesn't give us a big feeling of security."

"How would you suggest we handle the senator and his little worm?" Amir asked.

"Twist them harder. You have the power on your side if we take away the hitmen."

"And all you want is us to consider doing business with you?" Zangar was still skeptical.

"Well," Clint stretched out the word. "It would be nice for us to have a senator beholden to us as well. And I would like the lunch you promised."

This time both Zangar and Amir laughed. "You are funny. I would like to do business with you. I would consider telling you even more than you already know about the senator, if your deal sounds lucrative."

Clint pushed at Drake with the toe of his Italian leather shoe. "You awake yet?"

"Huh?" Drake said drowsily.

"You might want to get your ass up off the floor. We're talking business and you're going to miss lunch."

Zangar gave a chin tilt to Thug Number One who took his foot off of Drake's neck.

"Your plan?" Amir asked.

"You have the opportunity to make just as much money with us as you ever did with the senator. You realize the US can't sell crude outside of the States and Mexico. Our employers are losing out big. We have a way to sell it internationally, but it requires your help."

"You have a way to smuggle out the oil, to Kazakhstan?"

"That's the beauty of the operation. At sea, we would just change over the tankers to Kazakhstan ownership. That allows us to ship overseas. There's no need for the ship to ever go to Kazakhstan—it goes straight to the buyer. You take the money and funnel it back to the consortium. You're just the men who can get this done for us."

"That has possibilities," Amir said.

Possibilities my ass. Amir was practically drooling. Good, if Drake and I can pull this off without fucking up our covers, all the better.

"The Russian mafia is going to be a small problem. Do you have any ideas on how that might be taken care of?" Clint looked back and forth between the two oligarchs.

"We just might have some old friends who can assist with that," Zangar smiled.

23

BY THE TIME THEY GOT BACK TO THEIR HOTEL ROOM, THERE were three new bugs to deal with. Clint decided to leave them as they were until they were ready to call Lydia and update her. At that point, he would again turn on the blocker.

First, he wanted to go over everything she had found in the WhatsApp chats and see if he agreed with all of her analysis on this deal and if there was anything else the little demon spawn was working on that needed to be stopped.

"I'm calling for room service," Drake said. "Lunch sucked."

"What are you talking about? It was great," Clint grinned.

"Sure, for you. You didn't have a headache from hell. I could barely eat, and that's not like me." Drake threw the room service menu at Clint and he grabbed it. He told Drake to order him a steak, then he hopped back to it. Drake placed the orders and managed to sit still and quiet for almost ten minutes.

"Whatchya doing?" Drake asked.

Clint shrugged his shoulders and lifted his eyebrows. Drake went to Clint's suitcase, found the blocker, and turned it on. "Give. I missed shit while I was unconscious. So what are you doing?"

"I'm checking in with Lydia and seeing if weasel dick has any other side gigs going on that we should know about. I'm telling her about me making up the Russian Mafia connection."

"Yeah, I heard that part, it was brilliant," Drake grinned as he crouched in front of the mini-bar.

"I'm worried that part might blow up in our faces. They might have too many contacts in Russia and might find out it's not true."

"Sounded good to me, my man," Drake said as he unwrapped a huge chocolate bar. "I especially liked the plan our supposed consortium came up with to sell crude oil worldwide. You have the makings of a supervillain."

Clint grimaced. "Great, just what I want on my resume."

"Clint, that's really good news. Dude, your brain is at one-hundred and ten percent capacity of what it was before the explosion. That was classic Clint Archer in action."

For just a second Clint allowed himself to feel good about what Drake was saying. He had felt pretty pumped as he'd come up with that shit off the cuff. It had seemed to impress the Kazakhstani men.

After Drake put in the order for food and ate some nuts and cheese from the mini-bar, he sat back down with his feet up on the coffee table. "So tell me what's eating you. Is it Lydia? Is it this op?"

"Nothing big, I just want to make sure that we have all of our ducks in a row for tomorrow's meet. When we talk to Lydia tonight, I'm positive she'll be able to give us all the backstory we need to make the bullshit I came up with solid. I just want to ensure that Amir and Zangar give us everything, and I mean everything, they have on the senator's activities. We can't leave a stone unturned if we want to double-back on them and give them the squeeze. I want them so goddamn scared of us that they'll be puckered up at the idea of your tape being out anywhere. They need to know you are the Big Dog."

Drake laughed as he finished up his food with some mineral water. Any kind of liquor wasn't advised at this point, since they needed to be on top of their game at all times. Which just made Clint all the more pissed at himself for working too hard on the code.

Not smart.

"I'm going to turn off the blocker, we've had it on long enough," Clint said as he bent to switch off the blocker. Then his phone rang before he could. He grinned when he saw it was his woman.

"Hey, Lydia, it's three in the morning there, I just e-mailed you what went down in our meeting, I figured you could work on that while we were sleeping."

"Yeah, I read it. That was damn good thinking. Now I want to talk."

Clint took his hand away from the switch and settled back into the couch. "Okay, talk. I'm going to put you on speaker, okay?"

"Yep."

"So what do you want to know?" Clint asked.

"Why was Devon going to arrange the hit? Why not just have the senator arrange the sanctions?"

"Beats me. As far as I'm concerned, these guys are on par with the Russian mob. I wouldn't want to be on their bad side," Drake said after he swallowed.

"It has to be that the senator can't get the sanctions lifted, and he and weasel dick know it, and they know that there is no other alternative but a slow death if they fail for a second time," Clint said thoughtfully.

"He's the majority leader, why would he fail?" Drake asked. He was looking at his watch, obviously waiting for the food.

"Could it be someone in Congress or the DOJ has him under watch?" Clint mused.

"You know who would be good to ask?" Lydia sounded excited.

"Conroy," Clint said. "I haven't talked to him in over a year. Does he still know what's going on in D.C.?"

"Are you talking about Declan's guy?" Drake asked.

Clint nodded, but his focus was on his conversation with Lydia.

"He definitely knows what's going on, especially now that he's working with Liam McCallister. Between the two of them, they have D.C. and the Pentagon gossip covered."

"Okay, go fishing," Clint said with a smile. "If for sure Senator Leonard can't deliver, then we know the reason for the hit on our new Kazakhstani friends. In the meantime, besides Devon's ick, ick love life texts, what else have you found?"

"He's a gambler. Plays poker. Loses. He needs this money bad. So when you said that the Russian mob was out after the Senator and him, you weren't far wrong. It's the American mafia that is out to get Devon if he doesn't pay up soon. They too are being promised a piece of the senator. I'm telling you, the way Devon works, he has divided up that guy like a California sushi roll."

Clint heard a knock on the door. "Hold on a minute, Lydia." Drake got up to let the waiter in with the food. Out of the corner of his eye, he watched as the man took two covered trays off the crowded trolley and put them onto the table in their room. Clint motioned for Drake to come back to the couch. He wanted him to listen to this next part.

Drake signed the check and ushered the man out, then came back to Clint and the phone.

"So, we need to figure out why or if the senator can't deliver on the sanctions to the Kazakhstanis," Clint said. "If that's what's going on, then we know why they want them killed. But Drake will still be on the hook because the next thing you know he'll be asked to kill mob guys who own his gambling debts."

"Got that in one," Lydia agreed.

"Fuck me. Can't I just kill him and be done with it?" Drake complained.

"Maybe that's for the best," Clint started to say.

"I can't be listening to this. I don't care if I'm using a secure satellite phone, I can't be hearing this, so shut up Drake. The answer is no." Lydia was getting pissed, and Clint was getting a hard-on. "Let me get with Conroy, I'll find out what's going on in D.C. In the meantime, you two stay safe. I love you guys."

"But you love me more, right?" Drake asked.

"Ahhhhh, not really?" Then Lydia laughed.

"Love you, Clint." Then she hung up.

Drake tilted his chin to the blocker, and Clint shut it off. They got up to get their dinner. As soon as Drake took off his lid, he started swearing. "Really? Who would order clam chowder while in Kazakhstan? Where the hell is my meal?"

Clint stared at his lid, hoping his steak and mushrooms were underneath. He uncovered it and found what looked like Kazakhstan's version of SpaghettiOs. "Ah, damn. Me too. See if you can flag down the trolley guy. He's probably giving our orders to someone else."

But Clint was talking to thin air. Drake was already out the door. "Hey!" he yelled down the hallway of the hotel.

He heard Drake yell again, but this time it was different. He watched as clam chowder and SpaghettiOs spewed up into the air like they were spat out by geysers, then he was slammed to the ground. The splat of gooey mess hit him as he was scrambling to get back to his feet. He looked around the room in a panic.

Why was he seeing a concrete building?

Why was he seeing himself falling?

He was going to die.

"Clint!"

Someone was calling his name. But it didn't matter. He didn't know where he was. He was standing covered in red and white. Was that blood?

He smelled smoke.

"Clint, hurry. If they're alive, they don't have much time!"

He heard the words above the roaring in his head.

He jabbed at his clothes, trying to get the blood off him but only managing to smear blood and brains into the fabric.

Oh God.

He looked at his hand and the smell of clams hit his nostrils.

Clams.

Kazakhstan.

Explosion.

Drake!

He headed for the hotel door that was askew and slammed through it. There was smoke pouring out of a room at least six doors down. Drake must be in it. SpaghettiOs? Kids.

Clint ran as fast as he could to make it to the door.

"Drake!" he yelled.

He heard crying. The room was filled with smoke. It had to be a suite laid out like theirs. The table would be in the far corner near the window. He could feel the bite of the bitter winter air coming in, which was just making the fire worse.

Drake came out through the smoke carrying a small body. *Please God say they're alive.*

"There's a baby in the other room."

Drake tried to hand off the injured child, but he was holding onto Drake like a little monkey, his arms and legs wrapped around him.

"I'll go," Clint said as he sped by them.

The fire was going to engulf the entire room and soon spread to the other rooms on the floor. Where were the sprinklers? Where was the alarm?

Just as he was thinking that, the sprinklers came on and frigid cold water doused him. He heard a young child or baby screaming at the top of their lungs as he opened the door to the bedroom. Not much smoke, so he easily found the crib. When he picked up the child, they squalled and squirmed and did everything possible to get out of his hold.

"Not now," he muttered, as he plopped the kid onto the bed with the now-wet sheets. He swaddled him or her up, and made a run for the entrance to the hotel room. It was an inferno. It seemed to take forever to make it the four meters.

People were milling outside the room. A woman grabbed the child from Clint. Another woman was still trying to extract the child from Drake. "The parents?" Clint demanded.

"It's too late," Drake said as he finally handed off the child with a look of grief.

"Steak?" Clint asked.

Drake nodded.

Clint started toward their room. He knew that Drake would be behind him. They had outstayed their welcome and two kids were orphans because of it.

24

THEY'D TAKEN THE TIME FOR A CAMP BATH IN THEIR ROOM AND changed their clothes. Drake and Clint's eyebrows were both singed, and Drake was bleeding from his knee and his elbow where he had been slammed into the food trolley. The waiter, long gone.

Patched up and cleaned up as best as they could, they high-tailed it to the airport to catch the next flight out of Kazakhstan. They didn't care that it was going to Chicago instead of California—anything to get them to America. Clint left Lydia a message about what was going on.

Not even seeing Drake stuck in a middle seat, squished between two equally large men could bring a smile to Clint's face. Face it, he was still shocky from going through another explosion, and the idea of the mom dying in the explosion was killing him. *Devon and the senator are going down!*

He didn't trust himself to close his eyes and get some sleep. He knew damn well he'd wake up with a nightmare, and the last thing they needed was Clint trying to take one of the passengers down in a choke-hold. Knowing this, he'd picked up five magazines at the kiosk at the airport before boarding the airplane. There wasn't even one about cars or computers; all five of them were gossip rags.

God, what he wouldn't give to be playing on his computer right now. Just playing. A video game, something that he and Lydia used to do all the time. He shoved his thumb and forefinger along the bridge of his nose. What was it that Lydia needed to tell him? Didn't she know that he lived with life and death all day long? His priorities were straight. Loving Lydia was set in stone and nothing on God's green earth was going to change that. Unless...unless...she didn't love him?

He swallowed, and it felt like shards of cut glass were coating his throat.

God, Lyd, just tell me.

He looked down at the magazine and started to read about who wore it best.

LYDIA WAS READING the report of the explosion in the Kazakhstan local newspaper with a translation app. It was devastating. They still weren't divulging the names of the victims, but they did say that two unidentified heroes had gone in and saved the two children, then disappeared. There were searches out for the two men so that they could be rewarded.

Sure there were. They just want to take them in for questioning, don't you lie to me.

The guys should be landing in Chicago in three hours. Clint hadn't booked them any further than that, probably just ecstatic to get the hell out of the country before another attempt was made on their lives. One that actually worked. Lydia had scored them tickets from Chicago to Palm

Springs. No need for a rental car when they got there because they would be met with an oh-so-happy-and-not-happy welcome party.

Me!

She had nine hours to get to Palm Springs, and it was a four-and-a-half-hour drive. Enough time to try to figure out why Clint's new best friends tried to off him. Now that Richards had solved the Satanic Voices case—*Score Richards!*—Lydia had time to focus on Alice's case. Maybe she could bring Melvin in on things.

"It feels like an oven," Drake groused.

Clint was so tired, he was having trouble walking a straight line, but even so, he had to agree with his friend. After the frigid temperatures of Kazakhstan, the sunny day and almost seventy-five degrees felt almost sweltering. This was not helping him to stay awake. But at least he hadn't fallen asleep on any of the flights and had a nightmare. What's more, he was pretty sure he knew everything there was to know about the Kardashians.

Since this was the first time they'd had an opportunity to really talk since they'd left Kazakhstan, they compared notes.

"Russian connections?" Clint asked Drake.

"That's my take. They must have reached out to their friends and realized that nobody was in league with Devon or the senator, so our entire story broke down."

"That's the reason they tried to kill us."

"It's either that, or Lydia's background fell apart when they dug deeper," Drake said.

Clint glared at Drake.

Drake held up his hands. "Just exploring all the options. It had to be the Russian angle. That means they're going to be back to twisting weasel-dick and the senator."

Clint nodded and sighed.

They went to the baggage claim to pick up their empty suitcases. They'd known that traveling without one would be a red flag, but they hadn't had time to pack. Clint spotted his first. The silver tape on the handle made it easy to recognize. Since they hadn't packed their normal duffel bags, Drake's bag was easy to recognize by the ZZ Top, Allman Brothers, and Toby Keith stickers.

"You know, that suitcase could have blown our cover, now that I think about it," Clint complained.

"Hell no. It added realism."

Maybe he was right. When he picked his suitcase off the conveyer belt, it was so light that he damn near swung it around and hit the lady next to him. Drake smirked.

Clint looked at his phone. He was checking his texts to find out which rental car company Lydia had arranged for their car, when Drake let out a hum of appreciation. Clint did a side glance up from his phone so he wouldn't be obvious, and saw a pair of familiar legs balanced on red stilettos. His gaze meandered upwards and he took in the black pencil-skirt paired with the red silk tank top and damn near swallowed his tongue. By the time he got to the scarlet lipstick and deep brown eyes, his temperature had gone through the roof.

He stood still, praying he would get to see her walk toward him. And she did. God, did she. One slow, sexy step at a time, she sauntered his way, never losing eye contact, her sexy lips tilting up into a wanton smile that had him hard as a rock. God, how could he ever think of her as a

Dork Queen, when she was the sexiest goddess known to mankind?

Every other person in the terminal had disappeared, she eclipsed them with her presence. Mere inches from his body, she tilted her chin upwards. "Nothing to say?"

"I'm tongue-tied."

She wound her arms around his neck and pulled him down for a kiss. It was beyond hot. It was scorching. His hand wound in her hair, luxuriating in the silken strands as he caressed her cheek, her jaw, her neck.

She pulled back then hid her face in his neck. "I needed this."

His touch changed, and he began to stroke her hair.

"I was scared. So scared."

She snuggled closer, her arms encompassing his waist.

"I'm here, Baby." His arms instinctively clutched her closer. This was Lydia—all he ever wanted to do was comfort her, soothe her. She was the sun in his sky.

After long moments ensconced in the warmth of Lydia's body, Drake's voice penetrated the bubble.

"You're impeding traffic, son."

Slowly, ever so slowly, he tilted his head back so he could see the love in Lydia's eyes. Never, ever had anything been more beautiful.

"Honey, we've got to go," he whispered.

She nodded.

He lifted the non-existent weight of his suitcase and tangled his fingers with Lydia's, pressing his palm against hers. She dropped her head against his shoulder and they headed toward the parking lot.

"So, Finn bailed on us?" Drake asked casually as they crossed the street to the parking lot.

"You could say that." Lydia peeked around Clint to answer.

"You told him how it was going to be, didn't you?" Clint chuckled.

"Maybe." She smiled up at him. *Ooops, now here comes the woman who is the ballbuster.* He exchanged a glance with Drake, who had heard the same thing he had.

"What car are we looking for?" Drake asked.

Lydia pointed and Clint saw his blue truck standing out amongst a sea of sedans. "Give me the keys, Lydia, I'm driving."

"Are you cleared to drive?" she asked as she fished in her purse.

"Lydia," was all he said as he held out his hand.

"Fine." She handed him the keys. She looked at Drake. "Are you okay with this?"

"Sure am. He's spent damn near a month at rehab. He's doing good Lydia, real good."

Clint hit the key fob and Drake beat them to the truck. Before Lydia could protest he tucked his big body into the back behind the passenger seat.

"I would have sat back there," she protested.

"Just pull up the seat. I don't want to do anything to get in the way of you and Clint. He'd do the same thing if it were Karen picking me up from the airport."

Clint saw Lydia about to protest. He claimed her lips for a short, sweet kiss. "It's true, Baby, I would."

He opened her door for her and couldn't help but stroke his hands down her smooth thigh and leg as she settled in. When she shivered, he prayed he could make it back to the resort.

"Lydia, did you get us a separate room at the resort?"

"Nope."

Damn.

Lydia grinned. "As soon as Finn saw what I was wearing to pick you up, he arranged it. He apologized that he couldn't arrange a suite."

Drake chuckled from the backseat. "As long as it has a bed, I think you'll be fine."

Clint put on his sunglasses and got into the driver's seat for the twenty-minute drive. Lydia played with her skirt for the entire drive, inching it slowly upwards. He was so damned aroused by the time he pulled up to the resort it was a wonder he could manage to move his foot from the gas to the brake.

"I'm going to go say hello to Finn," Drake said as he opened the back door before the truck had even stopped. Lydia's laugh was hell on Clint's libido.

She undid her seatbelt and reached for the door handle.

"Hold up, you know the rules."

She slanted a grin his way. "I wear a dress, you get the door."

"Uh, uh, uh," he disagreed. "Our rule is everything but jeans. That's the deal. Even then I'm not happy with the deal, but you browbeat me into it."

Lydia let out a throaty laugh. He couldn't get to their room fast enough, but then again, he liked walking slowly with her when she was in heels. It was a form of foreplay all on its own. By the time they got through the lobby and up the elevator to the room Finn had reserved, Clint was beyond aroused—he was on fire.

He closed the door behind them.

"No recriminations we need to work through?" he asked before he touched her.

She shook her head, her luxurious black hair flowing like silk around her shoulders. Part of him wanted to ask why, but he wasn't a stupid man. He took her hand and led her to the bed. The bright sunlight was softened by the sheers. *Perfect.*

"I need to see you. I need to know that you're all right."

He frowned. "I'm fine, Honey." What was she talking about?

As if reading his mind, she said, "The fire."

He shook his head and smiled tenderly. "I'm good," he attempted to reassure her. It didn't work because she was pulling his t-shirt upwards so that it skimmed his abdomen, his chest.

"Raise your arms," she pleaded.

He yanked the shirt over his head with one hand.

Her fingers traced every bit of his front, starting at his sternum, then trailing to his nipples which she scraped with her fingernails, and continued down to his stomach. She kissed his chest, then pushed him to turn around, which he gladly did. Anything to keep her kissing and caressing him.

Her nails softly scored his back as she took inventory.

"Enough," he growled softly. "I'm good, now I think it's my turn to make sure you don't have any 'owies.'"

Lydia giggled. "Did you just say 'owie?'"

"Yep, because if you do, I get to kiss it better. It's a rule."

He turned around and picked her up, gently depositing her onto the bed. "Did I tell you I liked the outfit?"

"Maybe not with words, but yeah, I got the message."

His hands skimmed over the silk of her top, toying with the buttons.

"Don't tease."

She was right, who wanted to tease when there was so much more he could be doing? After the buttons were undone, he parted the silk to see a red lace bra covering her breasts. He traced over the lace while watching her eyelids shutter close. He moved and then suckled one nipple deep into his mouth, laving the tender flesh hidden behind the frothy material. Lydia squirmed and arched, not making a sound. Before switching to her other breast, he looked up in her face and saw her arms spread wide above her head, her face suffused with passion. He licked and blew on her tender nub until her hands slammed against his head and she spoke.

"Harder."

He laughed and pulled out of her grip. He quickly got her out of her blouse and bra, sucking in a deep breath as he did so. It was as if someone had reached into his mind and created the perfect woman for him. Not just her body, but her mind and soul. He rested his big hand against her stomach for a long moment and stared into the liquid depths of her eyes.

"Clint? Are you okay?"

"Knowing you're mine makes my life worth living. Did you know that?"

She struggled to sit up.

"Don't, I've got you," Clint whispered as he lowered himself. Their bodies met and he took her mouth for a breathtaking kiss. It was a meeting of mouths, hearts, and souls. Her lips were soft under his, and Clint enjoyed the warm glide of his mouth sliding against the plump feel of her lips, savoring the innocent play. Then he felt her nipples pebbling against his chest, and Lydia moving ever so slightly against his chest hair to get the sensation her body craved. It was time to take her further.

He wrapped an arm around her waist and rubbed himself against her plush breasts the same time as he plunged his tongue into her mouth for a deeper kiss. The carnality was exhilarating, and she was with him every step of the way. She was fierce in her passion. She tugged at his short hair while her nails scored his back.

He broke the kiss and slid downwards. She moaned at the feel of her nipples being abraded by the hair on his chest.

"So good."

He grinned; she'd like this better.

He grazed her areola with his teeth and she bucked beneath him. He continued his play until her head was rolling back and forth on the duvet, her brown eyes glittering with need. Her need was a thing of beauty.

He sucked the pebbled nub into his mouth and twirled his tongue around and around until she let out a breathy sigh that was his name. When he kissed his way to her other breast, he continued to touch and tease with the nipple that he had abandoned. Plucking and tweaking with his fingers, in a rhythm that he knew his lover liked. He could do this for hours, keeping her on a knife's edge of release, pleasuring her until she didn't know her name. His fingers roamed over the silky, plump flesh and he knew that he was torturing them both.

"Clint, you've got to give me more," she sobbed.

When he looked up, he saw that her overbright eyes were glistening with tears. He glided upwards and cupped her cheeks. "I'm here, are you okay?"

She pushed up and bit at his lower lip, then sucked it into her mouth, laving it with her tongue. He didn't feel her hands on his body and realized they were above her head in supplication.

"You're right, I need more too, Baby."

He slid off the bed and shucked off his shoes, socks, and jeans.

Her eyes crinkled. "Commando? What if they searched you at the airport?"

"It'd be their problem, not mine," was his lazy response as he concentrated on sliding down the side zipper on her skirt.

"Shoes," she reminded him.

"Oh no, those stay on," he grinned.

He pulled off her skirt and the red thong in one sweep. He would have taken a moment to admire the tiny piece of lace, except there was something far more beautiful to admire underneath it.

Clint guided her thighs to open wide, not that it took much effort. Lydia shoved herself up onto her elbows, and her eyes were greedy as they feasted on his erection. His damn cock bobbed up and down, preening under her gaze. When she went to reach for him, he took her hand and kissed her palm, then placed it against the wet flesh between her legs.

"Touch yourself, not me."

He was greeted with a husky laugh as she opened herself to him. His legs turned to water at the glorious sight. She swirled her finger, then reached out to him. He gripped her wrist and brought her hand to his lips. He sucked the sweet taste that was all Lydia from her dainty fingers. He wasn't going to last. Then his sexy siren lifted one foot and took the heel of her shoe and drew a line from the top of his hip down to his knee. His entire body shuddered.

Game over.

He grabbed her ankle and yanked off her shoe. He kissed the arch of her foot, then pulled it around his waist. He did the same thing to her other foot before she could do something even more evil with that shoe and he lost control and wasn't able to bring her the pleasure she deserved.

Carefully, tenderly, he pressed the tip of his cock to the well of her vagina and she flowered open. He was lost in the beauty of their joining, but when she sighed, he looked at her face and saw an expression that could only be labelled love. He was enthralled.

He continued to push forward, until her body enveloped him in her silky, tight warmth, all the while staring at her face as her eyes welcomed him home. He was lost physically and emotionally in the woman who owned his heart and soul.

Every move forward he made, she countered with a push upwards, until they were caught up in a dance as old as time, but one that only they had ever perfected. Clint tried to make it last, but when Lydia's velvet sheath shuddered around him for the second time, and he watched her eyes close in ecstasy as she cried out his name, he had no hope but to follow her into a place that existed just for them. A place that would always contain love and hope, no matter how pain-filled or ugly the world that spun around them got, they would always be safe together.

25

LYDIA WOKE UP HAPPIER THAN SHE HAD BEEN IN MONTHS. SHE didn't open her eyes, instead, she let herself bask in the feel of Clint's arm around her waist and the tantalizing smell of his soap and that other aroma that was all him. Finally, she allowed herself to take a peek and found him staring at her.

"How long have you been awake?" she asked in a hushed voice.

"Awhile," he whispered back.

She pushed up on her elbow. "Why didn't you wake me? Shouldn't we check in with Drake and Finn?"

"Honey, it's three o'clock in the morning. Finn's probably asleep. Drake might be up because of the few days we were in Kazakhstan, but you and I need to talk."

She shut her eyes. He was right. She tried to work up a head of steam, but she couldn't. Clint was her hero. He would always be her hero. It didn't matter if he went traipsing off to a foreign country when he should be in therapy, not when he was helping a friend. That was who he was.

But that didn't mean she wasn't going to give him ever-living hell for it...eventually. Somebody needed to keep him in line. Somebody needed to take care of him, and that was her job. A job she took seriously. Because that went right back to him scaring the hell out of her because no matter how much of a hero he was, he still was just a man—a man who almost died, a man who was still recovering.

"Uh-oh," his lips twitched.

"Damn right we need to talk," she said as she scrambled out of bed. She'd checked into the room late last night, so she had jeans thrown over a chair somewhere, she just needed to remember where. She looked over her shoulder at Clint who was watching her with his hands behind his head.

"Get dressed," she ordered.

"Can't."

"Why not?" she asked as she put one leg into her jeans.

"Too busy enjoying the show."

"You are such a man."

He chuckled. She sighed. It wasn't much of an insult, considering how much she enjoyed all that hot manliness a few hours ago.

"Seriously, Clint, get dressed. We have a lot to talk about."

"And this requires clothes, why? Do you have to put on a t-shirt? Can't you stay topless?"

Lydia yanked the t-shirt over her head and glared at him. At least when she was dressed it propelled him out of bed. She stalked over to the desk and grabbed her backpack. She undid the locks and pulled out her laptop.

"You left that here in the room?" Clint asked.

"Finn had it. I texted him to bring it back when we were on our way back to the resort," she explained. She booted it up.

"Where's yours?"

He picked up his light carryall that he'd had with him. "In here."

"Put. On. Some. Clothes."

Clint really chuckled. "Gotcha hot and bothered, don't I?"

"Clint, be reasonable, we have to get to work. For all I know your manly bits," she waved her hand at his semi-erect penis, "will get in the way of the computer monitor."

Clint threw his head back and laughed. It did her heart good to hear it. He grabbed his jeans off the floor and tugged them on.

"So, when are you going to go for the jugular about me leaving for Kazakhstan with Drake?"

"Never," Lydia said. "It's water under the bridge. You did it. You came out none the worse for wear. I still think it was foolish, and I don't want you to do it again, but it's done. But can you tell me what you think of your therapy at the clinic? Do you still think you need it?"

"Hell yes," he said immediately. "I lost it when the explosion happened. I spaced out and didn't know where I was, or what to do. We'd said two months; that's only five more weeks. I don't know if that's going to be enough. My hope was to be team-ready, but after the fiasco with the bomb in Kazakhstan, I'm not sure that will ever happen."

Lydia turned away from the computer and looked up at him so she could watch his face. "What happened exactly?"

"We called for room service, but our order had been screwed up. Drake went into the hallway to call back the waiter to get our right food. I was still looking at the dishes when the explosion happened. I think I was remembering Syria. I thought I had been wounded, there was blood all over me, but it was just marinara sauce. I couldn't get it together for a while.

When I finally remembered where I was a few minutes had passed. Drake was already rescuing one of the kids from the fire by the time I got there. I don't know if I'd gotten there sooner if we could have saved one or two of the parents."

"But you helped to save the other child, right?"

Clint nodded.

"Thank God for that."

He didn't say anything.

"Clint?"

"Lydia, that's not who I am. That's not what a SEAL needs to be. I'm not sure what the outpatient place is going to be able to do for me. If it can really get me back to where I need to be. Finn was out of commission for six months before he went to sniper school. We all thought he'd never crawl his way back."

He looked so devastated. She wrapped her arms around his waist and held him for all she was worth.

"Lydia, I'm trying to come to grips that it's not the end of the world," he said as he stroked back her hair. She tilted her head so she could look up at him. "Being a SEAL is a young man's game. I'm getting up there. I'm thirty-three. I'd be looking at leaving the teams in a couple of years anyway."

She never thought she'd hear him say that.

"But..."

Her eyes narrowed. "But what."

"I've got to finish what I started with Drake."

"This thing with Devon and the senator? I wouldn't expect anything else. But you're going to take into consideration the things you can and can't do, right?"

"Lyd, SEALs work in teams. Drake is always going to need someone at his side, and it can't be Finn. Finn's career would be in jeopardy. Drake's ass is already on the line, and now that you're in on this thing, it just makes it easier for me to be playing hooky from the clinic. You can help with that, right?"

"Don't expect me to only help with that. I'm going to be working all of our contacts, and doing a shit-ton on the comp. You know that, right?"

He bent down and kissed her lips. "Yes," he kissed her again. "I know that."

"Good," she sighed. "I didn't want to have to break your arm, or shoot you or anything."

"Speaking of which, what about your assignments? Aren't you back on the job? How are you going to square things with Eddie?"

"I've got seven new cases, and one special one I'm babying along. Three I've already closed, two are close to being closed. That leaves two more that will take some thought, and one special case that I'm doing on the side. I was hoping to pick your brain about that one, if you have time after the weasel-dick stuff is done. Do you think you will have time?"

"Always."

"I'VE BEEN WORKING on breaking into your boy's bank since you went to Kazakhstan. It's been a little tough."

"How many hours?" Clint asked.

"I've put in at least twelve, and I've had Melvin and Rylie helping me."

He whistled.

"Come look at this." She pointed to another trapdoor on her screen. "This is pretty sweet. It's a trap. If I try to open it, it's going to come back and bite me and totally blow up my hard-drive."

"I have pants on, can I take a crack?"

She snickered. "Good pun." She got up and waved him into the chair.

It felt good working with Lydia again.

He heard a buzzing sound coming from his carry-on. He jumped out of the chair to go grab the phone.

Lydia watched as he found the burner phone.

"Drake's getting a WhatsApp. The Kazakhstan fire didn't make it to the American papers, did it?" he asked as he fished out the phone.

Lydia shook her head. "I was tracking activity in Kazakhstan because you were over there."

"Yeah, so must've Devon. Call up the WhatsApp program on your comp," he directed Lydia.

She had it up by the time Clint had fished out the phone. They looked up when there was a banging on their door.

"Drake," they said in unison.

"You better be dressed," he yelled through the door.

Clint let Drake into the room. "We were just reading the message. Where's Finn?"

"He should be here in another minute. I just woke him up."

"Are you seeing this?" Lydia asked.

"No." Drake answered, "I was too busy hightailing over to your room." Clint and Drake moved to stand over Lydia's shoulder.

"Fucking weasel-dick. Now I'm going to kill him."

Lydia looked over her shoulder. "You're not. We're going to play him, and put him and the senator behind bars. From everything you told me, that would be a much worse punishment for this little piece of slime."

"Nope, he's going to die slowly."

Clint closed his fist and hit Drake on his shoulder, hard enough to make an impression. "Stop talking about murder in front of the cop, you dumbshit."

There was a knock on the door.

"Go answer it," Clint told Drake.

Messages continued to come up on Lydia's computer screen fast and furious. Obviously, wherever the prick-weasel was, he couldn't talk on the phone.

"What is he saying?" Finn wanted to know.

"To sum it up, he's assuming that Drake fucked up the hit on one of the bankers because of the explosion at the hotel. But somehow, he knows they're both alive, and he's pissed. He's demanding to know where Drake is. He's telling him to get his ass back to America because he has bigger fish to fry right now."

"Lydia, ask him what the job is."

IT'S PERFECT FOR YOU.

WHAT IS IT?

YOU JUST HAVE to take one shot, and I burn the tape. Get to D.C.

WHEN?

. . .

As soon as possible. When can you get here?

Tomorrow.

What time?

I don't know. Tomorrow. Eighteen hours, maybe. What's the job?

There was no answer.

"Shit, one shot means he wants you to play sniper." Finn shook his head.

"Yep," Drake agreed.

"If the Kazakhstanis are after them again, it has to be to lift the sanctions. This has to be about that," Clint said as he frowned. "I'm going to start researching the Senate Foreign Relations Committee, see what's up. I know Amir and Zangar were convinced that Senator Leonard could force the others in the group to go his way, but maybe there's trouble in paradise."

"Good, I have to work on my work-work," Lydia said as she yawned.

"Anything we can help with?" Finn asked.

"Yeah, while Clint's checking out the Committee, we have nothing to do," Drake complained.

She bent down and picked up her backpack and put it onto the unmade bed. She pulled out three files.

"These two I'm having trouble solving. I'm going to work on these. But this one," she tapped the top file. "I've been working on for two months. It would be great to have fresh eyes look over this."

"What's it about?" Drake asked.

"Alice is twenty-five, she has plenty of reasons to believe she's being stalked, and it's escalated. It's been thrown into the round file because she insists that it is her former step-father."

"Former?" Finn asked.

"Her mother died four years ago. I think that something must have triggered it, but I can't wrap my head around it. I sure would appreciate anybody with a new perspective."

Drake took the file. "We'll look at it in our room. Why don't you get some more shut-eye?" he grinned. "Doesn't look like you got a lot," he said as he gave the bed a long glance.

"Shut up, Avery," Finn groaned. "Ignore him. He just hasn't seen Karen for too long and is suffering from envy. Let's go."

The two men left the room, then Lydia settled in an armchair to go over the two remaining files while Clint worked. She'd stop him in two hours.

26

CIVICS CLASS WAS NOT SOMETHING HE'D ENJOYED. EVER. BUT digging into the Senate Foreign Relations Committee and seeing just how much power they wielded was fascinating. Senator Leonard was certainly in the know about things, and through the years could have easily profited on some of this insider knowledge. But to actually sway the committee to do what he wanted, now that was a whole new level of dirty pool.

Clint read deeper into the sanctions that were currently stopping Kazakhstan from doing business with the US, specifically the banking business. He understood why this hindered Amir and Zangar in their world domination plans. So far the Secretary of State was the big roadblock to their plan. She'd been against the US doing banking business with her country for some time despite Kazakhstan's improved score on the World Trading Economics Index. It was due to the ongoing investigations the British currently had going against some of the oligarchs in the country for their shady business practices. From what Clint read, nobody was out and out saying it, but it sounded like the country was rife with money laundering, corporate fraud, fraudulent accounting, and operating as a tax haven just to name a few issues.

"I think I know who the target is," Clint said as he rubbed the back of his neck and stretched his back.

"Who?" Lydia asked.

"The secretary of state. She's been against lifting sanctions since she got into that role, and Leonard's committee is going to have to go head-to-head with her."

Lydia closed her file and came to stand behind him. She started to massage his shoulders. "So, we've got fifteen hours to figure out how to implicate Leonard and Devon on an attempted assassination of the Secretary of State. Should be easy," she said, tongue in cheek.

He picked up the hotel phone to call Finn and Drake. "See if you can get ahold of Conroy. He would be great to have looking into this for us. Also, would you mind booking us all tickets to D.C.?"

"I'm on it."

THEY WERE ALL BACK in the suite by the time Conroy Lake called.

"Do you need more info about the ins and outs of D.C. politics?" he asked.

"Maybe, we're not sure. It's a long story," Drake started.

"Give me the CliffsNotes," Conroy said.

"After a mission in Syria, Drake is being blackmailed by a senator's aide named Devon Cron. He wanted him to assassinate two Kazakhstani businessmen first because they were demanding payment after the senator wasn't able to lift tariffs," Clint started. "You with me so far?"

"Yep, easy enough," Conroy said over the phone's speaker.

"Drake and I went to Kazakhstan and met with these two, pretending to be businessmen who could offer them a shady deal. In the course of talking to them, they admitted the tariff deal went south but that the senator now needed to lift some sanctions against their country. Soon after, these two guys figured out our cover and tried to blow us up. We left town. Now Devon wants Drake to do a one bullet assassination in D.C. We figure it has to be the secretary of state since she's the one blocking the senator from lifting the sanctions." Clint took another deep breath to continue.

"I'm assuming money was in it, for the senator to lift the tariffs and now the sanctions?" Conroy asked.

"Yeah, both Devon and the Senator were going to make a pretty penny with the Kazakhstanis if either of these were lifted. My guess is they invested with them on a show of good faith, but it was a paltry investment as to what these two oligarchs are on the hook for," Clint answered.

"Makes sense. The secretary of state, she's a stickler for the rules. She will have wanted Kazakhstan to really have cleaned up their act before lifting the sanctions. I doubt they have. So you're looking for ways that the senator and Devon can implicate themselves, right?"

"We already have Devon implicated on a phone call," Drake said.

"You do?" Conroy sounded surprised. "He was that stupid?"

"It was over a WhatsApp call," Clint explained.

"How'd you record it, a recording app?"

"Nope, directly off of WhatsApp. We have all his current chats monitored."

"Lord save baby Jesus, you've cracked WhatsApp?" Conroy exclaimed.

"Yep," Clint said with a smirk.

"That's huge. I'm impressed."

"Look, can you techies concentrate on the problem at hand?" Drake thrust his hand through his hair and glared at Clint and then at the phone.

"Sorry," Clint said. "So Conroy, what do you think? Do you think the secretary of state is the target?"

"Absolutely. She's due to leave the country in two days. She'll be gone for three weeks. Your guy is going to want her offed before she leaves."

"Do you know where Devon is going to tell us to make the hit?" Drake asked.

"I'd do it when she's boarding her plane. With a sniper rifle, you could definitely do this outside of the airport."

"Before that, we have to get the senator to implicate himself too," Finn mused. It was clear he was deep in thought.

"You got an idea?" Lydia asked.

"We can flush him out if there's money involved. Either the threat of losing it, or making more of it."

"We need to set up a sting," Clint said excitedly. "I have just the plan. Conroy, just how much security do senators have?"

"None, unless they request it because there's a threat."

"Perfect."

"You don't get to kill him, only capture him. Are we clear?" Clint asked for what seemed like the thirty-eighth time.

Drake rolled his eyes. "This is an actual mission, I know my orders."

That had been twelve hours ago. In that time, they had used their time wisely. They had figured out how to divide and conquer. Clint and Finn would tackle the senator, Drake and Lydia would handle the weasel-dick.

Lydia had loved the story that Clint had provided to the Kazakhstanis, so she decided to capitalize on it. With a wicked-good special effects store and Melvin's help, she set Clint and Finn up with the perfect way to handle the senator. Lydia had traced Devon's credit card to the seediest casino in Baltimore known to mankind. The air wasn't fit to breathe, and the slot machine handles were slimy to the touch. He was at the craps table...losing.

Lydia was in the crowd watching his efforts. He had a blonde and a brunette on either side of him. She'd bet anything that they were paid companions.

The guy was throwing money around like it was water. How in the hell was he doing that if his money was tied up with the Kazakhstanis? Not for her to figure out. What mattered was that they finally found him.

And it was time to squeeze the little prick.

When Devon had lost almost all his money, he grinned like it didn't matter and gave the croupier a big tip and had the nerve to shove chips down the dresses of the two women. Ick. Ick. Ick.

The guy then went over to a blackjack table and pulled out another wad of cash. Dammit, they didn't have time for this. When he dumped it on the table, with the ladies standing behind him, he got another big pile of chips to start playing. Lydia looked at her watch. They had this planned down to the minute. Devon needed to be in his room in thirty minutes to take a call, so enough with the gambling already.

Lydia looked around and found exactly what she needed —a three-quarters full Mai-Tai cocktail in between two slot machines. When she got closer she saw a cigarette butt floating in it. She winced, but it would do the job. Dressed in a tight top with a Victoria Secret bra that had the ladies pushed up to her chin and a red wig, Lydia swayed slowly toward weasel-dick's blackjack table.

She saw the spot next to him open. She stood behind it as if considering whether to play or not as the hand was dealt. Dammit, Devon was winning, he'd never leave. Yep, time for action.

Lydia pulled at her minuscule cross-body purse, and in the process spilled the Mai-Tai all over the front of Devon Cron.

"Hey! Look what you did, you dumb bitch."

"Mister, calm down," the dealer said.

"My suit is ruined."

The blonde found some napkins and started dabbing at his white shirt. He shoved her hand away as he glared at Lydia. "Get the fuck out of here," he yelled at the blonde.

"What about me?" the brunette asked.

"You too!" Then he turned on Lydia.

"What the hell are you going to do about this? Not only is my suit ruined, I had a winning hand. Now they'll have to cancel the bet."

She looked at the dealer.

"I'm sorry," she mumbled. She easily made her escape while Devon gathered his chips.

As soon as she was mixed in with the crowd of people she headed for the hotel elevator. She punched the number for Devon's floor. When she knocked on the weasel's door, Drake let her in.

"He's coming?" Drake asked.

Lydia grinned. "Oh yeah, and he's not going to be happy to see me. Put your mask on. Have you practiced your Russian accent?"

"Da," Drake winked at her. "Love vodka, borscht and caviar."

"Passable." She watched as he put on a harlequin mask. Hopefully, weasel-dick would be so scared that he wouldn't notice Drake's size and put two-and-two together.

He pointed to a chair that had seen better days for her to sit in. "Finn checked in. They're at the Senator's house."

Drake positioned himself behind the door. When the hotel room door opened, he grabbed Devon around his neck.

"Don't make sound," he growled.

Hell, the Russian accent was more than passable, it was pitch-perfect and downright scary.

27

"No bodyguards my ass," Finn breathed into his mic. "I count three."

"You're losing your touch, son," Clint huffed out a laugh. "There's a shadow coming out from behind the pillar out front of the mansion—bet you ten to one, that's a fourth bodyguard."

"Shit, you're right."

The senator's house was surrounded on one side by a state park. Finn was up in one of the trees with his sniper rifle, surveilling everything. Clint had made it onto the grounds and was behind the water feature that was made up of hundreds of pieces of granite. Seriously, who thought that would be a good idea? It made for a prime launching point for an attack. With his cammo garb and face covered in black paint, he was going to be impossible to spot, especially when he was behind the lights that shone onto the fountain. Currently the three guards were stationed up at the house and only one guard strolled the perimeter of the fence, and he took his sweet time to do it. Clint clocked him at twenty minutes for each rotation. Finn had caught a big ole whiff of marijuana, which meant he was toking up when he was in the shadows. So he wasn't going to be a problem.

"Finn, you have to be right, because that guard patrolling the perimeter is getting slower and slower. He hasn't made it back to the front for a half-hour. I think he's napping."

"Probably."

They watched as a burly man in black slacks and a t-shirt stepped out of the shadows and talked into a walkie-talkie. It was obvious when he got pissed. He motioned for one of the other guards to go around to the back of the mansion.

"I'll go wrap up those two," Finn said. "You can take care of the two in front," he said to Clint.

"I'm on it."

Their plan was no blood, just a peaceful in and out, with the senator so scared he'd turn on his mother. Clint waited a long five minutes until Finn said he had the two men subdued, then he pushed one of the granite stones off the top of the water feature into the pool of the fountain. It made a god-awful noise.

"Go check it out," Shadow Man said to the other guard.

The other man pulled out his gun and slowly made his way to the fountain.

"Come on, don't be a pussy, it was probably a racoon, but you have to check it out."

The other man didn't speed up. He continued to wave his gun back and forth as he crept forward. Clint was on the other side behind the lights, watching the man as he got closer. It took him long moments until he finally looked into the pool. Clint was careful as to the position of the next rock and the man. Then pushed it so it hit his back and he plunged into the water. He was going to be out of commission for a minute.

"What the fuck?! Jason, what happened?" The man on the porch didn't move an inch. From the back of the fountain, Clint broke the two lights that shone on the fountain's pool, then pulled the bodyguard from the pool. He gasped for breath as Clint applied zip ties to his wrists and feet.

"If you stay here and shut up, you won't die tonight. Got it?"

The man nodded.

"Jason!" Shadow man yelled again.

What a shitty leader. Not even bothering to help his man. He pulled out his walkie talkie. "Mike, can you hear me? What's the status on Lou?"

He was met by silence.

"Somebody answer me."

Clint saw Finn at the corner of the mansion's porch.

Perfect.

"Jason's over here," Clint yelled out. "If you want him alive, you need to come and get him."

"Who are you?" Shadow Man demanded to know, but he didn't move a step. So much for a diversion.

"We want to talk to the senator. Either let us in, or you'll be in the same boat as Jason, Mike and Lou. Is that what you want?" Clint asked.

Clint saw him hesitate. Then he turned around and ran for the massive front door. They couldn't let him inside the house. He'd be one more obstacle between them and getting to the senator, but they didn't want to kill him either. Finn pointed his rifle and took a shot. The man fell to the ground, yelling in pain.

It took a moment for Clint to figure out what had

happened. Finn had shot off the top of one of the ornate large door handles and it must have hit Shadow Man.

Score for Finn.

Clint and Finn rushed the man.

"How many more guards inside?" Clint demanded to know.

"None," he said weakly.

Finn kicked him in the ribs where the handle had hit, and he shrieked in pain.

"Tell the truth."

"Two. But they'll have heard everything on the walkie-talkies. You're toast. There's no way you'll get to the senator."

"Where does the senator sleep?"

"Upstairs, third bedroom down the hall on the right."

God, he wasn't bright. Clint picked him up, not caring if his ribs were broken. He pulled him out into the yard. "Point to a window."

"It's on the other side," he whimpered. "He likes to look over the park."

"God save me from idiots." He hauled him around to the other side of the estate and made him point. It was perfect, plenty of stone handholds to get to the window. He shoved the guard to the grass and zip-tied him after throwing the walkie-talkie into the bushes.

"Finn," he said into his mic.

"Yeah?"

"I can make it to the senator's room. I'll meet you there."

"You're leaving me to take out the bodyguards. You are a true friend." Clint could hear the smile in Finn's voice.

Lydia and he had done a lot of research on the senator. No family, no women or men friends who might be spending the night. Nope, this guy was totally boring. So, they felt safe confronting him.

But, Clint was cautious because the bodyguard intel was totally off. You never knew. He climbed up to the third-floor window. It was February, so the window wasn't open, but when he looked he saw that it wasn't locked either.

He could see the senator sleeping soundly by himself. So at least something was going right tonight. "How you doing Finn? Can I go into the senator's room yet?"

"Give me three more minutes, I'm still searching for the second guard."

Clint waited three minutes. Still nothing.

"You okay?"

"I don't think he's on the first floor, I'm going to check the basement."

Clint watched as the senator rolled over and made a grab for a pitcher of water beside his bed.

"Can't wait. Gotta go now," Clint said.

So much for stealth, time for surprise.

Clint slammed the butt of his pistol against the glass. It shattered and he saw the senator drop the pitcher. Clint used his gloves to pull out the shards of glass that would otherwise rip his hands to pieces, then dropped and rolled into the room, his gun at the ready. He was met with the senator holding a peashooter.

"Really? I don't think that's going to do much against my Kevlar, you greedy son-of-a-bitch. But you can try while I shoot you with my Glock. We'll see who wins and who loses," Clint laughed.

"Who are you?" the Senator demanded in a supercilious nasally tone.

People voted for this asshole?

"I'm your worst nightmare."

"I pressed my panic button. In less than one minute, six

men will be in here to blow you to hell. Then we'll see who is whose nightmare."

"Like they haven't been dispatched," Clint said sarcastically. "Seriously, hiring people from Rent-A-Cop was not your best choice."

Clint was watching the senator carefully so he saw the second he twitched. Clint moved, but he moved into the shot. Not only had he shot low and to the left, he'd shot two feet to the left.

Goddammit.

Clint's shoulder hurt like a motherfucker. He lunged and wrestled the goddamn senator to the floor.

"Didn't anybody ever teach you how to shoot, you dumbass?"

The senator looked up at him blankly.

The pain, the rage, the adrenaline overwhelmed Clint. He wanted to kill the man who was cowering below him.

"What do you want?" he finally whispered. "I'll do anything."

"I want you dead. Isn't that what you've been planning for others? You fucking puppet master. Isn't that what you do? Arrange things all your way, for nothing more than money, not caring who you hurt, or who you kill?"

Shit, he was so fucking off script. Reign it in. Get it back in line. You can do it, Archer.

"So you want me to repent? Is that it? You want to toss me into jail?"

"Maybe I do." Clint stared at him for a long time, trying to get his head back in the game.

"Tell me!" The senator screamed up at him, spittle hitting Clint's face. Clint kept thinking of how to dig himself out of this hole. He knew his lines.

Wait.

Maybe.

"I understand being in a jam. But you're not in a jam, you're a greedy fuck who is screwing over everybody and doesn't care who you kill. I'm doing this for my family. I don't have a choice."

"What do you want?!" The senator screamed again as he looked frantically at his bedroom door.

"They're not coming. All your bodyguards are gone. It's just you, me, and the Russian mob."

His eyes got so wide, white was showing all the way around. Yep, nothing like the Russian mafia to put the fear of God in someone. Then the man swallowed. "How do I know you're telling the truth?"

"Your secretary is dead. But we have a souvenir for you." Clint rustled around in his backpack and pulled out a smallish-sized box. He opened it up with a flourish and allowed a hand to fall out on top of the Senator.

"Ahhhhhhhhhh, get that off of me! *Please.* Get that away from me." Clint picked up the fake hand with his gloved thumb and forefinger.

"Recognize this ring? Isn't it Mrs. Sugarman's?"

The Senator started to cry. "Please don't hurt me."

The door to the bedroom opened and the senator looked at it with such hope. But it was Finn. He looked like he had gone a couple of rounds with someone. "Found the guy. He's down for the count. Oh good, is the senator going to come through for our bosses?"

"I was just going to find out." Clint continued to hold the hand just inches away from the man's face.

"Anything. Just let me live. What do they want?"

"They want the deal you're planning on giving the Kazakhstanis."

"But I can't get the sanctions lifted off of Kazakhstan, the secretary of state won't allow me to lift them," he whined.

"That's bullshit. We know what your boys are planning. Tell us how it's happening, we want to make sure nothing goes wrong."

"I can't."

Clint dropped the hand so that it palmed the senator's face. He screeched like a little girl. His hands were trapped by Clint, so he could only shake his head back and forth to dislodge it. "Anything, I'll tell you anything."

Finn had his phone ready to record everything. "Talk."

"I was going to make a killing with the Kazakhstanis once the tariffs were changed, but then they weren't. They were pressing me for their investment. When Devon and I couldn't deliver, they demanded that I remove the sanctions against their country. They thought I could just wave a magic wand since I was the leader of the Senate Foreign Relations Committee. The goddamn bitch of a secretary of state is standing in my way. Unless I can get rid of her, my life is worthless. Devon swears he has someone who will assassinate her before she goes on her trip to Africa. I've given him money to arrange it."

Clint laughed. Of course Devon asked for money, the little shit was always finding ways to get his palm greased.

"Well, now you're going to do the same thing, only for our bosses. I need you to make a call to Devon, right now. I need you to explain that the bosses have changed. I need you to tell him that we need to know all of the details. Got it?"

"He won't tell me," the senator whined.

"I don't care if you go to the Senate floor missing three toes. You'll get this done."

Clint's shoulder still ached, but he was damned proud of

himself for having pulled off the con, despite the initial slip. He looked up at Finn who gave him a thumbs-up. They got it all on tape.

"DON'T MAKE ANOTHER SOUND."

Lydia loved keeping to the script of the Kazakhstani meeting. Devon was hog-tied in front of her and the heel of her very sharp stiletto was positioned close to the little shit's eye.

"I would like to kill him," she said in Spanish to Drake.

"English!" he snapped at her.

She repeated herself in English.

"I know. But the boss might need him. It depends. We will see."

"What do you mean?" Devon begged. "I swear, I can help. Please. Trust me."

Drake laughed. It was the evil villain laugh from the Bond movies. Devon trembled. Lydia's heel scraped his nose and drew blood.

"You will take phone call," Drake said as he held up Devon's cell phone. "If you are good little boy, you might be allowed to live and serve my bosses. If you aren't, I will allow Carmen to kill you."

"Do you promise?" Lydia said throatily. "I haven't done anything fun in weeks."

"If he screws up, you can take your time with him, *Milaya.*"

"I love it when you speak Russian to me," Lydia cooed.

Drake had unknown talents coming up with Russian endearments. She just knew he was smirking underneath the mask. She wondered what was taking Clint and Finn so long to call. *Please God, say everything is okay.* It should be simple. No bodyguards, no family, just snag the senator and have him call.

The phone in her hand started to play the first few bars of the Stars and Stripes. She looked down at the display and saw that it was Senator Leonard. She put it on speaker as she answered. "Yes?" she asked in a thick Spanish accent.

"Carmen?" Clint asked.

"Yes, my love. My Russian darling is here with me as well and he has this little man tied up at my feet. I want to kill him. Slowly. Painfully. May I?"

Lydia looked down at Devon, his trembling even worse than before. But she kept her foot up so she didn't actually take out his eye. *More's the pity.*

"Where's....where's....what..."

"Do you have something to say?" Drake yelled at Devon. "If so, just say it!"

"What happened...to the..."

"My love, I think this little worm wants to know why you have the senator's phone," Lydia purred.

"Oh. Is that what he's stammering about. Well, let's have him talk to the senator."

"Devon," a new voice came on the phone. He sounded as scared as Devon. That fake severed hand must have done the trick. Seriously, one trip to the costume store and everything falls into place. Lydia tried to make her grin look evil.

"Senator," Devon responded. "What's going on?"

"Never mind. You have to tell me what plans you've made in regard to the secretary of state."

Lydia watched Devon closely. Scared as he was, she saw him start to scheme. Little shit. She scraped her heel from the corner of his left lip, up over his scratched nose to the corner of his right eye.

"Please, be careful," he wailed.

Drake knelt down beside Devon and pulled out the knife he'd used to cut the rope that he had used when tying up the little man. "You think her heel is scary?"

Drake used the tip of the knife to pluck the first three buttons off his orange-stained shirt. Then he scraped off some of his wispy chest hair.

"I'll do anything, please don't hurt me."

"Answer the senator's questions," Lydia said in the thick Spanish accent.

"Devon, listen to me." The senator sounded more in control. "I need all of the details of what you have planned. It is imperative that you tell me everything right now."

"We agreed you wanted plausible deniability, sir."

Drake yanked open Devon's shirt and played the knife around Devon's nipple.

"I'll talk. I'll talk." Weasel-Dick cried.

"I have the SEAL; you know the one. I've been blackmailing him."

"How?" The senator demanded to know.

"I faked the tape of when we were in Syria. I threatened to take it to the Navy Brass to get him arrested, kicked out, or something. Anyway, I've got him by the balls now. He's going to be in D.C. in a couple of hours. I'm going to tell him that his target is the Secretary of State. I have all the details of where she is flying out, the whens, the wheres, the everything."

"You really think he can kill her?" The senator asked.

"Absolutely. They're trained to kill. This be a cakewalk for him. I saw what he accomplished in Syria."

"Tell me the whens and wheres," the Senator demanded.

"She's leaving tomorrow at midnight out of DCA."

"Security is damned tight at that airport, how in the hell is your SEAL going to accomplish a kill there?"

"Not my problem," Devon defended himself. "He'll get the job done. You know their motto, the Few, the Proud, the SEALs."

"That's the Marines, you moron."

"It doesn't matter. He's going to get her off your back, and then you'll be able to lift the sanctions, and the Kazakhstanis won't kill us," Devon said breathlessly as he looked between Drake and Lydia.

"Our plan has changed. The Russian mob is going to take care of our friends in Kazakhstan, and instead, we're going to lift the sanctions in Russia."

"Will we get our money?" Devon whined.

"We'll come out of this with our lives, is what we'll get. They want to be in charge of your asset."

"I figured everything out. I have the tapes. He's mine," Devon cried out.

"They're there with you, right? I have men here in my goddamn bedroom. I have my secretary's severed hand on the carpet beside my head. They're not fucking around. You give them everything they want, or we're both dead."

"But..."

"Devon!" The senator shouted. "You will do this, or I will kill you myself. Give the Russians what they want. Give them all copies of the tape. Do. Not. Fuck. Around."

"I wouldn't," Devon lied.

"Bullshit. But if you do, not only will they come after you and probably cut off your feet and hands, I'll make sure you never work in this town again!"

"But..."

"Devon! Where is everything?"

"At my mother's house, in her safe."

Lydia scraped her heel against Devon's cheek. "Of course it is," she laughed. Evilly, of course.

28

CLINT WAS EXHAUSTED BY THE TIME FINN GOT BACK FROM Mrs. Cron's Georgetown apartment. She was in the Hamptons, so using Devon's key and instructions, it had been easy enough to get all of the original and doctored videos of the events in Syria. Additionally, Finn found a fake passport, two overseas bank accounts, and the evidence of what weasel-dick had been using to blackmail the other two aides and the reporter. Finn gave all of that information over to Conroy so that he could disseminate it how he saw fit.

"You okay?" Lydia asked quietly as they sat together on the redeye back to California. Clint said yes, but he really wasn't. It had been far too much stimulus for too short of an amount of time. Yeah, they might have come out on top, but he had almost blown the mission with the senator.

Lydia lifted up the armrest between them and rested her head against his chest. That was something that *did* make him feel better.

"Are you ever going to tell me what is wrong? What's *really* wrong?" he asked Lydia. He mentally kicked himself as soon as the words were out of his mouth.

"It's not wrong anymore," she whispered softly. "It's been my problem all along, but yeah, I'll tell you when we get home."

His head jerked as he looked down at her. Was she finally going to tell him the truth? *The big reveal?*

She stroked her hand over his heart. "Let's just be like this until we get home, then I'll tell you everything, okay?"

He picked up her hand and kissed her palm, amazed that his heart didn't jump out of his chest. "Okay," he whispered back.

GETTING home takes a lot longer than you would think, especially when you've been shot. Thank God it was a through and through or he never would have made it through TSA.

"I don't know why you're making such a big deal out of this," Drake muttered as Darius leaned over Clint's arm, watching him put in stitches.

"I'll tell you why," Mason Gault snarled. "It's when I find out that my men have been fuck-all over the world, pretending to be Russian gangsters, threatening senators, breaking and entering, and specifically bringing in a civilian on a situation that I said was to be handled only by the team. That makes me ready to murder the three of you just on principle. And Finn, as the adult in the room, I'm holding you responsible."

That hurt. Usually, I'm considered one of the adults in the room.

Mason must have seen the look on Clint's face. He took it down just ever so slightly.

"Tell me you got everything that this worm had on Drake. How do you know he doesn't have any more copies?"

"They're pretty scared of the Russian mob," Drake answered.

"Yeah, and when the secretary comes into the office just fine on Monday morning, her hand intact?" Mason said derisively.

"Actually, this was Clint's idea." Finn grinned. "He got her promoted to a new job working with the director of Walter Reed. One of the conditions of the promotion is that she had to start on Monday. She went for it."

"Is there actually a job?" Mason demanded to know.

Clint grinned. "Sure is. Lydia and I created it two days ago. We found funding for it, and the director is going to be thrilled to have extra help. We did the check on the senator's secretary; she has a daughter and two grandkids in Maryland, so she was happy to take the move package."

Clint watched Mason's lip twitch. "You got her a move package, huh?"

"That was Lydia's idea. My idea was getting the senator the no-nothing airhead from rent-a-guy assistants. Bart is going to make the senator's work life a living hell until the FBI comes and takes the senator away in handcuffs."

"So, how'd you get your video to the Feds?"

"Conroy," Finn and Clint said at the same time.

"Ah, shit. So now we have Lydia and the Shadow Alliance in on this thing. What part of keep it in the family do you not understand?" Mason glared at the three of them. "Darius, I hope you're sewing his arm without anaesthesia."

"Whatever you say, lieutenant. Just trying to stay out of the line of fire." Darius kept his head down, but Clint could see his grin.

"Mason, don't you have someplace more important to be than here?" Drake asked softly.

"Yes, goddamnit, why do you think I'm so pissed at you asshats?"

"Do you have pictures?" Clint asked.

Mason pulled out his phone and scrolled through until he found what he wanted. "Here you go." He handed the phone to Clint.

"She's beautiful, Mase. Did you two finally decide on a name?" Clint asked as he stared at the pretty baby with the unfocused blue eyes.

"We're naming her Amelia, after Sophia's mother."

"That's perfect." Finn clapped Mason's shoulder. Clint nodded in agreement.

"Hey, quit moving around. I'm almost done," Darius complained.

"So am I. Just wait until I get the two of you on the exercise yard." He glared at Finn and Drake. "As for you, Clint, what's your prognosis? How much longer at the rehab center?"

He handed Mason back his phone. "I just don't know. I had some problems on the op. I'm not mission-ready," he said quietly, as Darius rolled down his sleeve.

"Clint, with time—" Mason started.

"No guarantees with this one. I can't go into this thinking there are." Clint stood up and smiled at his boss. "It's a one-day-at-a-time type of deal. I've got at least five more weeks, if not more, at the center. Then I'm home for good, and it's just a matter of me doing my exercises and letting nature take its course."

Mason put his hand on his shoulder, "I'm here if you need me, anytime you need me."

"Ah, hell, Mase, I know that."

"We all are," Darius piped up.

"I'm probably going to be doing push-ups, so don't count on me," Drake said.

"Whatever you need, just call," Finn said as he came over and put his hand on top of Mason's.

"Well, now that you mention it," Clint grinned at Finn. "Can you square another two days away from the rehab place while I say good-bye to Lydia?"

"Ah, shit, you mean I can't go home to Karen?" Drake whined.

"It's not the same situation now," Clint said. "If need be, I'll sleep on the couch. But I won't require your sorry ass at my house."

"Thank God."

IT WAS RAINING when he walked up the stairs this time, so no yellow sundress for him. But maybe...finally...some answers. He listened as Mason's new SUV drove away and he knocked on the door.

"Clint." Lydia's smile was glorious as she drew him inside.

"You're wet," she laughed as she threw her arms around him. He noticed she was careful of his shoulder. "Tell me how it went. How soon do I have to have you back to Palm Desert?"

"Not until Friday," he whispered into her hair.

She dragged him towards the couch.

"Not the bedroom?" he teased as he followed her. He knew this was it, and it was all on her time, and he wasn't going to make it hard for her. He sat down first, then pulled her onto his lap.

"This is bad," she whispered into his shirtfront.

"Do you love me?"

She nodded.

He speared his fingers through her silky hair.

"Are you going to leave me?"

Her head shot up so fast it hit his chin. Dark, panic-filled eyes stared up at him. "Never."

"Then we'll get through this."

"Clint, I realized just how damned stupid I've been since your injury. It's like it jarred everything into place. You're going to be over-the-top crazy mad about what I have to tell you, plus you're going to be mad at me for keeping it from you, and you're going to be mad at me for allowing it to keep us apart, and—"

"Lydia, slow down," he cupped her face and gave her a soft kiss. "It's going to be all right. You need to breathe."

"It's not all right."

"I love you. It *is* all right. I'm not going to be crazy mad. You don't intend to run away with Melvin, so I'm good."

She snorted out a big laugh. Her eyes danced. Just what he wanted.

"He's tempting, but I'm kind of set on you." She rubbed her cheek against his hand.

"Rip the Band-Aid off, Baby."

She swallowed. "I haven't confronted him, but since the trial, I know. I know deep in my gut that my father set it up so Berto could molest Beth while he was visiting Dad's accounting office."

He jerked so hard, he almost dislodged Lydia from his lap. Clint looked down at Lydia, unable to fathom what he was hearing. Beth's own father gave his sixteen-year-old

daughter to a drug-dealing murderer to be sexually abused
—all but raped—by a Mexican drug lord?

"That can't be right." His voice was hoarse.

Lydia didn't respond. She continued to hold on tight to
Clint and stare at him solemnly.

"Lydia, tell me that you're wrong. Tell me the man who
has been living next door to us for the last five years isn't
that much of an animal."

Clint watched as one lone tear streaked down her soft
cheek.

He didn't say any more, trying hard to process the sick
feeling in his gut. As he tried to wrap his head around the
type of man who would knowingly do that, he felt his brain
swirl. It was incomprehensible. He wanted—no, he *needed*—
to go to the adjoining duplex and rip the door from the
hinges and beat the man to death. It was only Lydia's hand
stroking his chest, telling him to breathe, that was keeping
him sane.

Long, long moments later. Minutes? Hours? He gained a
semblance of control. His mind finally slipped back into
gear.

"But I don't understand. Why has this been keeping us
apart?" He was desolate. Five years without Lydia as his
wife. They could have had a child by now. It made no sense.

"Guilt. Shame. I was lying by omission. I was tainted.
You name it, I was feeling it. I can't explain it. It was a roiling
ball of emotions that all resulted in me not wanting you to
tie yourself to me. You could have done so much better."

Again, Clint felt the ground drop out from underneath
him. He loved this woman for all he was worth, and he felt
betrayed.

He breathed in through his nose.

He breathed out through his mouth.

Why would Lydia betray him?

Another breath in.

Another breath out.

"Why, Lydia?"

She bit her lip and wiped at her tears. "It seemed right back then. It seemed honorable even. But you almost dying made it clear. I was wrong. I was so wrong." More tears.

"You should have known better, Lyd. You should have." Clint shook his head when he heard the desperation in his voice.

Keep it together. This is Lydia. She needs you.

"I know I should have. I'm so sorry, Clint. Can you ever forgive me?"

His thumbs tried to stem the tide of her tears, but there were too many. He pulled her close and rocked her.

"Say you forgive me."

He took another deep breath.

"There's nothing to forgive."

"How can you say that?" she wailed. "I've been so wrong in the head."

That startled a laugh out of Clint. "Now that I can understand, Honey."

She sucked in her breath. "Don't make fun of yourself," she admonished.

"Lydia, we're us again. I hate that this has kept us apart. It's over now, right? We're finally moving forward?" This time Clint held his breath.

"Yes, Love. We're finally moving forward."

"God, I adore you." He tipped back her head for a loving kiss.

CLINT, God bless him, went over to her parents' house to back Lydia up when she finally confronted her father. She made sure that her mother was home because she needed to be able to look both of her parents in the eye when she made her accusation. Her mother was stoic while Lydia spoke, then started to cry while her father denied everything. But despite his denials, Lydia had no doubt that she was right. It was her mother who ended it. "You need to leave now. You're upsetting your father," she choked out, as she held her husband's hand.

Clint wrapped his arm around her shoulder and guided her out the door.

Her relationship with her parents, such as it was, was forever ruined.

"What do you want to do?" Clint asked her when they returned home.

"I can't live here anymore," Lydia said. "You should stop giving him such a big discount on the rent, and Jack should stop supplementing him."

"I'll talk to Jack," was all Clint would agree to. "But I agree, it's time for us to get a bigger place. While I'm at the rehab center, that's something you can work on."

Lydia hated to see him go, but she agreed with him, he needed to do this. In the interim, she had house hunting to do, a trip to San Antonio to visit Beth.

She wanted to visit Alice in person to let her know that her stepfather had been apprehended. It was due to Finn and Drake's help, they had figured out the trigger that had started the whole thing. Alice had been mentioned in the paper for her award as Teacher of the Year and that had started his fixation on her. It coincided with him losing his job, and with that evidence Lydia could question him and he broke down.

"What do you mean you knew?" Lydia stared at her sister, then looked over at her brother-in-law.

"It's the only thing that made sense," Beth said gently. "I figured it out years ago."

"Then how could you stand to be in the same room with him?"

"I rarely do. I only really spend time with Mama."

Lydia thought about it and realized it was true. But...

"Beth, our father served you up, he—"

"I've come to terms with it," Beth sighed. "He'll have to face God. I'm healed." She turned and smiled up at the big man beside her. "I have my husband, my life, my children." Then she smiled back at Lydia. "And my sister. I'm blessed."

Lydia felt tears well, and then fall. "You are so beautiful, inside and out."

"She absolutely is," Jack concurred. He hugged Beth close as they sat on the couch together. "Lydia, I agree with your decision to move. I think that's healthy. I'm just sorry this has been eating at you all these years."

That was Jack, so gentle and compassionate. Just the man that her sister had needed.

Beth leaned forward and grabbed Lydia's hands. "What are you going to do now?"

"I'm going to pray for Clint's recovery. He's really come to terms with the fact that he might not return to the team."

"Don't count him out yet," Jack reassured her.

"Still, all I care about is him. I just want him healthy and happy."

"He's got five more weeks, right?" Beth asked.

"I think he's going to stay longer," Lydia said. "He doesn't want to rush this."

"Good for him," Jack's approval was apparent.

"I need to ask you both for a favor."

"Anything." Beth practically bounced on the couch, eager to help her sister.

"Okay, let me tell you my plan."

EPILOGUE

IT HAD BEEN GREAT TO SEE MASON WHEN HE WAS DISCHARGED today. But he had to admit, he was disappointed when it wasn't Lydia who was waiting outside the rehabilitation center. He was dying to see her, plus he wanted to hear her take on Senator Leonard and Devon Cron's takedown. Luckily, Mason was more than happy to talk about it—as a matter of fact, he had a lot of questions.

"I saw it on the news, but how in the hell did Conroy Lake arrange to have Senator Leonard arrested on the stairs of the State Capitol?" Mason wanted to know.

"Hell, Mason, I thought you would have realized that wasn't Conroy, that was Declan," Clint laughed.

Mason shook his head as he pulled onto the I-10 freeway. "I should have known that. Did Liam help?"

Clint shrugged. "Probably. Since he joined the Shadow Alliance I noticed that they've had a little more muscle with the military and all the D.C. types, and can play a little more above-board when they want to."

"God, it was a thing of beauty. First, he was protesting all charges, but when he saw Devon being dragged out of the building, pointing at him, the senator actually started to cry. My God, they've used that clip to make hundreds, if not thousands of memes."

"Really?" Clint laughed at that. He bet Melvin and Lydia had been holding a contest or something. When he suggested it to Mason, he disagreed.

"Nope, turns out that guy was universally despised, so it was easy. Then there were the side-by-side mug shots of the two of them. They actually pulled off Devon's toupee for that one—he had three Homer hairs sticking up, and the senator's eyes were puffy from crying."

"More memes?" Clint asked.

"You got it."

"What are the charges?"

"You and Finn did good. With that tape, showing them plotting to assassinate the secretary of state, they're throwing the book at them. The trial won't be for a couple of months, but it should be good."

Clint sat back with a sense of satisfaction. It had been a long haul—not just the mini-mission, but the time at the rehab center. He was damn near at his peak physical condition thanks to Arnold, but he still hadn't really tested out his computer capabilities. Let's face it, Palm Desert Renewal didn't have the type of equipment that he and Lydia or Uncle Sam had for him to play with. He was anxious about his abilities. He sighed.

"You okay?" Mason asked as he looked away from the road for a moment.

"Yeah."

"How did it really go out there? I know you filled me in and so did the center, but how was it really?"

Clint snorted. "Don't lie to me, you got reports from Dex Evans too."

Mason grinned. "Well, I wouldn't be doing my job if I didn't."

This time Clint laughed. "I would have done the same thing. Hell, normally I'd be the one getting you the info."

"And soon you will be," Mason assured him.

"Not necessarily," Clint sobered up.

"We'll see what the Navy docs have to say."

Mason changed the subject to his favorite topic, which was his daughter Amelia. He passed over his phone and had Clint look through pictures while he told stories. It was a good thing that he had progressed as far as he had, otherwise an hour of listening to the antics of a baby a little over a month old would have driven him batty. Seriously, she couldn't even sit up yet.

When they pulled up to Clint's house, the first thing he noticed was the For Sale sign in his yard.

"Thanks for listening to me. All the other guys have said that they'd string me up if they had to hear another word. Except for Jack. He's still willing to listen."

Clint barked out a laugh. "Sounds about right."

"Well, Lydia's probably waiting. I'll let you go. See you on Monday."

Clint got out of Mason's SUV with a spring in his step and headed up the stairs. The door was locked, so he knocked. Lydia opened the door, and he stepped into another world.

SHE WAS TREMBLING. *Please say I got this right.* She'd turned off all the real lights in the room, covered all of the windows, and decked out the living room with strings of tiny white lights. She'd covered damn near every surface with baby's breath flowers, interspersed with red roses. She was wearing another frothy sundress, only this time in white.

"Lydia—" Clint started.

"Let me talk, okay?"

She pulled him over to the large, overstuffed chair that they had, and pushed him down so she could kneel down in front of him. He looked perplexed.

"Honey, what's all this about?"

"I want to get this right, okay?"

He must have realized her seriousness because he nodded.

Out of the pocket of her dress, she pulled out a small jewelry box. She hesitated. "I've taken a long time to get here, and you've been the most patient man in the world. I've loved you for five years, and they've been the best years of my life."

"Mine too."

She couldn't help but smile. She knelt up high and cupped his cheek with one hand as her other hand tightly gripped the box. She brushed his lips with a tender kiss. He lifted his hand, but she pulled away before the kiss went deeper. She had more to say.

"I'm so sorry for putting you off, for not standing before God and marrying you years ago. It will forever be the biggest regret of my life."

"Baby—"

"It will," she interrupted. "There's nothing you can say or do to change it. But, I'm hoping that from this day on, we can move forward and be the family we were always destined to be."

Her hands were trembling as she lifted up the box and opened the lid. Nestled inside were two wedding rings, one for him and one for her.

She watched through her tears and saw his eyes glisten.

"Are you asking me to marry you, Ms. Hildalgo?"

"Yes, I am."

He pulled her off her knees and stood up with her. He pulled her into an embrace of a lifetime.

"Yes, my answer is yes."

"Are you sure?" she breathed.

"I've adored you since the first moment I saw you." He tenderly kissed her lips. "I'm sure."

He picked her up and twirled her around their own little slice of heaven. Their lives were headed for the stars.

If you haven't read Her Loyal Seal, the story where Clint and Lydia first met, pick up your copy today.

Her Loyal Seal (Book #2)

ABOUT THE AUTHOR

Caitlyn O'Leary is a USA Bestselling Author, #1 Amazon Bestselling Author and a Golden Quill Recipient from Book Viral in 2015. Hampered with a mild form of dyslexia she began memorizing books at an early age until her grandmother, the English teacher, took the time to teach her to read -- then she never stopped. She began re-writing alternate endings for her Trixie Belden books into happily-ever-afters with Trixie's platonic friend Jim. When she was home with pneumonia at twelve, she read the entire set of World Book Encyclopedias -- a little more challenging to end those happily.

Caitlyn loves writing about Alpha males with strong heroines who keep the men on their toes. There is plenty of action, suspense and humor in her books. She is never shy about tackling some of today's tough and relevant issues.

In addition to being an award-winning author of romantic suspense novels, she is a devoted aunt, an avid reader, a former corporate executive for a Fortune 100 company, and totally in love with her husband of soon-to-be twenty years.

She recently moved back home to the Pacific Northwest from Southern California. She is so happy to see the seasons again; rain, rain and more rain. She has a large fan group on Facebook and through her e-mail list. Caitlyn is known for telling her "Caitlyn Factors", where she relates her little and big life's screw-ups. The list is long. She loves hearing and connecting with her fans on a daily basis.

Keep up with Caitlyn O'Leary:

Facebook: tinyurl.com/nuhvey2
Twitter: @CaitlynOLearyNA
Pinterest: tinyurl.com/q36uohc
Goodreads: tinyurl.com/nqy66h7
Website: www.caitlynoleary.com
Email: caitlyn@caitlynoleary.com
Newsletter: http://bit.ly/1WIhRup
Instagram: http://bit.ly/29WaNIh

ALSO BY CAITLYN O'LEARY

Her Passionate Hero (Book #3)

Her Wicked Hero (Book #4)

Her Guarded Hero (Book #5)

Her Captivated Hero (Book #6)

Her Honorable Hero (Book #7)

Her Loving Hero (Book #8)

THE FOUND SERIES

Revealed (Book #1)

Forsaken (Book #2)

Healed (Book #3)

SHADOWS ALLIANCE SERIES

Declan

Made in the USA
Monee, IL
07 March 2021

61247004R00167